MW01071518

Full Circle

Full Circle

Mary D. Brooks

Renaissance Alliance Publishing, Inc.
Nederland, Texas

Copyright © 2002 by Mary D. Brooks

All rights reserved. No part of this publication may be repro-
duced, transmitted in any form or by any means, electronic or
mechanical, including photocopy, recording, or any information
storage and retrieval system, without permission in writing from
the publisher. The characters herein are fictional and any resemblance to a real person, living or dead, is purely coincidental.

ISBN 1-930928-25-4

First Printing 2002

9 8 7 6 5 4 3 2 1

Cover art and design by LJ Maas
Illustrations by Lúcia A. de Nóbrega

Published by:

Renaissance Alliance Publishing, Inc.
PMB 238, 8691 9th Avenue
Port Arthur, Texas 77642-8025

Find us on the World Wide Web at
http://www.rapbooks.com

Printed in the United States of America

Acknowledgments:

I would like to thank LJ Maas for her help with this novel, Angelica London for her invaluable advice and friendship. To Maggie & T.Novan for their friendship and to Madame President, Taylor Rickard - you know why.

Many thanks to the Eva & Zoe Fans for giving me so many laughs. To Lucia de Nobrega for her artwork which only inspires me even more.

— Mary

This novel is dedicated to Katelin Welles. You rock lady.

Chapter
1

The quiet street greeted the postman as he trudged up his usual route. Jack was a portly man in his late fifties, who enjoyed his work. He had been walking the same route for over twenty years, and had watched the suburb, and the people in it, change and grow as the years passed. He enjoyed talking to all the different people here and listening to the different accents and languages, even though half the time he didn't understand a word that was spoken. Walking his route, he was greeted in English, Greek, Italian, Polish, and even the occasional German tongue.

He hefted his large postal bag, thankful that it was a beautiful summer's day–a little on the warm side, but he was used to that after so many years. He came up a small hill and stopped when he heard a familiar rumble coming up behind him.

An older motorcycle with sidecar passed him, the rumbling stopping as its diminutive driver manoeuvred the old bike into the driveway of number 56, a few houses down from where he was. The rider practically jumped off the seat, then took off her helmet and shook her short dark hair, running her fingers through it a few times in a useless attempt to bring order to chaos.

Spotting the postman walking toward her from the next house, she jogged up to the gate and leaned on it, waiting for him to arrive.

"Hi, Jack! Anything for us?" Zoe Haralambos asked.

"You're going to kill yourself on that thing one day," the postman replied, making the same comment he did every time he saw the young woman on her bike.

Jack had "adopted" the petite young woman soon after she had moved in, and loved her artwork, which he bought from her on occasion. He had even commissioned a portrait of himself and his wife for their 25th wedding anniversary, which took pride of place in their living room.

A secret part of him enjoyed the attentions of the pretty young woman, her green eyes always seemed to twinkle with mischief when she saw him. She lived with another, older woman, whom he seldom saw and rarely got to speak with.

Where Zoe was short, the older woman was tall and intimidating. He had spoken to her only a couple of times and was quite surprised the first time she had conversed with him. He hadn't expected to hear a German accent, since Zoe spoke with a soft Greek accent.

"Nah, Mabel is not going to kill me," Zoe replied, looking back fondly at the old motorcycle Earl had given her a few years earlier.

"I don't know, young lady, the way you zoom about on that thing–"

"Jack, you worry as much as Eva does!" Zoe laughed.

The older man grumbled good-naturedly and handed Zoe a letter. "You be careful now."

"I will," Zoe promised as she watched Jack walk back down the sidewalk to continue his route. As she walked the sandstone-paved walkway to the front steps, she patted her jacket to see if she had the house keys.

She stopped to admire the jasmine that Eva had planted near the steps leading up to the house. The climber was growing, and was soon going to wind itself around the steps. The garden was beautifully cared for–one of Eva's other passions, apart from photography.

With its two large palm trees and the beautiful garden in the front, Zoe loved the old house that was nestled away from the road. It had a lot of character.

Eva had fallen in love with the house on her way home from work one day, and had returned to their flat excited that she'd finally found the house they were looking for. They had already spent many hours house hunting, much to Eva's frustration. Her idea of shopping was going in and getting what she wanted as quickly as possible, and house hunting was on her list of least favourite activities.

The three bedroom wooden house was built at the turn of the century and was known as a Federation house, based on the year that Australia had become a nation, or so she was told by the real estate agent. Zoe was totally charmed by the house.

They'd both spent considerable time in restoring it to its original colour scheme. Inside, the walls were white with dark green skirtings, and the painting was done by the two of them, with Earl, Elena, and Friedrich lending a hand. Elena's youngest at the time, Albert, also joined in, getting paint all over himself, much to the amusement of everyone present. Zoe grinned at the memory of little Albert sitting on Eva's foot, covered in green paint and sucking his thumb.

It was their home, or as Eva described it, their "little patch of Australia." She surprised Zoe one day when she came home with a sign that read "Haralambos" and promptly mounted it to the wall on the left hand side of the door. Zoe laughed when Eva said that no one would forget whose house it was.

Zoe entered their home and dropped her keys on the small table in the hallway, then took her jacket off and placed it on a hook near the door. She was happy to be home, even though she really enjoyed her job at the art gallery. Buying new artwork for the gallery was a great way to spend her time, and she also had the opportunity to show off her own work occasionally.

Zoe was content with her life. She was married to the love of her life—she and Eva would be celebrating their fifth wedding anniversary in a few weeks. Every time she saw her "other half," as Eva had taken to calling herself, her heart still skipped a beat, and she hoped that feeling would never stop happening. Eva had been her first love, and her first—and as far as Zoe was concerned, her last—lover. She could never contemplate a life without the tall, older woman.

Zoe looked down at the letter in her hand, noticing the postmark was Greek. She smiled when she recognised the handwriting. Her father-in-law's bold script was unmistakable. Deciding not to open the letter yet, she placed it on the counter to wait until her wife came home so they could share it together.

She took off her shoes and padded into the kitchen to start preparing dinner, hoping Eva would be home soon.

"If I see Mr Sitiropoulos again, I think I'm going to explode," Eva Haralambos grumbled to her friend and assistant, Debbie. She was standing beside her assistant, who was seated at her desk going over the rest of the day's schedule.

Debbie nodded, having heard that particular grumble many times from her boss, who was her direct supervisor in the translating section. Debbie's job was to take care of Eva and let her get on with the day-to-day running of the department.

Debbie wasn't surprised when Eva had been promoted to deputy director of the unit. She was good at her job, courteous, and had diplomatic skills that their boss, Richard Farmer, lacked. Though she normally wasn't very talkative, she did go out of her way to help people, and she was well liked by almost everyone. Of course, there had been some grumblings from others in the unit about seniority and the like, since Eva had only been working there a little over four years, but the decision to promote Eva was met with general approval.

It was a great surprise to Debbie when Eva requested her as an assistant or, as Zoe called her, Eva's Girl Friday.

Debbie quickly turned her attention back to her disgruntled boss. "He'll be back," she warned, getting a scowl in return.

Before Eva could respond further, the main door to the office opened and Richard Farmer, the director of the unit, walked in. Richard was a tall man, with salt and pepper hair and a jovial demeanour.

"Eva...good, you're in. I need to have a little chat," Richard said as he smiled down at Debbie. He followed Eva into her office, settling into one of the comfortable chairs. "We have a problem."

"Which problem are we talking about?" Eva asked, thinking of four different things she had to sort out.

"You know I was going to go with the Immigration Minister to Europe?" Eva nodded. "Well, there has been a change of plans."

"Oh?"

"I need someone to go with the Minister to Greece, France, Germany, and Italy. Do you know anyone who can speak Greek, German, and Italian?"

Eva looked at her boss with a tiny smile on her face. "I think I may know someone who meets those criteria, although they can't speak French."

Richard scratched his chin in thought and grinned. "Not to worry about the French, the Minister is fluent in French. Would this person be available?"

"She might," Eva replied.

Richard chuckled. He liked his deputy. She was "good people," his mother would have said about her. Always honest and hardworking.

"When does the Minister leave?"

"In a week. Is your passport up to date?"

"I got my Aussie one the other day, so I'm ready," Eva replied. Both she and Zoe had become Australian citizens, and they'd been very proud to get their citizenship papers and their passports altered. Zoe still had her Greek passport, but Eva had renounced her German citizenship. Eva didn't think Zoe would ever give hers up altogether. Zoe was a proud Greek who loved her heritage, but she recognised that she now lived in Australia, and her newly adopted country was giving her opportunities she'd never have had in the old country.

"Excellent, I'll send the paperwork over this afternoon. I'm relieved that you can take this on."

"It's going to be great to go back home for a visit," Eva mused. She knew Zoe was going to be thrilled at this latest news, and suddenly she couldn't wait to get home and talk to her wife.

"Will Zoe enjoy a trip back home?" Richard had met the younger woman, who he'd initially thought was Eva's sister until he'd accidentally walked in on them together in Eva's office one day. He was shocked to find out they were lesbians and married to each other. It had taken him a few days to mull it over, and he finally decided it was none of his business what they were. He liked and respected Eva, and although he didn't approve of their choice, he wasn't going to be judgmental since it had nothing to do with her job performance.

"I would like her to be with me," Eva responded, wanting to add that she wouldn't be able to stop Zoe, even if she had to travel by herself and meet Eva there.

"Good, then that's settled," Richard said, getting up from his chair and walking to the door, Eva following. He opened the door and turned to her. "As I said, I'll send the paperwork to you as soon as I get back to my office."

Eva thanked him, walking him out of the office and back to the lobby.

Debbie watched as Eva returned to her office. Eva was counting as she waited for Debbie's inevitable interrogation.

"So, what was that about?" Debbie asked, following Eva into her office.

"Hey, you only took 10 seconds that time," Eva grinned.

"Ha, ha, funny lady."

"I'm going to Europe with the Immigration Minister."

"So," Debbie said, and sat down with a smug grin on her face, "the rumours were true!"

"Huh? What rumours?"

Debbie shook her head. Sometimes her boss had her head in the sand when it came to office politics and the rumours that circulated.

"I heard that Richard and the Minister's wife were having an affair!"

Eva was incredulous. "Where did you hear that? That's ridiculous."

"You think so, Miss Head-in-the-Sand? Why isn't he going with the Minister, then?"

Eva shrugged. "I don't know."

"There you go," Debbie said brightly, as if it were conclusive evidence. "Are you going to take Zoe with you?"

"I would love to, since we're going back home. And I could show her a little of Germany as well."

"That will be nice," Debbie sighed. "Oh, Mr Zimmerman has cancelled. I'm sure you're heartbroken by that news. I know I was."

Eva gave her assistant a grin. Mr Zimmerman enjoyed teasing Debbie, and, much to Debbie's disgust, would take every opportunity to pinch her behind when he could get away with it.

"Richard is sending over the paperwork for the trip. Can you make sure we get all the papers and then start filling out the requisitions?"

Eva drove the white Holden slowly up the hill and turned into the driveway. She smiled when she caught sight of Mabel. The presence of the motorcycle indicated that her wife was home. Eva parked the car, taking her briefcase from the front seat with her as she got out and locked the door.

She was happy she had learned to drive and no longer had to

rely on public transport, as that had totally aggravated her. Earl had patiently taught her how to drive, though she gave him a few scares, and she got her licence on her first try. She was rather proud of that and didn't let Earl forget it.

She stopped to take a sniff of the jasmine and sighed contently as she climbed the stairs to the front door. As she entered, she was greeted by the sound of jazz music and a wonderful aroma coming from the kitchen. Putting her briefcase down, she took off her jacket and hung it up.

She stood in the hall grinning as she watched Zoe, oblivious to Eva's presence, dancing and singing to the music while stirring the pot. Eva walked up behind her wife carefully, not wanting Zoe to notice her yet.

"I could ravish you and no one would hear you," Eva whispered in Zoe's ear as she put her arms around the petite woman and nuzzled her neck.

"Oh, my...please, no. I mean, yes!" Zoe played along, and they both laughed. She turned in Eva's embrace and looked up into twinkling blue eyes. "So, you want to ravish me?"

"That's the plan," Eva said, waggling her eyebrows.

"Well, I have to let you know that my wife is due to come home at any moment."

"Is that so?"

"Uh huh. And you know, she's quite the jealous type."

"Is she now?"

"Oh yeah. She is also the most beautiful creature God put on this earth." Zoe grinned and reached up to caress Eva's cheek before teasing her dimpled chin.

"Can't be. I'm staring at the world's most beautiful creature," Eva replied, getting a tender kiss from her wife. "Hmm, I should remember that line; it gets me kissed."

Zoe playfully slapped her arm and giggled.

"So, Miss Zoe, what have you been up to today, apart from letting strange women attempt to ravish you?"

"Well, Miss Eva, I spent the morning buying some new artwork, which was really nice and expensive," Zoe chuckled. "Then I had lunch with Elena, Albert, and Elizabeth."

"That sounds nice."

"Hmm, it was," Zoe said wistfully.

"Something wrong with El?" Eva asked, noticing the change in her wife's emotions.

"No. Well, yes–that is, not really."

"Clear as mud, love. Want to try that again?" Eva teased.

"Well, she's expecting again."

"That's wonderful. Isn't it?"

"Yeah, it is," Zoe said quietly.

"Not so wonderful?"

"Um...I've been thinking about this for a long time...um..."

"I'm confused now, Zoe."

Zoe looked up and gave a tiny grin. She wasn't sure what Eva would say, but she really wanted this badly. She felt she was ready for it. "Um, I would like to have some children."

Eva wasn't expecting that revelation, and she took in a deep breath. "Um, Zoe, you may not have noticed this, but I don't have the right equipment for that."

Zoe giggled nervously. "I know, and I would be extremely worried if you did."

"Yeah, me too," Eva deadpanned, then broke out in a grin. She took her wife's hand and led her to their sofa and sat down. Zoe chose to sit on Eva's lap.

"I think I'm ready to be a mother."

"Hmm, you would make a wonderful mum, but we may have a problem."

"I've been thinking about that, too."

"Mmm, and what have you come up with?"

"Well we need a...um..."

"A donor?" Eva offered and watched a pink blush travel up Zoe's face, which she found quite endearing.

"Yeah, a donor. I want a baby that looks like you." Zoe smiled at the look of mild shock on her partner's face. "I want a baby with blue eyes, beautiful dark hair, and..." she traced the dimpled chin, "a dimple." She leaned down and tenderly kissed the woman she loved so much.

"Oh, Zoe, um...that would mean we have to find someone who looked like me; but I would love a baby that looks like you. Green eyes that twinkle when she smiles, a child that would have her mother's beauty inside and out."

"God, I love you," Zoe whispered, giving her a long and sensual kiss. She laid her head on Eva's chest and let out a sigh. "Where do we find a donor?"

"Plenty walking around," Eva joked and got a slap on the belly for her wit.

"You can't find many blue eyed, dark haired men around here, can you?" Zoe giggled.

"Well, it doesn't have to be dark hair, does it?"

"Absolutely," Zoe said resolutely. She was determined to have the baby look like Eva.

"Okay, so you want to ask Earl?"

"You have noticed Earl's colouring, haven't you?" Zoe cupped her partner's face and gave her a mock glare.

"He's blond and blue eyed."

"Right," Zoe nodded and then nibbled her lip.

"What's going on up there?" Eva tapped the dark head lightly and smiled.

"Well, I was thinking about the other man in our lives. What about Pat?"

Eva's smile grew as the realisation sank in that Pat did indeed fit Zoe's requirements in the looks department. He was tall, had thick black hair and blue eyes. She remembered once Zoe had remarked that they looked so much alike they could be siblings. "I like that idea."

"How do I fall pregnant? I don't particularly like the idea of having sex with Patty," Zoe frowned.

"I think there are other ways to fall pregnant, love."

"There are? How?"

Eva wanted to laugh, but her wife's innocent look stopped her. "A turkey baster."

"Oh, so you mean I don't have to...um...have sex with the guy?"

Eva shook her head and grinned when Zoe exhaled loudly. "You were worried about that?"

"Yeah, I want a child, but I don't want to have sex with a man."

"I should hope not," Eva teased.

"Seriously, Evy, I wouldn't want to do that to you."

Eva was touched by Zoe's loving concern for her feelings. She didn't want to think of Zoe in anyone's arms except hers. "Thank you, love."

"So how do we get a donor?"

"Well, first we ask Pat, and hope he doesn't fall over," Eva said and chuckled when Zoe snuggled up against her.

"When?"

"Well, it will have to wait for a few weeks," Eva said and watched as Zoe frowned.

"Why?"

"Well, Miss Zoe, how would you like to go home?"

Zoe looked at her wife in puzzlement. "I am home."

Eva shook her head. It never ceased to amaze her how this young woman could say a few words that made her love her even more, if that were actually possible. "No, love, I meant back home to Greece."

"Really?"

"Really. Richard asked me to accompany the Minister to Europe–"

"Ah, so the rumours are true!"

"What?"

"The rumours that Richard and Carla, you know, the Minister's wife, are having an affair," Zoe said matter-of-factly. Every time she went for a visit, Debbie always caught her up on the latest gossip going around the office.

Eva shook her head. "I think everyone knows everything in that office except me."

"That's because you stick your head in the sand, love. There was this juicy rumour about you and Richard that was going around about six months ago."

"What?"

"Just kidding," Zoe teased and collapsed onto the sofa as Eva's fingers began tickling her mercilessly. "Oh! I give, I give!" she cried out until Eva relented.

"So the Minister needs a different interpreter?"

"Well, he is taking more than one with him, but Richard wants me to go in his place."

"Hmm, being in the same place as the Minister while Richard is having an affair with the Minister's wife is tricky," Zoe muttered.

"We have some money saved up, and I thought you might want to take the trip with me."

"Um, can I get back to you on that? I have to check my schedule and–" Zoe didn't finish as Eva started the tickle assault again. "Oh, that's not fair! Okay! Stop it now!"

"So, Miss Zoe, do you want to come with me?"

"Try and stop me," Zoe replied. "Are we going by ship?"

This was going to be the fun bit, as Zoe was scared of flying. They had taken a hot air balloon ride with Earl and she had been glued to Eva all the way, with her eyes firmly shut.

"Nope."

"Well we can't swim there–oh no! We're flying?"

"The Minister doesn't have three months to play with. Yep,

we are flying."

"Oh, yuck!" Zoe scrunched up her face, and then a thought occurred to her. "We're going to celebrate your 30th birthday in Greece!" Zoe grinned. She had been planning on a huge party for her wife. She then remembered the letter they'd just gotten from her father-in-law. "Oh, Evy, we got a letter from Dad!" She quickly got up from the sofa and retrieved the letter. "Me, or you?"

"You can," Eva replied as Zoe settled back onto her lap and ripped the letter open.

"Save the stamps for Albert," Eva reminded her partner.

With his father's help, the young child had started a collection of stamps and always asked her if she had any. She usually remembered to keep the ones from the office. Debbie had caught her cutting out stamps one day. When she told her assistant what she was doing, Debbie began to save them and give them to her. Albert now had a huge collection of stamps from around the world, which he treasured.

Zoe straightened out the letter and began to read aloud. "My dear daughters, I hope this letter finds you both well and happy, I pray every day that Zoe hasn't crashed Mabel."

"What a funny guy," Zoe commented dryly, as Eva chuckled.

"Ally sends her love. We are both well. The weather has been good for our health, and the change in climate is just what we needed. We are going to Trikala for a dip in the artesian waters, which should help my leg a bit. Eva, I haven't forgotten your birthday, my dear child. Thirty years ago I wondered what you would look like, and whether I would ever be in your life to see you grow, or if you would never know who your real father was. Your mother raised a very beautiful person. Your gentleness and kindness are a blessing to me." Zoe stopped and wiped the tears that were running down her face. She glanced at her wife, who had her head bowed, then continued to read. "I am blessed with two daughters who have made me a very happy old man. I love you both, more than you will ever know. Here I am, crying like a baby. Zoe would call me mushy now. I wish I could be there for your 30th birthday, Eva, but know that despite the thousands of miles between us, I am with you. I have some exciting news to report–Thanasi is getting married! I never thought I would see the day. His fiancée is a lovely young woman. Her name is Althea and I have enclosed some photographs of the lovely couple. The wedding is going to be a huge event here. Larissa loves her hometown heroes, and all the town will be at the wedding. It will be a wedding to remember for a long time. I wish you could be here to enjoy the festivities, but alas, I know getting to Larissa would be impossible. I dream of the day when you can come home for a visit. Give my love to Earl, Elena, and Friedrich. Kiss little Albert and Elizabeth for me. I keep both of you in my prayers every night. I love you both. Love, Dad." Zoe finished reading and sighed. "I miss him."

"Yeah, so do I, but I think the Greek climate is better suited to his health."

"Hmm, I can't wait to see his face when we get to Larissa!" Zoe grinned, imagining her father-in-law's surprised face. She laid her head on Eva's shoulder. "Are you hungry?"

"I am a bit. What's for dinner?"

"Your favourite." Zoe smiled when Eva smacked her lips, knowing Zoe had made stuffed capsicum, and peppers with rice and minced meat.

"Let's eat!" Eva picked her wife up and carried her into the kitchen.

Chapter
2

Eva sat back, enjoying the warm evening on the sofa they had put outside in the back, one of only a few things they'd brought with them from their apartment to the new house. Zoe had insisted on bringing the sofa, and Eva couldn't figure out why she needed it. The sofa was old and had seen better days, but Zoe wanted to keep it, so along it came. The large four poster bed and the oversized bathtub also made the trip over.

She scratched her arm and scowled, noting where a mosquito had taken another bite from her. She was wearing a short sleeved, apricot coloured cotton shirt and a pair of shorts, and her feet were bare against the cool timbers of the balcony.

Their house was set on a large block of land, and from the backyard balcony they had a perfect view of the Pacific Ocean. Eva found the view very soothing, another reason why she'd wanted to buy the house. She had practically dragged Zoe down to see the latest prospect, hoping her partner would fall in love with it, just like she had. Zoe took one look at the kitchen that overlooked the garden, and she was in love.

The three fireplaces added to the charm of the house, and Zoe made sure their bedroom had the biggest one. During the winter, she usually found herself on the floor in front of the fireplace sitting on the rug with her wife at her side, enjoying the warmth and feeling content with her life.

The garden was also very important to Eva. She enjoyed gardening, letting her mind wander. Zoe's gardening skills were non-existent, and she gladly ceded that particular task to her eager partner. They'd planted several trees on either side of the garden. A fig, a pomegranate, and an avocado tree lined one side, and on the other were an olive, a plum, and a lemon tree, whose branches were heavy with lemons at the moment. *I will have to get a bag and pick the lemons before they fall,* she idly noted.

In the back, the fence was reinforced to stop anyone from falling over the cliff. "I'll have to reinforce it more rigourously when the babies come," Eva mused to herself.

I'm going to be a parent! Eva thought to herself and sighed. She'd never thought she would have children since she couldn't have any of her own. No man was going to marry a barren woman, and Eva had reconciled herself to that fact. She wasn't sure what kind of parent she was going to be, and she had to admit she was a little terrified at the prospect.

Zoe watched her wife for a few moments as Eva twirled her wedding ring around her finger. *She's worried,* Zoe thought. She knew her wife well enough to know when she was worrying about something. She had discovered in the years since they'd been married that Eva would play with her ring whenever she was thinking about something important and wasn't quite ready to voice her thoughts, or when she was scared or concerned. Zoe didn't think she would tell her about that little idiosyncrasy. Besides, she was sure Eva had worked out her own little "worried" signs.

Zoe stepped out onto the balcony holding two steaming cups of tea. "Want some company?"

Eva turned and smiled as Zoe gave her a cup. Zoe set her cup down on the small table and tucked her legs under her as she got comfortable on the old sofa beside Eva. She picked up her cup of tea and leaned on Eva's shoulder.

"Want to talk about what's worrying you?" Zoe asked her wife, looking up at the clear night sky and watching thousands of stars twinkle back at her.

"Hmm." Eva sighed and sipped her tea.

"You're scared." Zoe quietly stated the obvious.

"Am I that transparent?"

"Only to me," Zoe assured her.

"I'm a little scared about having children...well, you having the children–"

"Don't you want children?" Zoe asked with concern.

"Oh, I do want children, Zoe!" Eva exclaimed and was quite annoyed with herself that she'd led Zoe to think she didn't want to have children. It wasn't fair to her partner since she had thought about it for so long. "I'm just not sure what kind of parent I will make. I had reconciled myself to the fact that I couldn't have any, and...um...I never thought I would get the opportunity."

"You know, when I fell in love with you, I gave up the idea of having them as well," Zoe said and took a sip of her tea.

Eva couldn't help herself and she smiled. "When did the idea come back to you?"

"Well, one of our regular customers had a baby last week–"

"Zoe, women have babies every day," Eva interrupted.

"You're funny, you know that?" Zoe teased back. "Stacey is a lesbian."

"The shock of it," Eva said, and got an elbow in the ribs for her trouble. "Ow!"

"Oh, you poor baby. Want me to kiss it better?" Zoe asked, and lifted Eva's shirt, giving her a little tickle and a kiss. "There, all nice and better."

Eva chuckled. "Okay, Stacey is a lesbian and has a baby."

"Yeah, so I started thinking, 'If Stacey can have one, then what's to stop me from having one?' But then, I thought of one very important obstacle."

"You had no...donor?"

"Give the gorgeous woman a gold star," Zoe joked. "But like you said, we can find a donor with exceptional good looks and a dimple, and we can use the turkey baster, which is extremely unromantic, but there you go."

"Who says it will be unromantic? We're going to have a baby, so it must be done right. We can go up to the Hydro Majestic and do it right."

Zoe sighed, thinking about the hotel that had become a traditional stopover for them, visiting every year for their anniversary and birthdays.

"Do we have to take Patty with us to keep the stuff fresh?"

Eva was sipping her tea and snorted at Zoe's question, getting tea all over herself as she coughed. Zoe patted her on the back as Eva dissolved into helpless laughter, pulling Zoe into her lap. "Oh God, Zo, please warn me next time you're going to do that!"

Zoe grinned; she knew she was going to get Eva relaxed. The idea of taking the man with them made her chuckle, as well.

"I promise to warn you next time I try and be funny," Zoe promised. "So you want children, huh?"

Eva tightened her hold on her wife and nodded. "Very much."

"That's good, because I can't do it without you."

"I'm sorry, love, I don't mean to be..."

"I know, Evy, you're scared; and I am as well. But, when I was holding little Albert today, it just felt so right. I think you'll make an excellent mother. You're kind and gentle; you can teach them so much."

Eva was touched by Zoe's words. She scooped the small woman up in her arms and gave her a quick kiss, because mere words were inadequate to explain how she felt. They sat cuddling together in silence, listening to the cicadas chirp away in the warm evening.

Eva looked at her watch. Elena and Friedrich were going to the opera and were due to arrive soon to leave their three year old son, Albert, and their two year old daughter, Beth. The two children were adorable. Eva didn't like to play favourites, but little Albert stole her heart. His big brown eyes and the sweet expression on his face won her over. The little boy looked so much like his mother, while his sister resembled their father.

"Elena and Friedrich are going to see Joan Sutherland tonight. I hear she's very good," Eva said just as the doorbell chimed. "That's probably them."

Zoe got off her wife's lap and let the tall woman get up, following her to the front door. "Well, lookee who is here," Zoe cooed and Beth ran to her as soon as Elena put her down. "Hi there," Zoe greeted the young child, who giggled.

Elena smiled fondly at her daughter with her best friend, and then turned as Friedrich put Albert down. The boy attached himself to Eva's leg and looked up, his big brown eyes blinking at her.

"Aunty Eva, up!" Albert demanded imperiously, not at all intimidated by the tall woman. Eva grinned down at him. "Your wish is my command, young man," she said, picking up the boy, who squealed with delight, and settling him on her shoulders.

Zoe looked on and grinned. From what she could see, Eva's fears about being a good mother were unfounded. Albert absolutely adored Eva; the little guy loved to jump on her and go on tall rides, trying to touch the ceiling. Zoe watched her wife making horse noises as she walked around the living room carrying him on her shoulders, then took him outside.

Friedrich followed the pair outside, chuckling.

"I guess I'm going to be stuck with you tonight, little lady," Zoe said to the two year old in her arms, as the child gave her a sloppy, wet kiss.

"So, did you tell her?" Elena asked as she watched Eva's antics outside, holding Albert up to the laundry line and hearing her son's delighted squeals as she let him swing on it.

"Uh...yeth," Zoe tried answering, but Beth had two fingers in Zoe's mouth.

"And?"

"And we're going to be parents," Zoe said as she wiped the little girl's fingers.

"You're going to make great parents, Zo."

"I hope so, El."

"So have you thought about...you know..."

"You still can't say it?" Zoe teased her friend. "It's called sex."

"I know that!" Elena gave her a slap on the behind as Zoe passed her. "Who is it going to be?"

"That's one thing we haven't figured out for certain, but I want him to look like Eva."

Elena wasn't sure her friend could find someone who looked like Eva and would agree to father a child, but who also wouldn't want to have any obligations as a father. "That's a tall order, isn't it?" she asked.

"Yeah, I would like him to be tall," Zoe joked.

Elena shook her head, figuring she had walked into that bad joke. "So are you going to ask Wiggy?"

"Not unless his hair has gone dark. It was still blond the last time I saw him."

"Um...no, is that important?"

"Of course, I want the baby to look like Eva. We're going to ask Patty," Zoe responded. "Pat looks like Eva."

Elena's smile spread across her face. "Have you asked him yet?"

"Not yet."

"Zoe, even if you get Pat to agree, the baby could turn out to have dark hair and green eyes like you. Just look how different Beth and Albert are."

Zoe watched Eva come back in with Albert hanging on, his arms around her neck, and hoped that their children would take after Eva. The secret was to find the right man.

"Mummy, we saw the Big Cross!" Albert cried out to his mother, getting a confused look from her.

"The Southern Cross," Eva mouthed, setting him down. The young boy looked back and gave her a grin.

"Aunty Eva, why don't you have a picture?"

Eva frowned and looked at Elena and Zoe, who both shrugged. "I have lots of pictures."

"Not like mummy's. See the picture on her arm? You don't have one. Maybe Aunty Zoe can paint one for you," Albert said, then went back outside to bring his father in.

"Out of the mouths of babes," Elena said quietly and watched her son jump on Friedrich. "One day we are going to tell him. Friedrich wants to take them to Germany and show them where we came from."

"That would be nice. We're going over there ourselves," Eva said as Zoe put an arm around her waist.

"You're going back home?"

"I'm officially going to be there to replace Richard in the Minister's group."

Elena turned to Zoe. "So it's true, huh?"

Zoe nodded and chuckled as Eva rolled her eyes as she realised yet another person was aware of the rumours she had never even heard.

"So, where will you go?"

"We're going to Greece, Germany, Italy, and France. Can you housesit until we get back?" Eva asked.

"I don't see why not," Elena said, looking down at her watch. "Oh, we're going to be late!" She leaned outside and called to Friedrich, who came in with Albert attached to his leg.

"Thank you for babysitting tonight," Friedrich said as Albert ran over and attached himself to Eva.

"Don't worry about it, good practice," Eva replied, taking Albert on another ride around the living room.

"Huh?" Friedrich said, looking at Elena.

"I'll tell you later. Come on, Mr Jacobs, we're going to be late."

They said their good-byes, and Zoe closed the door then took Beth in her arms. Albert's squeals brought a smile to her face.

"Aunty Eva, let's go and see the Big Cross again!" Albert said, tugging on Eva's hair.

Eva gave Zoe a grin as she took the young boy outside to gaze at the stars.

Chapter
3

Debbie sat at her desk and looked up at the wall clock for the third time in as many minutes. Eva was late coming back from a meeting, and the man inside her office was not going to be at all pleased. She was about to pick up the telephone handset when the door opened and the tall deputy director walked in with a stack of files in her arms.

"Eva! I am so glad you're back!" Debbie exclaimed as she went to her side.

Eva smiled. "Nice to see you, too, Debbie," she joked. "What's up?"

"He's in there!" Debbie whispered to her.

Eva looked at her office and then back at Debbie. "Who?" she whispered back.

"The Foreign Affairs and Immigration Minister!" Debbie hissed. She picked some stray lint off Eva's jacket, straightened it, and took the files from her.

Eva looked on, bemused at her flustered assistant. "Really?"

"Yesss, now go in there. He's been waiting for half an hour!" Debbie turned her towards the door and pushed. She let out a relieved sigh when Eva entered her office.

Eva entered to find Richard, the Foreign Affairs and Immigration Minister, Percy Hester, and his assistant gazing at her photographs on the wall. On hearing the door open, they turned.

The Minister was a portly man, quite short, with a shock of black hair which Eva assumed was a very bad toupee. She resisted the urge to straighten it. His black framed glasses were perched on the tip of his nose, and he gazed at her from over the top of them.

"Ah, Eva, you're back," Richard said as the Minister looked up at her with a grim smile.

"You are a tall one, aren't you?" Hester said as he took over Eva's chair and sat down. He had heard a great deal about this woman and was eager to meet her. *She is quite a good looking woman*, he thought to himself. *A bit on the tall side.* But it was her eyes that captivated him. He did like his women a little shorter, but those blue eyes were quite enticing. He mentally shook himself from his admiration of the young woman who pulled up one of the visitor's chairs and sat down.

"Sir, this is Eva Haralambos. Eva, this is the Minister, Mr Percy Hester."

Eva stopped herself from grinning. The Minister's first name reminded her of the old icebox that Zoe had nicknamed Percy and would occasionally kick when it failed to work properly. She wondered if the Minister ever needed the same treatment. His surname gave Zoe the giggles every time Elena mentioned him. It wasn't until Zoe had explained what it meant in Greek that Elena had understood her friend's reaction to it. Eva hoped Zoe wouldn't laugh when she met the man on their trip.

"I think she figured that out, Richard," the Minister grumbled, motioning for the director to sit down.

"Pleased to meet you, sir," Eva said, gazing at the Minister. She also smiled at the young man sitting next to her, who, she assumed, was the assistant.

The young man gave her huge smile. "Hi, I'm Michael Kremer." Michael extended his hand. Eva smiled back at him and shook his hand.

"Michael, I think you can do the meet and greet later, okay?" Hester said impatiently as he placed his hands on top of a file in front of him.

"Yes, sir." The young man gave Eva a tiny smile and turned his attention back to his notebook, his dark hair falling into his eyes.

Percy Hester took off his glasses and used his handkerchief to clean them while he stared at Eva. "So, Miss Haralambos, Richard tells me you are going to be taking his place on my team. As you know, this is going to be a very sensitive mission."

"Yes, sir."

"As it is of such a delicate nature, I need to get to know you a little better, both personally and professionally. We need to work as a team, and I don't like surprises. It would be very embarrassing to find out when I'm in Germany that you were a Nazi or some other silly thing like that. I understand you have been working here for four years?"

Eva nodded.

"You're not a Nazi, are you?" Hester asked, hoping she wasn't since her file indicated that she would make a great addition to his staff.

"No, sir, I never joined the Nazi party."

"Oh, that's good. I've heard a lot of good things about you, and I hope by the end of this little chat you will be able to join my staff for the duration of our tour. Now," the Minister opened a file on the desk, which Eva assumed was her personnel record, "you are German, yes?"

"No, sir, I'm Greek."

Puzzled, the Minister rechecked the fact sheet in front of him. "You were born in Vienna and raised in Berlin, were you not?"

"Yes, sir."

"Then you're German," he concluded.

Eva did not feel it was her responsibility to educate the Minister on the nuances of being Austrian-born but considered German, so she sat back with a neutral expression on her face. "No sir, I'm Greek. I was born in Vienna of Greek parentage," Eva replied. She was beginning to dislike the boorish man.

The Minister snorted–much to Eva's surprise. "Your accent is German."

"I grew up in Germany."

"You are German when we go to Germany, and you will be Greek when we go to Greece. Do you want to be Italian when we go to Italy?" Hester laughed as Richard and Michael smiled weakly. Both men were used to the crude humour of the man. Eva sat there with a frown on her face. "You have no sense of humour, Miss Haralambos? No need to answer. I've never met a Kraut with a sense of humour yet." He gazed at her for a few moments.

Eva's dislike of the man increased with the racist taunt. She was going to have a hard time dealing with the Minister, but she would have to if she wished to go on this trip.

"So, what were you doing during the war?"

"I was in Larissa in Greece with my stepfather, Major Hans Muller of the Germany army," Eva replied. She never lied about her whereabouts during the war; when she was asked, she told the truth.

"Hmm...the Communist Resistance movement was operating in Larissa in 1944. Are you a Communist, Miss Haralambos?"

Eva was furious at the questioning. The Minister sat back in the chair looking at her over his glasses, which annoyed her even more. She took a deep breath and calmed down. It wasn't going to help to get angry and lose her job. "No, sir. I've voted Liberal since I was eligible to vote."

"Really?"

"Yes."

"Hmm...who is your local Member of Parliament, Miss Haralambos?"

Eva wanted to grin. Zoe had gathered information on all the candidates in the last Federal election, and they'd debated the merits and policies until they decided they were going to both vote Conservative. Their local Member was the man sitting in front of her, and she was sure the Minister was aware of where she lived, since it was listed quite prominently in her file. She made a mental note to herself that in the next election she was going to vote for someone other than the man in front of her.

"You are, sir," Eva replied.

Hester grinned for the first time since Eva had walked in. "So I am. Fancy that," he chuckled. "I see you are a stickler for detail," Hester said, thinking of her responses to his previous questions. Then, looking down at Eva's file laid out in front of him, he added, "And you are an honest person. I like that." Hester made a show of reading the file in front of him. "I have a report here from the War Crimes Tribunal investigators that you were involved in Resistance activities during the war...hmm?"

Eva pursed her lips. She wasn't sure whether she should answer or sit there.

"Well? You were involved in the Resistance?"

"Yes, sir."

"You were working against the Germans?"

"Yes, sir."

"Hmm." The Minister took off his glasses and twirled them in his hand. "Why?"

"I hated the policies of the Nazi party."

"I see. So if you don't like the policies of the Australian government, based on your actions during the war, you will also work against the interests of Australia?"

Richard was horrified at the Minister's question, as was Michael who sat stunned, his pen frozen over the notebook. He turned to the woman next to him who had a very calm expression on her face.

Eva was shocked by the question, but showed no outward sign of her surprise. "I would if the Australian government sanctioned genocide," Eva replied quietly. Michael hid a grin as he noted her reply.

Hester nodded his head. He wasn't quite sure how to respond to that, so he decided to leave it. "Would you have a problem with dealing with the German government?"

"No, sir. They are not Nazis, as far as I know."

"Yes, that's quite true," Hester replied. "Do you have a boyfriend, Miss Haralambos?"

Eva looked at Richard for a moment. She didn't think she was going to get the sack for revealing her relationship with Zoe, but anything was possible with the racist, arrogant Minister in front of her. "No, sir, I don't. I'm married."

"Oh? Your file says you are single. Which is it? Married or single?"

"I'm married to a woman, sir."

"Really?" Hester's eyebrows shot up. He was really enjoying himself. He was quite taken by the woman's honesty, even if she was a Greek Kraut. He had known about her so-called marriage to this Zoe woman through the reports he had obtained. He was surprised when he first read the reports, not expecting a beautiful young woman to be a homosexual. From the various police enquiries he had commissioned, he found out she was a devout Greek Orthodox woman who was honest and trustworthy. He had decided to overlook her sexual preference.

"Yes, sir. We've been married for almost 5 years," Eva replied, unconsciously twisting the ring on her finger.

"Zoe Lambros, correct?" Hester continued the questioning. "Hmm, she's Greek?"

"Yes, sir. Zoe was born in Larissa."

"Is she as tall as you?" The Minister grinned, knowing the answer since he had seen photographs that had been taken by the federal police. He was a thorough man, not leaving anything to chance, or as his wife called him–a super perfectionist.

Eva refrained from telling him that Zoe was taller than him. "No, she's quite petite."

"Hmm. Did she have a problem with you being the step-daughter of the Nazi commander?"

Eva looked at the Minister and angled her head a little to the left, a slight smile playing on her lips. "With all due respect, sir, that's none of your business."

The Minister was taken aback and coughed. It was a question that had come to him when he was reviewing the files, and she was right, it had nothing to do with the line of questioning he was pursuing, but he was curious. He chose to overlook the woman's remark. "For security purposes, is Miss Lambros–"

"It's Haralambos," Eva corrected him. Zoe had changed her name to Haralambos three years earlier, a loving gesture by her wife which touched Eva a great deal. "She changed her name three years ago."

"Ah. Why?"

"She thought we should share the same last name."

"Oh, how quaint. Just like normal married couples, huh?" The Minister chuckled. Eva didn't bother telling him her marriage was as normal to her as anyone else's union, since it would simply be a waste of time and breath. "Is Zoe Haralambos a Communist?"

Eva wanted to roll her eyes. It seemed that the Minister was fixated on Larissa being a Communist stronghold. "No, sir. She voted for you as well," Eva replied. She was going to tell Zoe about this interrogation, just to see her reaction to it.

"Am I going to meet your little woman?" Hester found the punning in his question extremely funny and chuckled.

Eva wondered if Zoe would be able to keep her temper with the man long enough to last the entire flight. She hoped she wouldn't have to restrain her wife from hitting him, because she was close to doing that herself. "Yes, sir. Zoe would like to come with me. I understand we'll be going to Larissa?"

Hester looked up at his assistant.

"Athens, Larissa, and Salonika, then we head to Italy."

"Thessaloniki," Eva corrected him.

Michael looked down at his notes. "Yeah, that place," he said, giving her a grin.

"Excellent. I look forward to meeting Zoe."

"I know she's looking forward to meeting you, sir," Eva

replied and restrained herself from chuckling out loud. Zoe and Hester in the same room—it could get ugly.

"Did you take the photographs?" the Minister asked, watching the young woman look instinctively up to her pictures.

"Yes, sir. I'm a photographer."

"You're very good. What about the paintings?"

"Thank you, the paintings were done by Zoe. She is an accomplished artist and works for the New South Wales Art Gallery." Eva wanted to tell him more about her wife's talent, but she was quite sure he didn't really want to know.

"Nice," the Minister grumbled and made a show of looking through the file. "I think everything is in order. I do like your honesty, Miss Haralambos. It's very...refreshing." Hester got up and tugged down his vest that had inched up his large belly. "Richard, I want to see the paperwork on my desk by tomorrow."

"Yes, sir," Richard replied as he opened the door to let the Minister pass.

The portly politician turned to Eva as they approached Debbie's desk. "If your language skills are on par with your honesty, Miss Haralambos, then I'm happy to have you on my team." He turned and left the office, followed by Michael and Richard.

Eva let out a frustrated sigh and sat on the edge of Debbie's desk as the door closed.

"So, how did it go with the mouth-from-the-south?"

"Does 'getting hit by a semi-trailer and living' mean anything?" Eva replied with a grin.

Debbie grinned in return. "Want a cup of tea to aid your recovery?"

"That would be nice, thank you. Black, no sugar," Eva muttered. "You know what, Debbie? I don't blame Mrs Hester if she is having an affair." She shook her head and headed back to her office to recover.

Debbie gave her a bemused look. "Hey, Eva, why does Zoe giggle every time I mention the Minister?"

Eva turned around and grinned. "Hester is a Greek word."

"Yeah? What does it mean?"

Eva looked up at the ceiling for a moment, trying to suppress a giggle. "Well, if I tell you, you won't be able to speak to him with a straight face."

"Oh, go on!" Debbie urged.

"It means 'to shit on,'" Eva replied going back into her office, accompanied by the shrieks of laughter coming from her assistant.

"He said what?" Zoe hitched herself up on her elbow. She had been lying on the warm sand enjoying the cooler breeze that was blowing after another hot day. Eva was sitting on a low beach chair, her long legs stretched out catching the last rays of the sun as it set. They'd decided to forgo having dinner at home, so they'd packed the car and headed for the beach to enjoy the warm evening. Eva took a sip of her Coke as she ate the last remaining hot chips in the rolled up newspaper.

"He wanted to know if I was a Communist," Eva replied, licking her fingers. She opened her eyes to see Zoe's incredulous look.

"*You*? A Communist?" Zoe started to laugh. "The man's an idiot." She put her head back down and watched a few more clouds drift by.

"He also asked me if I had a boyfriend." Zoe snorted. "I told him I was married." Eva watched Zoe's eyes open and look up with a twinkle in her emerald coloured eyes.

"Did his toupee spin around on his head?"

"No, I didn't see it spin around." Eva grinned. "I wanted to straighten it though."

"What did he say?"

"He wanted to know if you were a Communist."

Zoe laughed. "He's got a one track mind...or maybe no mind. Are you sure we voted for him?"

"Yep, we voted for him."

"Remind me next time to vote for the Vegemite Only party," Zoe joked as she reached for more chips and discovered they were gone. "Hey, no more chips!"

"Sorry, I ate them," Eva replied. "I'm a growing girl."

Zoe gazed at her partner and grinned. "You certainly are."

"I think I ate too much." Eva grimaced and let out a button on her shorts.

"You want help with the rest of the buttons?" Zoe waggled her eyebrows.

Eva gave her wife a grin. "Yeah, I think I'd like some exercise."

Zoe looked up from where she lay and grinned back. "Here?"

"Yeah," Eva replied, deliberately not looking down at her smirking wife. "Want to?"

Zoe looked around the beach–which was still packed with people–and raised an eyebrow. She watched as Eva got up from the chair and stretched her tall body, making quite a show of it for Zoe's benefit, but also catching the attention of the teenaged boy nearby.

She extended her hand to Zoe and pulled her up. "Want to go for a walk, Mrs Haralambos?" Eva whispered.

"You are a wicked, wicked woman," Zoe replied, giving her wife a quick kiss.

"That's why you love me." Eva held her for a few moments, getting some stares from the people nearby, which she ignored.

"I knew there was a reason." Zoe playfully slapped her on the bum as they picked up the rubbish and placed it in the nearby bin. Leaving their towels near the chairs, Eva took Zoe's hand and they walked down to the shoreline. The setting sun created a crimson glow in the sky as the two women strolled along the water's edge, occasionally stopping to pick up a seashell.

Chapter
4

Zoe struggled to open her eyes as a noise invaded her sleep. Opening sleepy emerald eyes, she grimaced over Eva's bare shoulder at the clock. It was an ungodly hour to be woken on a Saturday. Another knock, this time more insistent, made Zoe growl with frustration.

She cuddled up against Eva's back, noting the touch of sunburn from their sun worshipping the previous afternoon. She warned her partner she was going to get burnt, but Eva wanted to get a tan. What she got was a pink hue instead. Zoe made a mental note to get the aloe vera to gently massage into her wife's back when they got rid of whoever was outside that door. She rested her cheek on the warm skin, giving the shoulder a kiss and putting her arm around her wife's waist. Zoe debated with herself about letting whoever it was stand outside and wait until they realised no one was going to get out of bed to come and answer the blasted door.

"Zo, what day is it?" Eva mumbled, turning slightly to see a scowling Zoe.

"It's Saturday. Go back to sleep."

"Okay." Eva closed her eyes, only to open them again when she heard the knocking. She winced a bit as she moved and the sunburn made her shoulders and back a little tender. "I think I got sunburnt."

"Your back is quite pink," Zoe informed her. "Are you warm?"

"Yeah, feels like I've got a heatpack back there."

"Nah, just sunburn. I'll get some aloe vera later to cool it down."

"Thanks, love," Eva murmured and curled up again, wanting to have a sleep-in. "Zo, I think someone is at the door."

"Yeah, I know," Zoe muttered under her breath. She gave Eva's shoulder a kiss before getting out of bed. "I hope it's not a salesman, or he is going to wish he hadn't gotten out of bed himself."

"I'll pray for him," Eva mumbled, closing her eyes and letting a smile play over her lips. She liked their arrangement of letting Zoe handle salesmen. What her partner lacked in height, she made up for in a no-nonsense attitude that scared most of the salesmen that knocked on their door. They were lulled into a false sense of security when they caught sight of the diminutive Zoe. That illusion was soon shattered, and they never came back.

Zoe padded out of the bedroom closing the door. She belted her robe and walked slowly to the door. Opening it, she found Earl standing there in overalls with a toolbox under his arm.

"Morning, sunshine," Earl greeted his friend and ruffled her hair as Zoe ushered him inside.

"It's not that I'm not glad to see you, but...*it's Saturday*!" Zoe growled.

Earl grinned. "Sorry, mate, but Eva asked me to see why the car was making funny noises."

"The car is making funny noises?" Zoe asked, running her hands through her hair.

"Yep, that's what she said," he reported as he put the toolbox down. "'Earl, the car is making funny noises.'" Earl tried to imitate Eva's accent, which only got Zoe giggling. "She's not in bed, is she?"

"Yep."

Earl grimaced, knowing how much they valued sleeping in on the weekends since they usually got up early on the weekdays. "I'm sorry, mate, I really am but she did ask me to come 'round."

"I believe you. I'll go and tell her to get her bum out here."

Earl watched as Zoe walked back to their bedroom. Zoe was a grouch in the morning, but Eva was even worse when she wanted to sleep in. He once knocked on their door at 5:00 a.m.

and got a very surly Eva at the door. She wasn't at all happy to be woken on a cold and foggy morning.

Zoe sighed and went back inside. She watched Eva sleeping for a moment, wishing she could join her. Going to Eva's side, she sat on the bed and leaned down. "Evy, Earl is here."

"Tell him to go away," Eva mumbled.

Zoe grinned and let her finger trace Eva's sunburnt cheek. Her face had a pink colour to it that matched the shade on her back. "He says you called him about the car."

Eva opened one sleepy blue eye and gazed at her wife. "The car?"

"Yeah, you know–that thing that goes vroom vroom. It's making funny noises."

Zoe got a lopsided grin from her wife at the description of their car, which had no name as yet since Zoe hadn't had time to bestow one on it.

"Argh...uh oh yeah, it was rattling." Eva remembered the noise the car had made as it went up a hill. It didn't sound normal and, since she knew nothing about cars, she'd called Earl to come and look at it.

"Well, he's here."

"Hmm," Eva mumbled.

Zoe leaned down and blew into Eva's ear. "Evy, get up."

"It's Saturday," she whined and gave her wife a pout that made Zoe giggle. Eva tossed the sheet off her body and slowly got up. Her long legs swung off of the bed, and her feet hit the floor. The coolness of the floorboards was a stark contrast to the heat in her face and back.

"Do we have some aloe around?" she asked as she scrunched up her face and felt it tighten.

"Yep, I'll cool you down when Earl leaves."

"Cool me down or heat me up?" Eva looked up at her wife with a smirk.

"Depends on whether you behave yourself," Zoe replied, hauling her partner to her feet.

"Promises, promises. Do I get anything for misbehaving?" Eva leaned down and whispered into her wife's ear. She got a slap on her bare bottom as she passed by to put on some clothes. Zoe admired her wife for a moment as Eva took out a pair of khaki coloured pants and matching shirt from the wardrobe.

"Aren't you lucky you haven't got a sunburnt bum?" Zoe teased as she put her hands over her wife's behind and squeezed, getting a little yelp from her partner.

"Zoe, Earl is here!"

"Yeah, I know," Zoe said as she took over buttoning her wife's shirt. She smiled and pulled Eva down for a quick kiss. "As long as he's here, are we going to talk to Earl about the baby?" Since they had known him the longest, they had decided to ask him to approach Pat with their request.

"Hmm, yeah. You want to get dressed first?" Eva asked, and untied Zoe's robe, pulling the garment off her partner's petite body and letting it fall to the floor. Eva put her arms around Zoe's bare waist and picked her up for a quick kiss. "Easier than leaning down," she whispered in her ear as she set Zoe back down.

"Oh, I liked that."

"Let's go and speak to Earl, and then you have a date with me, aloe, and my sunburn."

"I get to have my hands on you, I like that idea." Zoe grinned and watched as Eva picked up a brush and left the bedroom chuckling.

Earl sat on the sofa, his long legs stretched out, waiting for his friends to come out. He looked up when he heard the door open. Eva walked out, brushing her short dark hair.

"Morning, Earl," Eva greeted him and beckoned him into the kitchen.

"Hey, what happened to you?" Earl asked as he cupped Eva's face with his hand.

"Me. Sun. No protection. Sun won," Eva replied getting a chuckle out of her friend. "I didn't think the afternoon sun would be so hot."

"Yeah, well the sun does like fair skin like yours, so you're easily burnt. Is it just your face?"

"Nah, my back and shoulders, too. They feel really tight. Want some breakfast?"

"Are you cooking?" Earl joked, knowing Eva had indeed started to cook a bit and was quite good at it, but that didn't stop him from teasing her. He got a dirty look and a head shake in response.

"Hey, Wiggy," Zoe bounced into the kitchen.

"Ah, she wakens. Sorry I got you two out of bed."

"I forgive you, my friend, but don't do it again, or else," Zoe joked and looked up at Eva, giving her a little head shake.

Earl watched the two of them for a moment. "Okay, what's

up?"

"My car is making funny noises," Eva replied as she turned to take the kettle off the fire.

"Uh huh, and what?" Earl was suspicious. He was certain that the car did indeed need repairing of some sort, but there was something else going on.

Eva made the tea quietly as Zoe set the table, leaving Earl in the kitchen scratching his head. "Will you two tell me what's going on?"

"Eva and I are going to Europe. Eva's on the Minister's team," Zoe babbled and looked up as Eva walked out of the kitchen with the tea and muffins.

"That's nice." Earl was confused as to why his friends would be so secretive about this news. "And this is important for some reason, right?"

"We were going to bring up something that we wanted to discuss with you later when we got back, but, uhm..." Zoe looked at Eva and shrugged. She sat down and took her cup of tea.

"Uh huh, go on." Earl took a sip of his tea and was quite startled when Eva took it from him. "You two are acting weird."

Eva sat next to Zoe and took her hand. "Zoe and I have decided to become parents."

Earl looked at Eva and then Zoe with a puzzled expression on his face. "Unless I didn't pay attention when my father told me about the birds and the bees, that's impossible, unless you adopt. You're going to adopt, right?"

"No." Eva shook her head and noticed Zoe's hold on her hand got a little tighter. They had discussed this at length the previous night and tried to come up with the best way to ask Earl to discuss the matter with Pat. It was a convoluted way of dealing with it. Eva wanted to ask Pat directly, but Zoe felt shy about approaching their friend.

"You mean you're going to have sex with a bloke?" Earl's voice rose as his eyebrows went straight up in total surprise.

"Calm down, Earl, you're going to burst a blood vessel or something." Eva turned to Zoe and gave a small smile. "Well, um...would you consider helping us out?" Eva got a little flushed herself since it was a topic they hadn't discussed before with their friend. Judging by the look on Earl's face when he realised what Eva was asking of him, she wondered if he would have a stroke. His face was dark red, which didn't go well with his blond hair.

"You want *me* to have sex with *you*?" Earl squeaked out. The idea scared him half to death.

Eva and Zoe looked at each other with matching startled looks. Eva turned to her friend who was now so red she feared he was going to pass out.

"Calm down, Earl! We don't want you to have sex with anyone," Eva tried to soothe him.

Earl let out a deep breath and sagged against the sofa. "Jesus, girls, you are going to kill me one day!"

"I know it's not something you get asked about every day but, um...you are our friend..." Zoe found her voice and didn't look up.

Eva looked at her wife for a moment, she squeezed Zoe's hand. "It's okay." Eva whispered to her and kissed her gently. This was one side of Zoe's personality she found endearing. "Earl, we need to ask you if you can do us a favour."

"If it doesn't involve having sex with either of you, I can move mountains." Earl ran his fingers through his blond hair. He took a deep breath and let it out slowly before turning his attention back to them. "Look, girls, you really blindsided me."

"Well, we didn't know how else to go about it," Eva offered.

"What do you need from me?"

"Pat," Eva said with a grin.

"My Pat?"

"Your Pat," Zoe nodded.

"Uh," Earl scratched his head and took a gulp of the tea, then let out a relieved sigh when the doorbell rang. "That must be Pat." Earl muttered with relief. He had almost forgotten that he'd asked his partner to come over after he'd had a chance to wake the two women.

Earl got up and walked over to the door and opened it. Patrick Davis was Earl's partner of four years. A tall, broad shouldered young man with wavy black hair, piercing blue eyes and an adorable dimple in his chin. When he'd met Pat, Earl had finally understood why Zoe found Eva's dimpled chin so sexy. Pat reminded Earl of Kirk Douglas—with all the charm and without the American accent. They had met at a dinner party hosted by his two friends when they first moved into the house and invited their neighbours to the housewarming party.

Pat came inside and gave his partner a quick kiss. He was dressed much the same way as Earl, in overalls, but he didn't have a shirt on. Earl admired him for a few seconds, giving him a grin. Pat followed Earl into the living room where he noticed the tension between the friends.

Pat turned to Earl and shook his finger at him. "I told you not to wake them!"

"Nah, it's not that...we were discussing something a bit delicate," Earl muttered as he took a sip of his now cold tea.

"Oh yeah? Anything I can help with?"

Earl snorted the tea and inhaled it up his nose, giving him a coughing fit as Eva patted him on the back. Zoe went into the laundry to get the mop to wipe up the spilt tea.

"What did I say?" Pat looked around the room at his friends.

"Sit down," Earl muttered as Zoe mopped around him. She gave him a slap on the shoulder in passing. "The girls want to have a baby."

"Uh huh." Pat nodded.

"And they asked me if I wanted to help them out."

"Uh huh."

"They want me to ask you if you can help them out with having a baby."

Eva rolled her eyes at the indelicate way Earl sprang the news on the dark-haired man.

"Uh huh." Pat continued to nod.

"Is that all you can say?" Earl said to his partner, who grinned.

"Sure. I'd be happy to help out, if that's what you want." Pat looked up and met Eva's eyes and gave her a huge grin. Zoe leaned against the laundry door with her mouth open in total surprise.

Eva looked at Zoe, who was now grinning. She joined Eva and they both sat down opposite the two men. "Uh...yes, if you're sure you're willing."

"Sure, it's not as if I'm going to get Earl pregnant, am I?" Pat laughed and slapped Earl on the shoulder. "Might as well let the little guys have some fun."

A gentle breeze blew through the open window as Eva sighed contently. She was stretched out on their bed enjoying the soothing aloe that was being spread across her back by Zoe's gentle hands. Hands that were doing wonderful things to her back, she mused to herself.

"Hmm, this is nice."

"I'm enjoying it," Zoe grinned. It was indeed a nice view from where she was. Her wife was naked and in bed. Eva's broad shoulders still had the pink tinge to them. Zoe gently applied the soothing lotion as her thoughts turned to their most unusual morning after they'd gotten through the initial tense moment with Earl. Zoe thought Pat's offer was perfect. She had such a definite idea in her mind of what she wanted her children to look like. She knew the children might not have dark hair and blue eyes, that they could look like her, but she'd set her heart on wanting Eva to feel like she had a part in it all. Zoe rested her hands on Eva's lower back and daydreamed about little dark-haired children with blue eyes.

Eva twisted around when Zoe's hands stopped. "Zo, are you all right?"

"Oh yeah!" Zoe leaned down and gave her wife a kiss before Eva settled back down. "Evy, what do you think our kids would look like?"

"With you as their mother, gorgeous," Eva mumbled. She smiled to herself. She hoped that their baby would have green eyes and that chestnut colouring.

Zoe continued the massage in silence, her mind wandering to the conversation she'd had with Stacey, the woman she had met at the art gallery who had a child with her partner. She advised Zoe to get Eva to adopt any children they were going to have in case anything happened to her and Eva had to raise the children. Under the current law, Eva would not be able to get custody of the children unless she was their legal guardian. It scared Zoe. With all the excitement with Earl and Pat, she had forgotten about the conversation she'd had with Stacey.

"Zo, what's the matter?" Eva turned around fully to find Zoe with a very thoughtful look on her face. She opened her arms and Zoe settled down next to her, her hand resting on Eva's flat stomach.

"What are you worried about, love?" Eva stroked Zoe's face and turned her towards her.

"I want you to adopt them," Zoe blurted out, not knowing how she was going to bring up the subject. Zoe rested her head on Eva's shoulder. "I've been thinking about this, and if any-thing happened to me-"

"Nothing is going to happen to you," Eva reassured her, not

quite knowing where Zoe's mind was going.

"Evy, by law, if anything happened, you wouldn't have any rights. They could take our babies away from you."

Eva closed her eyes and sighed. "I know. I think we need to talk to Friedrich about getting some of the paperwork done."

"Can Friedrich draw up the papers?"

"He's a solicitor, so he would be the one to go to. I trust Friedrich, unless you had someone else in mind?"

Zoe shook her head. "Do you think adopting our babies is a good idea?"

"It's an excellent idea, Zo," Eva agreed.

"It scares me to think that if anything happened to me, you would not be allowed to raise our children." Zoe traced a finger around Eva's bellybutton and sighed. "It's not right, Evy. The law is wrong."

"I know, love, but there isn't anything we can do about it."

"That's wrong. Stacey–"

"Who's Stacey?"

"She's the woman that had the baby...remember, I told you about her yesterday?"

Eva nodded.

"Well, she told me that if anything happened to her, then the children become wards of the state and her partner doesn't have a say in their children's upbringing. That's the law. It stinks." Zoe was disgusted by that law when she'd heard about it, and couldn't believe how narrowminded and uncaring the laws were. "But if they were adopted by her partner, then she is the legal guardian. Stacey was telling me that we don't have any rights under the law!"

"Well, they don't recognise same sex marriages," Eva murmured, knowing that particular subject was one of Zoe's pet hates.

"That is so unjust. My love for you is real," Zoe whispered and put her head down. "My marriage to you is real; and the law is wrong, it should be changed."

"Zoe, I think, in time, the law will be changed. It won't happen soon, but it will happen. In the meantime, we know we love each other, we are married in God's eyes, and that's all that matters. Did you know that in 1936 Jewish weddings were not seen as legal in Germany?"

Zoe looked up, startled. Eva seldom talked about Germany or Hitler if she could avoid it. It was a subject that just was too painful to speak about. "Weren't they?"

Eva shook her head. "No, but that didn't stop the Jewish couples from getting married in the eyes of God. They were married, but they didn't have the blessing of the state with a piece of paper saying they were legally married. All that mattered was that they made the commitment to each other and to God. They didn't need Hitler's approval."

"But it would be nice to be able to declare that I'm Mrs Haralambos," she said wistfully.

Eva stroked Zoe's chestnut coloured hair and smiled. "Zoe, sometimes we can't have everything the way we want it. Our children will be able to grow up and marry anyone they want."

"Speaking of children...do you want to practice?" Zoe invited quietly, as she rolled on top of Eva's long body and stared into her wife's eyes, letting her finger trace Eva's strong profile and settle on the dimpled chin.

"Practice what?" Eva asked, meeting twinkling emerald eyes.

"Making babies," Zoe replied, entangling her fingers in Eva's dark hair. She leaned down and kissed her wife, who responded by scooping her smaller body closer. "I want to spend the rest of my life loving you and our children," Zoe whispered as she nuzzled Eva's neck.

"Uh huh," Eva replied, letting her hands roam over Zoe's shirt. "Zo?"

Zoe looked up. She grinned when she saw Eva's frustrated glare. "Hmm?"

"Off!" Her wife demanded, tugging at the shirt.

"Yes, ma'am!" Zoe said as a grin spread across her face. She slowly unbuttoned her shirt and watched Eva's eyes turn a darker shade of blue with desire.

Eva brought her wife down for a long and sensual kiss as she removed Zoe's shirt and tossed it away. "Let's make babies," Eva whispered.

Chapter
5

"Hit it out of the park!" Earl yelled at the top of his voice, leaning over the fence.

The cricket game was underway on the lush green oval. The woman standing on the outfield next to the fence gave Earl a dirty look before turning her attention back to the game. Earl sat down and watched the bowler steam in and bowl an ineffectual ball, which went wide off the crease. The ball was nowhere near where the batsman might have hit it, and therefore the umpire ruled it a "no ball." The fielding team wasn't happy, nor was the bowler who had to bowl the ball again.

The umpire indicated another no ball, and Earl groaned. "Sheilas can't bowl," he grumbled to Friedrich, who was seated next to him in shorts and a cotton singlet.

Dressed in a long sleeved, lightweight shirt, khaki pants, and wearing a hat on her head, Eva sat back enjoying Earl's outbursts more than the game. The looks he was getting from the woman near the boundary were getting fiercer. Eva had grown to love the game through osmosis. Zoe talked about it, Eva went along to watch her practice, and they listened to the game on the radio–so it was a natural evolution. By the way Earl was behaving, she had some idea that the bowler was not very good and the fielding team was hopeless.

They had come to watch Zoe bat on her debut as a batsman

for the Waratahs. The Waratahs were a women's cricket team that played in a league with other teams from New South Wales and around Australia. Zoe worked hard and had been overjoyed to be selected for the team.

"I swear my grandmother can bowl better than that, and she's dead!" Earl continued the tirade against the bowling team.

The fielder had had enough of the abuse and stalked over to the fence. "Listen you, galah, knock it off!"

Earl stood to his full height and glared at the woman. "If your bowler knew how to bowl–"

"Do you know who her brother is?"

"Do I bloody care who her brother is?"

"Harold Larwood, you windbag!"

Earl stood, put his hand up to his mouth in shock. "Oh my God, now I *know* she stinks to buggery!" he guffawed, much to the disgust of the fielder who trudged back to her place. Earl chuckled.

"Who's Harold Larwood?" Eva asked, watching the woman stalk off.

"A cheat," Earl grumbled.

"Uh huh, that tells me a lot," Eva mumbled, watching the bowler steam in again.

"England was trying to win the Ashes–"

"Ashes?"

"Goes back to one of the first matches Australia played against England. England lost, and someone wrote an obituary in the paper and then they had an urn, in which they burned a stump and called it 'The Ashes.' Australia plays England for the right to hold the Ashes."

"Uh huh," Eva nodded. She'd half listened to the radio one day while gardening and remembered Zoe getting excited over a game. Her wife was screaming about the "Ashes."

"The Don, well–"

"Back up, who is 'The Don'?" Eva asked, only to have Friedrich and Earl look at her in shock.

"Don Bradman," Earl said reverently. His hero, the man he called Poetry in Motion. "The greatest cricketer of all time, my dear girl. The man with a batting average of 99.99, where mere men couldn't average 65; the man who could hit a ball with such skill he made it look too easy. The Don."

Eva grinned. Zoe had talked about him, but she never heard of him referred to as The Don before.

"Oh, Zoe has mentioned him."

Earl rolled his eyes. "Eva, think of the best photographer you know about."

Eva didn't have to think too hard. Only one name sprang to her mind, Marianne Breslauer, a truly talented photographer whose work took Eva's breath away. "Marianne Breslauer," Eva simply said. "A true artist."

"Yeah, well Don Bradman is the BEST. In 1933, the English didn't know how to beat him, so they devised a plan where the bowler would bowl a ball that would swing into the body of the batsman. It was brutal to watch, and one man was lethal at it."

"Harold Larwood," Eva guessed.

"Yep, Harold Larwood. He was a fast bowler that steamed in and sent down balls that were aimed at the batsman's head. A few got hit in the head by it. They won the Ashes that year, all because of that disgusting tactic."

"Right, and the woman out there is Harold Larwood's sister?"

"Yep."

Eva shook her head. While they were talking, the batsman got out and boos by the small crowd indicated it wasn't a good decision by the umpire. Eva turned to see the next batsman head out of the dressing rooms, followed by Zoe who was dressed in white, her legs covered by the cream colored batting pads. She sat nervously next to the gate, her bat being used as a prop under her chin. Eva excused herself and went to Zoe's side.

"Hi there." Eva greeted her partner and tapped her on the leg.

Zoe looked up nervously. "Hi, I think I'm going to be sick."

"Nah, don't worry, you'll do fine," she reassured her wife. She wanted to give her a cuddle, but there were too many people around. Eva had another idea, which would work to make her partner relax before heading out. "Zo, you know what fair maidens used to do for their knights before a big battle?"

"Have sex," Zoe mumbled, watching the bowler start her run up to the crease.

Eva smiled. "Well, after that. They used to tie something of theirs to the knight's weapon, for good luck."

"Yeah."

"Hmm," Eva removed a gold pendent she wore around her neck and placed it around Zoe's neck. "There you go, my dear knight, go slay some cricket balls," Eva whispered to her.

Zoe looked down at the pendant and grinned. Before she had a chance to reply, the crowd shouted, alerting them that another batsman was out and it was Zoe's turn.

"Thank you, my fair maiden," Zoe whispered before getting up and opening the gate.

Eva grinned as she watched Zoe slowly make her way to the center of the oval for her debut, one hand around the pendant and the other holding the cricket bat.

"Yes! No! Yes!" Alice screamed as she flew down the pitch to get to the other side, the safe side where she didn't have to face the fast bowler. The stop-start fits were driving Zoe ,nuts as she grounded her bat, put her head down, and raced to get to the crease before the ball hit the stumps. She had barely made it back when she felt the ball hit her in the back, wincing as the hard red ball made contact. She dropped the bat in pain and doubled up, waiting for the ache to subside. Alice came running over from the other side of the pitch to help her if needed.

Eva was furious. She had watched the bowler as she turned with the ball in her hand–she could see that Zoe had made it back, but she still threw the ball. Eva let go of the camera with which she had been shooting the action. She leaned over the fence and yelled in German, forgetting herself in her fury at what had been done to her wife. "*Hafst du die Kugel herauf dein Arsch und verdrehst es!*" she screamed, and then stopped when she realised what she had said. She shrugged and followed up in English what Earl was yelling. "Stupid bloody bowler!"

Earl looked at his friend in total surprise. He didn't know what she'd yelled out in German, but it must have been good since Eva had turned a bright shade of red. He turned to Friedrich whose eyes had gone very wide at Eva's German curse. His mouth hung open.

"What'd she say?" Earl asked a clearly shocked Friedrich, who was trying to recover from hearing Eva swear.

".Uh...the bowler should stick the ball up her bum and twist it," Friedrich replied and shook his head.

"All right, Eva!" Earl said as he slapped Eva on the shoulder and laughed.

Eva looked across at her friends and made a face. She got so involved in the game that her naturally reserved personality was put on hold.

Zoe looked up when she heard the German curses and grinned. She picked up her bat and waved it in Eva's direction. The bowler took exception to being yelled at, even though she didn't know what was said, but seeing Zoe chuckle made her mad.

"Hey, shorty! What did that kraut yell?" The bowler, being taller and broader than Zoe towered over her for a moment.

"She's not a kraut, she's Greek," Zoe said and turned her back on the bowler. She stopped and turned back. "She said you could stick the ball up your bum and twist it."

The bowler scowled and muttered to herself before going back to her start. She turned to where Eva was sitting and gave her a glare.

Zoe tapped her bat on the hard turf, urging her heart to slow down from the galloping speed it was racing at. The wicket-keeper was making snarky comments to her from behind the stumps, and she tried to block her out. The additional two field-ers, placed close to her, were making her a little claustrophobic.

"Hey, shorty, do us all a favor and get out, I have a date!" the wicketkeeper muttered loud enough for Zoe to hear. She got a chuckle from her teammates nearby.

Zoe looked around and gave the wicketkeeper a glare, which only made the other woman laugh. She had been stuck on 49 for two consecutive overs, and she was running out of partners on the other end. Reaching 50 was a milestone in cricket that showed class. She didn't think she would reach 100, since her only other teammate that was out on the field with her was not going to be much help. Her batting partner was a good bowler, but her batting was horrendous. Twice Zoe thought the woman would get out and leave her stranded on 49. She looked up and spotted Eva, her camera pointed in her direction, and she sighed.

"Slay the dragon, Zo," Eva whispered, urging on her wife who was doing her best against what was good bowling, despite Earl's tirade against them.

"Huh?" Earl turned to her when he heard the muttering.

"Nothing, I was just talking to myself," Eva replied, bring-ing the camera to her eye again. "How many balls to go?"

"One in this over I think," Earl looked at Friedrich, who was keeping score.

"One more," Friedrich confirmed as he noted the chart and counted the balls. Each bowler was allocated an "over," which

meant they had six chances to bowl the batsman out before the
other bowler took over. "Hopefully the lass batting with her
won't get out. If she hits the ball straight and past the bowler,
she could get a run and get her 50."

"And if she doesn't get a run in this over?"

Earl looked over at the other batsman who was not very
good. She didn't need to be since she was a bowler and most
bowlers couldn't bat to save their lives.

"Well then, Alice is going to be batting, and we can pack up
and go home," Earl said grimly.

The only chance Zoe had was to retain the batting by running on the next delivery and then hoping to get a run from the
next over. If she remained where she was, it would mean that
Alice would have to face the bowler in the next over. Zoe looked
up and prepared, as the bowler came steaming in. She steadied
her nerves and watched the ball come out of the bowler's fingers,
and hit the pitch. She felt like she was in slow motion watching
the ball come towards her, seeing the seam of the ball spin. Zoe
came down the pitch and met the ball. She thumped the red ball
over the head of the bowler and it sailed into the boundary for
four runs, much to the disgust of the bowler who stood watching
it as it hit the boundary fence.

Earl, Eva, and Friedrich got to their feet and cheered as the
small crowd joined in. Eva was taking photos of Zoe, who had a
huge grin on her face, being patted on the back by her teammate.
They sat back down and watched as the next bowler began her
run up to start the over.

"Alice is a bunny. I think we can pack up now," Earl muttered.

"A bunny?"

"A hopeless batsman. Bowlers can't bat very well,"
Friedrich supplied.

Eva watched as the hapless Alice stood at the crease with a
scowl on her face. Zoe was urging her teammate on from the
other end. The bowler let the ball go and it slipped through,
between the bat and her pads, hitting the stumps. There was a
collective sigh from the small crowd as the game ended with the
fielding team winning.

Eva smiled broadly, the camera around her neck, as the
players were trudging off the oval. As the sun set over the
wooden stands, the long shadows fell across the cricket grounds.
Earl and Friedrich stood next to her, watching the various play-

ers enter the gate and go into the dressing rooms. Zoe was the third to last person to enter the gate. A tired smile played on her lips as she met Eva's eyes, her grin becoming wider. Her hand went to the pendant around her neck, and she brought it to her lips and kissed it.

"I slew the dragon, m'lady." Zoe bowed deeply and waved her bat in the air. She was tired but so high with the day's game. She'd scored 50 runs, and it had been a thrill to play against one of the best teams in the competition. She was sore from the hits she'd taken when the ball hit her, and was looking forward to a good soak in a bath.

"Good game, stretch!" Earl greeted her with a slap on the shoulder.

"Great game, Zoe," Friedrich chimed in.

Earl looked between his two friends and decided now was a good time to leave them alone together. "Come on, Freddy, let's go and get the car." Earl clasped Friedrich on the shoulder and they walked away.

Eva followed her wife under the stands, Zoe's spiked boots making a scraping noise accompanied by the tap, tap of the bat. The two women stopped just a little away from the dressing rooms and faced each other.

"I'm so proud of you," Eva whispered, as she wrapped her long arms around Zoe's waist. "That six over the stand was really a nice touch."

Zoe's grin split her face. She was rather proud of that shot. She'd heard Earl's booming voice berating the bowler a few times, which made her giggle. She was more surprised to find Eva's distinctive voice ring out, urging her on.

"I heard you, you know. Swearing in German at the bowler was quite interesting and inventive, though I don't think she could do that with a cricket ball," Zoe chuckled.

Eva blushed a bright shade of red as Zoe pulled her down for a quick kiss. "I don't think she was trying to hit me, Evy. I think she was trying to hit the stumps."

"She hurt you," Eva said quietly.

"A little bit, but I'm okay. I think I'm going to go and change. I want a good long soak in a bath."

Eva leaned down and kissed her tenderly, then swatted her on the behind as she walked into the dressing rooms. Watching her for a few moments, Eva finally headed out to the car, with her camera dangling from her hand and a smile on her face.

Elena had cooked them dinner, and it was waiting for them when they came home from the oval. She had also already enlightened her husband as to Zoe's desire to have children, so they took the opportunity to speak to Friedrich about the possible legalities involved. All in all, it was an enjoyable time spent with their friends. After dinner, the Jacobs' went home so that Friedrich could begin to look into the laws about adoption and other legal means to guarantee Eva's involvement with any children Zoe might have. Because his friends were so anxious, he agreed to return later that evening to discuss their options.

Zoe and Eva were seated outside enjoying the warm evening and light breeze. The soothing bath Zoe had taken to ease her tired muscles had made her very sleepy. It had been a long, tiring day, but they could not go to bed yet. They expected Friedrich to arrive at any time so they could discuss the adoption, and what they needed to do to get things in order. Zoe laid her head on Eva's lap and closed her eyes, resting while they waited.

Eva closed her own eyes and drifted for a while, until she heard a knock on the door. She looked down to see that Zoe had fallen asleep. "Zoe, Friedrich is here." Eva ran her hands through Zoe's dark locks.

"Okay," Zoe mumbled sleepily as she struggled to sit up.

Eva went to the door and greeted Friedrich, inviting him inside. Zoe yawned as she took a seat in the living room and waited for Eva to join her.

"That was a great game, Zoe," Friedrich said, noting her obvious fatigue. Opening his briefcase, he took out his notes. "All right, I did a bit of searching, and I have some good news and some bad news," Friedrich said, looking over the top of his glasses at them.

Eva rolled her eyes and took Zoe's hand. She hadn't thought it was going to be easy. "Okay, give us the bad news first."

"Well, it's not bad news really, but more like extremely-difficult-to-achieve news. Adoption in Australia is pretty difficult for single women. By law, you are both single and unmarried. You would have to meet certain guidelines to legally adopt Zoe's children. For instance, it would have to be proven that the children's father was not able to support them, and that Zoe was an unfit mother."

"That's stupid," Zoe mumbled. "Is there anything else we

can do?"

"Well, there is, but you're not going to like it," Friedrich replied. "You would need to draw up a will stating that Eva would be the legal guardian should anything happen to you."

"So I have to die for the law to recognize Eva as their mother?"

"Yes."

"Let's do it," Eva said quietly. It wasn't the ideal solution, but it was a way that they could get the law to recognize Eva's guardianship of any children they would have.

"Aren't there any other ways?" Zoe asked, hoping Friedrich hadn't exhausted every avenue open to them.

"If there are, I haven't found them." He paused, not wishing to possibly offend his friends. He drew in a deep breath and added in a rush, "Unless Eva wants to marry Pat; and then, by law, she does have guardianship of Pat's children."

Zoe scratched her head in confusion. "That is so convoluted! Wouldn't it just be easier to acknowledge Eva as my wife and give her the rights she deserves?"

Friedrich sighed. "Yes, it would. It would make perfect sense. But Zoe, our society doesn't recognize same sex marriages. Actually, you are both breaking the law by sleeping together."

"What!" Zoe looked at Eva who scowled.

"Homosexual relationships are against the law," Friedrich stated quietly. He felt sorry for his friends, who had to endure a law that was clearly discriminatory and arguably wrong.

"So if I kiss my wife, I'm breaking the law?" Eva asked quietly, putting her arm around Zoe.

"Technically, yes. I doubt any police officer would arrest you, but yes, it's against the law."

"What if we want to change that law? What do we have to do?" Zoe asked.

"Well, you would have to write a letter to your local Member of Parliament. Depending on where he stood on the issue, he could talk to the Justice Minister. If the Justice Minister agreed, then a private member's bill would be introduced in Parliament."

"Will it be changed then?"

"No, it gets debated and voted on by the House of Representatives, and if it passes, it goes to the Senate for debate and a vote. But, private member's bills seldom, if ever, get the chance to be sent to the Senate, since most of them are killed in the

House of Reps."

"So what are our chances if we go that route?" Eva asked, knowing she wasn't going to like the answer.

Friedrich scratched his chin. "A snowball would have a better chance of surviving in hell than you would of changing the laws."

Zoe looked at Eva and sighed. "So our only avenue is to have a will drawn up?"

"Yes, at the moment, but I will look into it further," Friedrich advised them.

"I guess that's what we will do," Eva said, quietly squeezing Zoe's hand.

"There is that other alternative." Friedrich pushed his glasses up his nose and looked up at them. "You could marry Pat, and then you would have all legal rights since Pat will be the father."

Eva looked at Zoe and grimaced. "I'm already married. I can't make a vow to anyone else when I've already done so. Marriage isn't something I trifle with."

"Eva, I think God would understand about this arrangement," Friedrich tried to reason, getting a stony glare from the tall woman. "It would solve your problems with the guardianship of any children."

"I don't like it," Eva mumbled.

Zoe turned to her wife who was scowling. "Don't frown, you'll get wrinkles." She smoothed the worry lines on Eva's brow and placed her hand on Eva's stomach. She could see her partner was getting angry.

"Well, Zoe marries Pat, has the children, and then they get divorced. Pat then marries you, and the guardianship problem is resolved. Legally, you are their stepmother, since Pat is going to be the father of Zoe's children." Friedrich presented the argument reasonably, oblivious to Eva's discomfort. "The divorce papers will say that Pat was cheating on Zoe, naming you as the other woman, and voila."

"Friedrich, marriage to us is not a game." Zoe tried to make her friend realise how they both felt about it.

"I know that, but it's a solution," he insisted.

"It's not the solution we want," Eva retorted angrily.

"I'm just trying to help."

"I know you are, Friedrich, and we really appreciate it, but there must be some way other than a sham marriage," Zoe said quietly, aware of her wife's anger. Eva took her vows so seriously that a sham marriage wasn't an option.

Friedrich looked at the quiet determination in the faces of his friends. "I'll find another way," he vowed, and the two women nodded.

Chapter
6

Eva stared up at the ceiling and sighed. They had discussed at some length the different ways for them both to have custody of their children. The idea of her marrying Pat was out of the question, no matter how many times Friedrich suggested a different version of the same scenario.

Eva looked at her sleeping wife. Zoe had gone through so much, and now a law which was homophobic in the extreme was depriving them of the happiness of being parents. Zoe had been only 15 when her mother was killed by Eva's stepfather and she was taken in and cared for by Father Haralambos. He'd adopted her as his own, giving her the love and care she needed.

Adopted. An idea formed in her head that she couldn't wait to investigate further, Eva quietly got out of bed. She looked at the clock, which read 3:00 a.m., and mentally calculated the time for Greece. She put on her robe and slippers and went out in the living room.

Picking up the telephone, she dialed her father's number from memory and waited a few moments for the phone to be answered.

"*Kalispera*," a man's gruff voice came from the other end.

Eva grinned. "Morning, father. It's Eva."

"Ah, Eva, is anything wrong?"

"No. Nothing is wrong. I just wanted to talk to you."

"Are you sure? Not that I'm not happy to hear your voice."

"Well, there is something I did want to ask you, but there's nothing wrong."

"Ask away."

"Father, when Zoe's mother died, you took her in, didn't you?"

There was a slight hesitation before Panayiotis Haralambos answered. Eva was quite certain his eyebrows had gone up in surprise at such a question.

"Yes, I was her legal guardian."

"Did you sign any papers to that effect?" Eva asked and crossed her fingers.

"Yes, I did. I had to in order to take care of her because she was under 16."

Eva grinned. She kissed the telephone handset. "I love you, Father!"

The older man chuckled. "I love you too, Eva, but what is this about?"

Eva wanted to tell him, but she would wait until they got to Greece. She wanted Zoe with her when she told her father he was going to be a grandfather. "Father, I can't tell you now, but in a week Zoe and I are coming to Greece, and we will tell you then."

Eva held the receiver away from her ear as the older man began whooping and yelling.

"You know, my child, if I pray hard enough sometimes it happens!" Panayiotis chuckled.

"I'm coming up with the Minister's team, and we'll be in Larissa for a few days. We leave on Saturday, so I guess I'll see you on Tuesday."

"Ah, I'm going to get the biggest pig to roast and have a huge party! Tell the Minister he is welcome to come!"

Eva grinned. A true Greek feast–that should impress the Minister to no end. "Yes, I will. Give Ally a kiss for me." She hung up the phone and spread her hands out. "Thank you!" she said aloud and went back inside the bedroom.

She leaned down to wake her wife. "Zoe, wake up!"

Zoe mumbled in her sleep but didn't wake.

"Zoe, love, I need to talk to you." Eva gently shook her smaller partner.

"It's not morning," Zoe mumbled.

"Yes it is. You have to wake up!"

"Why?" Zoe muttered and curled up against Eva.

"Zoe, please wake up!"

Zoe sighed and cracked open one eye and looked up. "I'm awake." She brushed aside her disheveled hair. "What's the matter?"

"Zoe, when your mother was killed, my father took you in."

Zoe frowned. *That's a very odd thing to say in the middle of the night*, she thought to herself. "Uh...yeah."

"I think we've found the solution to our problem."

"We have?"

"Yeah." Eva laid back down and let her smile widen as she looked up at the ceiling, feeling quite proud of herself.

"Evy?"

"Yeah?"

"Want to share it, since you got me up at 4:00 a.m.?" Zoe asked. Her wife looked like the cat that ate the canary, which made Zoe smile. She didn't know why she was smiling, but it was contagious.

"Zoe, by law, I'm your sister." Eva cupped her wife's face and grinned.

"Huh?"

"Okay, when your mother died, you were left an orphan right?" Zoe nodded. "Who was your legal guardian?"

"Father H."

"Right," Eva said to her very confused wife. Zoe frowned and used her hand to check Eva's brow for a temperature in case the older woman was coming down with a fever.

"Evy, explain to me what's going on up there." Zoe tapped Eva's head lightly.

"Okay, when you were left an orphan, my father became your legal guardian. In effect, he adopted you."

"Yeah."

"Right. You are my sister," Eva patiently explained, waiting for Zoe to understand the full ramifications of that fact. "I spoke to him just now, and he told me he signed papers to become your legal guardian. So, by law, you are my sister."

"Eww. I've been making love to my sister!" Zoe grinned.

Eva frowned and shook her head. "Zoe, as your next of kin, any children we have, I would have the legal right to decide about them if you can't be reached."

The realization of what Eva was saying finally sank in, and a huge smile split Zoe's face. "You know something, Mrs H?"

"What?" Eva asked, scooping up her wife.

"You are a brilliant, gorgeous woman." Zoe climbed up Eva's body and kissed her. "I love kissing my sister."

"We can call Friedrich later today and tell him to stop looking." Eva caressed Zoe's face. "I love you, Zoe," she whispered as the tears ran down her face. Zoe gently brushed away the tears. Eva brought down the younger woman's head and began kissing her passionately.

Debbie looked up as the door opened and smiled at the person entering the office. Friedrich doffed his hat as he came in. He was feeling very pleased with himself for finding a way for Eva and Zoe to get what they wanted. He'd stayed up all night poring over books and calling a friend who was a district court judge to get his view.

"Good afternoon, Debbie. Is Eva free?" Friedrich asked as he played with his hat. He never knew where to put his hands when he was talking to women. He still got nervous, even though he'd been married for 4 years.

Debbie shook her head. "She's with the Minister at the moment, but I don't think she will be too long. How's Elena?"

"Good. Thanks for asking," Friedrich said as he sat down on the visitor's chair and put his briefcase next to him on the floor.

Debbie smiled. "Was Eva expecting you?"

"No. I hope she can fit me in. It won't take long."

The door opened again, and Zoe walked in with two bags. "Hey, Deb, is Eva free?" Zoe asked. She had finished early at the art gallery and had promised to bring Eva some lunch. Sometimes her wife forgot to have lunch.

Debbie shook her head again and chuckled. It was beginning to resemble Central Station in the tiny office. Zoe looked around the door to find Friedrich waiting. "Hey, Friedrich. Did you find anything?"

Friedrich nodded and gave her a huge smile. She smiled back and turned to Debbie. "Has Eva had lunch yet?"

"No, she's been tied up all morning. What do you have?"

"Chicken salad sandwiches," Zoe replied, getting a grimace from her friend.

"Nah, don't want any," Debbie chuckled and answered the phone.

Zoe sat down next to Friedrich and turned to him. "We have

some news of our own."

"Yeah?"

"Hmm," Zoe responded.

Eva's door opened, and Percy Hester and his assistant exited to the main office. Eva grinned when she caught sight of Zoe and motioned for her to come over. Zoe left her packages near Friedrich and wiped her hands on her dark pants, giving Friedrich a look.

Eva made the introductions. "Sir, I would like you to meet Zoe Haralambos. Zoe, this is the Minister–Percy Hester."

Percy looked at Zoe and grinned. Finally, someone his own height to look at. "I'm pleased to meet you, Miss Haralambos."

"I've heard a lot about you, sir," Zoe said quietly, trying valiantly not to giggle. She couldn't help herself every time she heard his surname.

"You have? I hope it was good!" Hester laughed and slapped Zoe on the shoulder, causing her to nearly lose her balance. "You are a beautiful young woman, Miss Haralambos."

"Thank you," Zoe murmured. She blushed a little, feeling embarrassed by the man's attention to her.

Hester chuckled at the look on Zoe's face. "Hey, Eva, don't you tell Zoe how beautiful she is?"

"Every day," Eva replied and gave her wife a wink.

"Good, because such a beautiful woman deserves to be told every day. Don't you agree, Eva?" The Minister enjoyed watching the emotions flitting across the tall woman's face. So far he had seen the woman who was all business, but when she'd realised Zoe was there he noticed her eyes soften and a smile play on her lips. It was something quite different. He had never met any lesbians before, so this was a new experience for him.

"She is the most beautiful woman I've ever met," Eva replied quietly, looking down shyly.

The Minister looked between the two women, who were both blushing a little, and chuckled. He put his arm around Zoe's shoulders and looked at her over his glasses. "I hope you like long, long flights. Tell you what, I consider myself quite a good artist, but I would like for you to give me a few pointers. What do you think?" Percy smiled broadly. He was rather taken with the young woman, and her photographs didn't do her justice. He adored her eyes. They weren't a typical green eye colour, more emerald and twinkly, and she had such an expressive and beautiful face.

"I would love to," Zoe agreed quietly.

"Excellent! Zoe, can I call you Zoe?"

"Sure."

"You can call me Percy. Only my staff call me Mr Hester!" Hester laughed. "Now, Zoe, are you ready for the trip?"

"Not quite. I haven't packed yet, but I'll be ready."

Hester leaned in and whispered loudly, "Don't forget to pack for Eva." Hester chuckled. Zoe looked up at Eva and smiled. "Good, excellent in fact." The Minister rubbed his hands together and turned to Eva. "I'll see you on Friday for a staff meeting and," he turned to Zoe who still had a smile plastered on her face, "I'll see you on Saturday. Let's go, Michael. We have a lot to do."

Michael held the door open for the Minister as he walked through. He waved as he left.

"Friedrich, come in." Eva ushered her friend inside the office and stopped near Debbie's desk. Debbie had her hand out-stretched. Eva took a pound out of her pocket and gave it to her assistant.

Zoe frowned at the strange behavior. "What's the bet for?"

"The Minister likes you. He never lets anyone call him Percy!" Debbie chuckled and pocketed the money as Eva and Zoe followed Friedrich inside.

"I found it!" Friedrich said as he took a seat.

"So did we," Eva countered, as Zoe sat next to her and took her hand. "We're related."

"Huh?"

"Zoe's mother was killed when Zoe was 15 years old, and my father took her in. I spoke to him this morning, and he told me that he signed papers to be Zoe's legal guardian. I'm assuming that means Zoe is my sister."

"Not really. Well, not unless your father adopted Zoe."

"Isn't it the same thing?"

"No, being a legal guardian means he could make decisions for Zoe because she was under age. Once she reached the legal age, he didn't have any legal right to take care of her."

"Oh," Eva said quietly, disappointed.

"So we're back to square one again," Zoe sighed and looked at Eva.

"Well no, you're not. I spent a good deal of time researching this, and I spoke to a friend who is a district court judge. He told me that Zoe can give you Power of Attorney, which means Eva would have the right to make decisions about any children you may have if Zoe was not present."

"That's what we want," Eva said and looked at Zoe who nodded.

"A Durable Power of Attorney would be effective even in the event that Zoe passed away and you were left with the children. Now, when it comes to hospital treatments and so forth, you can claim you are Zoe's sister. If you have any problems, you can give them a letter stating you have Power of Attorney."

"Will that work?" Zoe asked, not quite believing it would be that easy.

"Yes, it should," Friedrich replied. He pushed his glasses up his nose and grinned at his friends who looked very happy. Eva had a smile a mile wide which made her look much younger, and Zoe was also grinning.

"Thank you, Friedrich. You've come through for us." Eva extended her hand and Friedrich shook it.

"Any time," he replied, feeling a little shy. When he was with the tall woman, he always felt like he was back in school. She reminded him of a strict teacher. Even though he'd gotten to know her over the years, she still made him nervous.

Zoe jumped up and hugged him tightly. "Thank you!" she said and gave him a chaste kiss on the cheek. Friedrich cleared his throat and blushed slightly. He picked up his briefcase. "I can draw up the papers tomorrow and have them ready for you to sign before you leave for Europe."

Eva opened the door and held it as Zoe gave him another kiss before he left. Zoe turned to her partner who enfolded her in outstretched arms and, putting her arms around Eva's waist, snuggled in her embrace.

"Are you happy?" Eva asked, kissing the top of Zoe's head.

Zoe looked up into twinkling blue eyes and beamed. "It's what we wanted. I'm happy."

"Then that's all that matters. If you're happy, I'm happy," Eva said quietly.

Zoe gazed into her wife's eyes, and she sighed contently. "Evy, I hope I spend the rest of my life loving you." She buried herself in Eva's embrace.

"We're going to grow old together, love. I promise we will." Eva leaned down and kissed her, putting all her love into the kiss and the promise she had made.

Chapter
7

It was a busy week for them both. Eva spent the week getting their passports in order, and Zoe packed for both of them. She'd had to tell Eva she couldn't wear her favourite sweater since it had seen better days and wasn't something Zoe wanted to see her wife in. She had even tried to get rid of it once, but Eva found it again. Now the suitcases were packed and the travelling papers were in hand. At last it was time for the journey to begin.

Zoe sighed. She looked up at the massive military plane from a little corner of the hangar and gulped. It was a huge plane that would take the Minister and his team to Europe. They would be stopping whenever necessary to refuel, and that would be the only time the plane would land. The large, grey metal bird made her nervous just looking at it. Zoe scowled as she watched the plane being checked by maintenance personnel.

Eva came around the corner carrying the small bag that they would have with them on board, then, seeing Zoe, stopped. She glanced around her to see if anyone was watching them, and put her arms around her younger partner.

"It's going to be okay, love," Eva whispered in her ear and gave her a quick kiss.

"Swimming is out of the question, huh?" Zoe replied, leaning back into Eva's embrace.

"Yeah, afraid so."

Zoe snorted. "Do you know what I'm going to hate about this trip, apart from being on that thing?"

Eva smiled. "No, what?"

"Not being able to touch you or sleep with you," Zoe said quietly. "It's going to be the first time in over five years that I haven't been able to put my arms around you and use you as my pillow."

Eva grinned. "Well, I've made sure we sit next to each other, so you can touch me under the blanket if you like," she replied, nuzzling Zoe's neck.

Zoe twisted around and gave her wife a grin. "You won't utter a sound if I do?"

"I'll be as quiet as a mouse," Eva chuckled. She could be in for some very uncomfortable, but enjoyable, moments and hoped that the Minister was well away from them.

Zoe snorted again. "I've heard how quiet you can be, Evy."

Eva smiled at her partner's reply, knowing she had succeeded in taking the younger woman's mind off the plane trip. She noticed the Minister heading their way and reluctantly let go of Zoe.

"All set, Eva?"

"Yes, sir. Just waiting to board."

"Excellent. I'm going to get everyone together for a briefing when we're up in that metal thing, just to make sure we have everything well in hand."

"Yes, sir," Eva replied and felt Zoe's hand rest on the small of her back.

"I have the seating plan here." He produced a diagram of the plane and showed it to Eva. "I realised you ladies would need some privacy from the men, so you've been assigned a section here." The Minister pointed to the diagram. "All the women will be in one section and all the men in another, except for meetings and so forth. Is that okay with you?"

"Yes, sir," Eva replied, not wanting to sound too disappointed. They would be sharing the same cramped space with the two other women on the Minister's team.

"Zoe, are you okay?" The Minister put his arm around her shoulders.

"Uh...I don't like flying," Zoe muttered.

"You don't? I love it. I was a pilot in the war, you know."

"Really?" Zoe feigned interest.

"Oh yes. Flew in the Battle of Britain, very exciting." Percy glanced at the plane with fondness. "This is the C-64 Skymaster transport ship. We bought this beauty from the Yanks." He admired the sleek lines of the plane that was quite a workhorse for the air force. "Do you know, Zoe, it's 117 feet in length with 4 engines that are a dream to fly. I hope they let me at the controls along the way."

Zoe rolled her eyes and tried not to show her lack of enthusiasm.

"So, don't worry your pretty little head over this, young lady. We'll be in Europe in two days, lickety split. My wife doesn't like flying, but you know what she does?"

Zoe shook her head.

"She dreams of me," the Minister chuckled. "Then her fears are gone."

"Okay." Zoe nodded, though the only thing she could think of that would be pleasant involved her wife, and she didn't know if daydreaming about Eva naked and in bed would be such a good idea. Well, it would, but she didn't think her travelling companions would appreciate it.

"Well, let's get everyone on board and settled." Hester let go of Zoe and gave her a pinch on the backside.

Eva put her arms around Zoe's waist and held her back as the Minister walked away barking orders to his assistant. "Don't. It won't get us anywhere if you do anything."

Zoe was outraged. "He pinched my bum!"

"I know," Eva whispered in her ear and got a scowl in return. "Just don't dream about him and I'll be happy," Eva joked.

"Oh that's gross, Evy," Zoe muttered as Eva hugged her.

The big plane's engines annoyed Zoe–they were loud and the roaring hurt her ears–but she would have to endure this and not be a baby, she thought to herself as she took her seat. A section of the plane was cordoned off to make it private for the women. A short plump woman, her dark brown hair pulled up in a bun, walked up and put her bag on a seat, then sat down with a thump on the one beside it. She was joined by a taller woman who sat next to her, and they began to chat between themselves.

Zoe closed her eyes and tried to get her pounding headache to subside. She tried to shut out the engine noise and the chattering women. Feeling a nudge, she opened her eyes.

"Hey, I'm Paula," the short, plump woman introduced herself.

"Hi," Zoe said softly and closed her eyes again.

Paula looked at her companion and gave her a scowl. She was about to shake Zoe again when Eva walked into the closed off section and knelt beside Zoe.

"Zo, I have some aspirin." Eva gave her wife the tablets and the glass of water and watched as her partner gratefully gulped them down.

"Oh, she's got a headache?" the other woman piped up.

When she realised where the sound had come from, Eva turned. "Oh, I'm sorry. Yes, she has a headache. She doesn't like planes all that much."

Paula chuckled. "I don't either. I'm Paula and that's Clarice."

"Eva Haralambos." Eva introduced herself and stood to place several pieces of their luggage in the compartment above them.

"Oh," Paula said quietly. Paula was Hester's secretary and all around assistant to Michael. She had typed up the reports of the meeting with Eva, and her eyebrows had gone up when she'd read about her "marriage." She thought Michael had made a mistake in his notes until she was told he hadn't. She had wondered what a lesbian looked like since she never met one before. The woman who was now standing before her was tall, not skinny, but not fat either, she mused to herself. Her father would call her well built, whatever that meant. The smaller woman must be her lover. She had made it a point to avoid meeting the tall woman ever since the Minister had first mentioned her, quite disgusted by the news that they would be included in the entourage, and not looking forward to spending so many hours in their company. What if they tried something with her? She would not have anywhere to go to get away from them. She would have to have a talk with the Minister. "I hope you don't try anything with me," she huffed.

Clarice sniggered at Paula's words. Before they came on board, they had discussed the two women lovers, and Clarice knew that Paula was quite upset that she had to spend time with them. She didn't understand why the Minister had agreed to bring these deviants on this trip.

Zoe opened her eyes and looked at Paula for a moment, trying to decide if it was a good idea to throw something at her. She caught Eva's eye and just closed her eyes again, since it was quite obvious her wife was going to handle this her way.

Eva sat next in the aisle seat next to Zoe. "I don't understand what you mean," Eva said. Zoe hid a smirk, knowing that this was Eva's way of dealing with idiots.

"You are a lesbian, right?" Paula asked.

"Yes, I am," Eva said patiently.

"That's disgusting. It's unnatural," Paula huffed. "I said that you shouldn't try to make a pass at me. I'm a God-fearing, married woman."

Eva rolled her eyes at the woman's statement. "Don't worry, I won't make a pass at you. My wife would kill me if I did." Zoe kept her eyes closed and smirked.

"Your what?" Paula asked, not quite believing what she had just heard.

"My wife." Eva pointed to Zoe. "Zoe Haralambos. Zoe is my wife and has been for the last 5 years. She doesn't like it if I make a pass at other women, gets me into trouble."

Paula's eyes went wide, surprised that Eva spoke of things so openly, as if they were quite normal. "Disgusting." Paula was outraged, and she struggled to get out of her seat and pick up her bags. "Come on, Clarice. I don't want to sit with these...deviants." She pulled Clarice by the hand and put her bags several seats in front of Eva and Zoe.

"Very diplomatic, Evy," Zoe said, giving her wife a knowing grin.

"I thought so," Eva chuckled. "She's not my type anyway." Zoe chuckled in response, then groaned as the plane began to taxi down the runway. Eva took her hand and squeezed it.

"Don't worry, love, you're my type." Eva smiled and bent down and kissed her.

Zoe yawned and stretched in the uncomfortable seat. She pushed back the blanket that Eva had wrapped around her and turned to find an empty space where her wife had been. She glanced down at her watch and grimaced. They had spent 15 hours travelling, landing only to refuel. Her back ached from the uncomfortable position she was in. She glanced down the aisle and caught Eva stretching out, leaning against the galley partition, her arms reaching the top of the door as she did some stretching exercises.

Zoe watched her for a few minutes and then saw the grimace on her wife's face. It could only mean one thing—Eva had sat down for too long in that cramped seat, and her back hurt. She shook her head and put away the blanket. "Oh, Evy," Zoe muttered. The cabin lights were dimmed, but she had enough light to go to where her wife was. As she passed through the men's section to reach the galley, she glanced at the Minister, who was snoring loudly.

"So, were you going to wake me?" Zoe asked, crossing her arms and leaning on the galley door.

Eva turned to find Zoe staring at her with a look she had seen quite a few times. "I didn't want to wake you?" Eva tried, but she could tell that wasn't going to be accepted. Her back ached from sitting in that cramped seat, and the lack of leg room also made life a little difficult for the tall woman. She truly hadn't wanted to wake Zoe, since she had just managed to fall asleep.

"Does it hurt?" Zoe asked as she went to her partner's side and placed her arms around the tall woman's waist.

Eva nodded. "Yeah, it aches."

"Come on, let me give you a massage."

"Where?"

"The galley. You can lean over in there, and I will work my magic. I'll close the screen so it will be private."

"I don't know..."

"Evy, don't argue with me. You're not going to be comfortable, and it's only going to get worse." Zoe took her hand and led her into the galley, pulling the screen shut behind her.

Paula yawned and looked around. It looked like she was the only one awake. She took a glance behind her to see if the other two women were asleep, and she frowned when she couldn't see them. She got up and was walking towards the bathroom when she heard a noise from the galley.

"Oh Zo, that's wonderful!" Eva's voice drifted out, her evident enjoyment causing Paula's eyes to widen.

"Magic fingers to the rescue," Zoe chuckled.

Low pleasurable moans could be heard, which made Paula blush. "I knew it was a bad idea," Paula muttered to herself as she went to find the Minister. She knelt beside the sleeping man and nudged him. "Sir, wake up!"

The Minister continued to snore and Paula sighed. "Sir, this is important. Wake up!"

"What is it, Paula?" Hester muttered as he removed the sleeping mask from his eyes.

She pointed to the galley. "They're doing it!"

"Who is doing what?"

"That Eva woman. She's in there doing God knows what!"

"Probably eating," the Minister mumbled as he put the mask back on his face.

"Sir, I think it's much more horrible. I think she's having you know..."

The Minister was tired, he was feeling very sore from the uncomfortable seat, and he was running out of patience with his secretary. He took off the mask and glared at her. "What is she doing?"

"Having sex!" Paula spat out. "She's moaning and stuff!"

"And stuff?" Percy Hester took a deep breath and shook his head. He would have to go and check this out so he could get his secretary to leave him alone. He pulled back his blanket, got up from the seat, and stretched. He winced as the muscles in his back complained. "God, I hate sleeping in these chairs," he muttered to himself as he was led to the galley. Paula pulled back the screen and waited for the Minister to start yelling. When he didn't, she turned to see Zoe's hands massaging Eva's lower back. Both women turned to find the Minister and Paula looking on.

Hester looked at Paula and then back at the two women. "Seat did your back in, eh, Eva?"

"Old injury that doesn't like cramped places," Eva muttered, as she straightened and grimaced.

Hester grunted. "Yeah, have one of those myself. Aches for days. I find a warm compress does wonders, and a good massage, of course," he added with a pointed look at his secretary. "I'm going back to sleep." The Minister closed the screen again and turned to his secretary. "Come with me, Paula."

Paula looked back at the screen and shook her head as she followed the Minister back to his seat.

"Not only was that stupid and embarrassing, you woke me from my sleep!" Hester hissed at her. "Now go back to your seat and leave me alone! Can you do that?"

"Yes, sir," Paula said quietly. She went back and sat in her seat and glowered at the galley. How was she supposed to have known that Eva had a sore back? She sure sounded like she was enjoying whatever was being done.

She watched as Zoe walked out of the galley with Eva. They stopped, looked up at each other and stood quite close. Paula frowned when Zoe's arms went around the tall woman. She was repulsed, but she continued watching as Eva leaned down and kissed her. "Disgusting," she muttered to herself. Zoe patted her taller companion on the stomach and said something which made Eva smile.

Zoe made her way back down to her seat and gave Paula a smile. She paused for a moment and then went back to where Paula was sitting. "You should hear her when she's really happy," Zoe whispered to her, getting an outraged look which only made Zoe chuckle as she returned to her seat.

Chapter
8

Zoe held Eva's arm in a death grip as the plane descended and the wheels touched down at the Air Force base. As the plane taxied down the runway, she let out the breath she had been holding.

"It's okay to breathe now, love," Eva teased gently, as her wife opened her eyes and gave a half smile.

The long journey had been difficult for the young woman, who hated heights of any kind. Eva looked at her and brushed away the errant bangs that fell across her eyes. Zoe hadn't complained at all, and Eva was proud of the way her wife handled herself. She'd had to contend with the flight and the bigoted and nasty comments from Paula which were spoken loud enough for Zoe to hear and which, Eva knew, had caused the young woman to break down in tears. Zoe tried to brush it off, but Eva knew her partner, and it was causing her pain. Eva vowed to have a word with Paula when they got off the plane.

Eva was also feeling very tired and achy from the long trip. Her back had complained about the cramped seating for the entire two days. On one of her trips down the aisle, the Minister had gently scolded her for not telling him that she had a back problem. He'd understood her discomfort, since he was feeling a little of it himself. The Minister promised that on the way back, they would find a better way of dealing with it. She'd slept little during the trip, which caused Zoe to stay awake to keep her company. The last 10 hours had been the most difficult when Zoe couldn't keep her eyes open to help Eva pass the time. Eva had paced down the aisle and talked to the Minister for a while, and then went up to the cockpit and chatted with the co-pilot until it was time to resume her seat for the landing. At long last, they were disembarking from the plane when she felt a hand on her shoulder and turned to find tired emerald eyes staring down at her from the step above.

The doors from the airport lounge opened to a very cold, rainy Athens day. Zoe looked around and grinned. She was back in Greece. The excited chatter of Greek speaking people flowed around her, and she gazed up at Eva who grinned. They took three cars, supplied by the Australian Embassy. The vehicles took them to the embassy where they would stay for the duration of their visit in Athens.

The cars pulled up to a red brick building, quite unremarkable in appearance, with one notable exception. Zoe gazed up at the Australian flag, the Southern Cross that was only visible in the Southern Hemisphere. It looked so out of place next to the Greek blue and white stripes with the blue cross in the corner; but Australia was her home now, and she had pledged allegiance to Queen and country when she became a citizen.

"Zo," Eva leaned down and whispered in her ear, "I just need to do something for a bit. Go on inside, I'll be there soon."

Zoe gave her a questioning look, but nodded. She followed a young man who was chatting away while leading her into the embassy. Eva waited until Zoe was inside, then she tapped Paula on the shoulder. The older woman turned around with a smile on her face that turned into a grimace when she realized Eva was standing next to her.

"Yes?" Paula asked, looking up into ice blue eyes.

"I'm only going to say this once, so I would like you to listen carefully."

Paula rolled her eyes and sighed in an exaggerated manner. "Yes, what is it?"

Eva took a step forward. "IF you ever taunt, belittle, abuse or in any way hurt my wife again, I will personally see to it you are sacked," Eva said very calmly.

"How dare you threaten–" Paula stopped in mid tirade at the look in Eva's eyes. The normally very quiet woman was looking at her with eyes that were shards of blue ice. To any passerby it would have seemed like the two woman were in deep conversation, but in reality, Paula feared she was seeing a side of the tall woman few people witnessed. Paula noted that Eva's German accent had become more pronounced. She had underestimated the tall woman, having thought of her as quiet and ineffectual. She had been totally wrong in her estimation. Paula tried to take a step back but hit the wall as Eva came in closer and looked down at the hapless secretary.

"That isn't a threat, Mrs Williams, it's a promise. I will get you sacked. Do I make myself clear?"

"Very clear," Paula said quietly and looked away.

Eva nodded and opened the door to the embassy and walked through, leaving a shell shocked Paula out on the pavement. The woman found she was holding her breath and let it out slowly. The door opened, and Clarice came out in search of her friend.

"Paula, are you coming in?"

Paula looked around and nodded.

Zoe was shown to her room, which was quite spacious and airy. Against the wall were two single beds and two small bed stands with a lamp on each. *The two beds could easily be moved together*, Zoe mused. She hated sleeping alone, and she had already gone two days without Eva's body to snuggle up to. There was a desk with a reading light near the window, and a comfortable looking recliner next to it.

She poked her head into the bathroom and grinned when she saw the tub. It wasn't as big as the one back home, but she thought Eva could stretch out in it. She would pamper Eva tonight and let her get some sleep. The dark rings under her wife's eyes were quite pronounced. She had mentioned to the young man who escorted her in that she needed some Hyraces gel. It was a jelly like substance that, when massaged into aching muscles, would relieve the tension and stress. The eucalyptus smell usually made her nose twitch, but she was determined to give Eva some relief.

She answered a light knock on the door and saw the smiling face of the young man that assisted her to their room. He held out the tube of Hyraces gel and grinned.

"Ah, thank you, Anthony, you found some," Zoe smiled at him.

"For a pretty lady like yourself, it's my pleasure," Anthony replied. Anthony was a little taller than Zoe was, with mousy brown hair and twinkling brown eyes. He was smitten the first time he looked at Zoe and was determined to ask if she would like to see the sights with him. His knowledge of the city was extensive, and he usually took the wives of visiting Ministers out while their husbands were occupied in meetings. "You're not with Mr Hester's team, are you?"

"No, I'm with my friend Eva."

Anthony gave her a blank look.

"The tall, dark-haired woman. You can't miss her," Zoe joked.

"Oh! Hey, she's a looker, isn't she?" Anthony grinned. He preferred women who were shorter, but the tall woman was a treat to look at.

"Yeah, she is," Zoe nodded and then looked over his shoulder and met Eva's eyes. "Speak of the devil."

Anthony looked around and smiled. He quickly turned back to Zoe. "If you have some time free, would you like to see the sights with me?"

Zoe smiled. She did want to go out and see Athens since it was her first time in the capital. And Eva was going to be tied up in meetings, so it would leave her days quite open. "I would like that, thank you."

"Great." Anthony flashed her a quick smile and quickly went past the tall, smirking woman.

Zoe took her hand and pulled her inside the room, closing the door.

"I think you've won another one, Zo," Eva joked as Zoe's arms went around her waist. "Not that I blame him."

"You're seeing things," Zoe replied. She snuggled up in Eva's embrace and sighed, then looked up into tired blue eyes. "Anthony brought up some Hyraces gel, so here's the plan. Let's take a bath." Zoe undid Eva's shirt buttons and pulled the shirt off her shoulders. She let the shirt fall and kissed Eva between her breasts, getting a little giggle from the tall woman. "Then I'm going to give you a nice soothing massage, and you are going to sleep." Zoe put her arms around Eva and unclasped her bra, letting it fall to the floor. Eva gave her a lopsided grin and pulled down her dark trousers. She stood naked in front of her wife, who brought her lips down for a sensual kiss, her hands entangled in Eva's dark hair. Zoe let out a contented little moan and broke off the kiss.

"Time for some pampering."

"Works for me," Eva replied, getting another kiss.

"Oh yeah, come with me, Mrs H," Zoe replied, taking her partner's hand and walking into the bathroom.

Zoe leaned against the window, gazing at the view of Mount Olympus–the home of the gods. She smiled to herself when she thought back to her childhood and the stories her brother used to read to her about Zeus and the rest of the pantheon. It was a lifetime ago; the child that believed in mythological gods and their deeds was long gone.

She gazed back at the bed and smiled. Her partner was sleeping soundly, dark hair framing a face that looked very tired. She was sleeping on her stomach in flannel pajamas that Zoe bought before leaving Sydney. The panama top was crème with pictures of little hearts, which amused Zoe the first time she saw it.

They'd had a bath in between kissing and cuddling. They were both too exhausted to go further, and Zoe was anxious to get Eva out of the bath and into the bed so she could give her a massage. It didn't take long for the tall woman to fall asleep while Zoe massaged her back. Zoe pulled up the blankets and watched her sleep. She was tired but too hyped up about where she was to be able to get any sleep. Zoe turned back to the window and watched the sky turn dark and the stars begin to twinkle.

"Zo?"

Zoe turned and met sleepy blue eyes. "Why aren't you asleep?" she gently scolded.

Eva blinked a few times. "I can't sleep without you."

Zoe smiled. She took off her robe and settled down beside her wife, who cuddled up next to her, letting her head rest against Zoe's shoulder. Zoe smiled. That was usually her position. She stroked Eva's hair and looked down.

"Much better," Eva mumbled and closed her eyes.

"Yeah, I think so, too," Zoe replied, giving Eva a kiss as she closed her own eyes.

They couldn't push the two single beds together, so they lay close in each other's arms. Zoe spent most of the night with her body cuddling up to Eva's back and her arm wound around the tall woman's waist. The incessant ringing of the alarm woke Zoe, and she lifted up her head to scowl at the clock that was on Eva's side of the single bed. Zoe wasn't complaining, but that alarm bell was going to wake Eva, and that was the last thing she wanted to happen.

Before Zoe could get out of bed, a long arm snaked out from under the blanket and smothered the alarm clock. Eva turned, her hair mussed up in a way Zoe found totally adorable. Sleepy blue eyes gazed at her, giving Zoe a smile.

"I couldn't throw it on the floor; it's not ours," she said sleepily and watched Zoe's grin widen. Quite a few alarm clocks had been broken during their marriage, either by Zoe flinging them out the door or by Eva doing the same.

"You are so adorable in the morning," Zoe said and kissed her soundly. "How are you feeling?" she asked, snuggling up.

Eva pursed her lips. She was feeling much better, even though her back was still complaining a little. The dull ache was better than the discomfort she'd experienced over the previous two days. "Better. I think the sleep helped, and I know your hands on my body helped." She grinned when Zoe waggled her eyebrows at her.

"I don't have a bad back, and your hands on my body help me a great deal," Zoe whispered, nuzzling Eva's long neck and giving her a gentle nip.

"Zoe, if you keep that up, I don't think I'm going to make my 8:30 meeting," Eva said a trifle breathlessly as Zoe slipped her hands inside her pajama top, cupping a firm breast and giving it a gentle squeeze. Eva let out a small gasp.

"What meeting?" Zoe whispered to her.

"The one Hester arranged...oh dear..." Eva stopped in mid-sentence as Zoe's other hand stroked her inner thigh. She wanted to go where Zoe was going to take her, but if they did make love, she would be late for the early morning meeting. "Huh...Zoe, please stop."

Zoe gave her an evil grin. "You sure?"

Eva lay back and groaned. "Huh, no," she grimaced. "Yes," she hissed. She'd missed having the freedom to make love to her wife over the course of the two days spent on the airplane. _I should have set the alarm clock an hour earlier_, she chided herself. Zoe undid the pajama top buttons and slid it off her wife's broad shoulders, kissing the skin as she took the top and threw it over her shoulder.

"Are you quite sure?" Zoe grinned as she placed gentle feather light kisses on her stomach then worked her way upwards. Eva looked down at her partner and groaned. Zoe took pity on her wife and stopped her gentle teasing. "Tell Percy to schedule meetings at a more reasonable hour."

Eva sighed. "And if he asks me why?"

Zoe looked up into the now very alert twinkling blue eyes. She loved everything about this woman. She tweaked the dimpled chin. "Tell him the truth–because your wife wants to make love to you."

"I don't think that would go down very well." Eva eyed the clock and sighed. She would have to get up and get ready. Pushing back the cover, she reluctantly left Zoe's embrace. Looking back down at Zoe lying on the bed, she sat back down.

Eva crooked her finger and Zoe crawled closer, letting her head rest against Eva's thigh. Eva leaned down and gave her a long and sensual kiss. Clasping her wife's hands with both of hers, she looked lovingly into emerald coloured eyes. "Good morning," she whispered and kissed her again before releasing her.

"Good morning." Zoe returned the greeting and watched Eva remove her pajama bottoms. "I think you've lost some weight, Evy. I should check, you know," she teased.

"You just want an excuse to come and put your arms around me," Eva replied, picking up a bath towel the embassy domestic staff had left for them.

Zoe grinned. "I don't need an excuse," she said, getting out of bed and wrapping herself around the tall woman.

Eva reluctantly disengaged herself from her wife. "Zoe, I need to go and have a bath."

"Want some help with it? I'm a good back scrubber."

Eva snorted. The idea of Zoe's hands on her body was warring with the need to be present at the briefing the Minister was going to be giving. Even though he had already gone over the itinerary so many times, she would have to be there, and on time. "You are wicked," Eva muttered as she headed for the bathroom, leaving a chuckling Zoe in her wake.

"And you are incredibly sexy," Zoe called after her, which caused Eva to turn around and give her a dazzling smile before

closing the bathroom door. Zoe heard the click of the key lock-
ing and wondered if there was a spare key lying around.

A gentle knock on the door dispelled any thoughts of attack-
ing her wife in the bath. Zoe put on her robe and opened the door
to discover a middle-aged woman with a fresh set of sheets in
her hand.

"*Kalimera,* I'm Evthokia," the woman introduced herself
and smiled.

Zoe smiled back and opened the door. "Uh, my friend is in
the bath."

"I just came to change the sheets and ask if you had any
laundry you would like to have done." Evthokia stripped the bed
Zoe and Eva had shared and began to work quickly and effi-
ciently. She looked over and noticed the other bed was already
made up. "You didn't need to make the bed, it's okay to leave it.
I will take care of it."

Zoe nodded mutely and watched the woman strip back the
bed and replace the sheets. "Um, what time do you normally
come around?" Zoe asked.

Evthokia looked over at the young woman. "Every morning
at 7:30 a.m."

Zoe rolled her eyes and sat down heavily on the seat as
Evthokia went about her chores.

Chapter 9

Zoe sat on a boulder overlooking the majestic monument and smiled. She was finally visiting a place she had vowed to see as a child. Her brother told tales of the wise goddess Athena and of the monument in her honor. For a while, she had called herself Athena, because it was richer sounding than plain Zoe was. Her head had been filled with plans for visiting Athens, a magical place full of adventures and wonder.

The child in Zoe was in awe that she'd finally arrived and was gazing at the site of one of her many long-held dreams. The sun shone brightly on the white marble columns of the ancient monument. Zoe fingered the hand knit sweater she had been coerced into buying by one of the gypsy vendors on the way up to the monument. It was the ugliest thing she had ever seen, but the gypsy was so insistent that Zoe gave in. *That would shock Eva*, Zoe mused, since she usually haggled and talked the ear off most merchants. She pulled the sweater out and grimaced. It was ugly. The multi colored pattern made her eyes hurt just looking at it. It was too big for Zoe, but it was perfect for Eva. Zoe doubted her tall partner would even wear it. She'd paid twenty drachmas for it, and she had no idea why she had done it.

"I hope you don't mind me saying this, but that thing is UGLY," Anthony said quietly and made a face.

Zoe turned and looked up. "Sure is; want it?"

Anthony shook his head. "I've been avoiding the gypsy traders here for a year now, and I wouldn't ever want to be seen wearing that."

"You're no help," Zoe good-naturedly muttered and stuffed the sweater back in her knapsack.

"How much did you pay for it?"

"Twenty drachmas," Zoe mumbled. Anthony let out a whistle and then laughed. "Okay, so she ambushed me," Zoe chuckled.

"Zoe, can I ask you a personal question?"

Zoe looked up and nodded.

"Have you got a boyfriend or anything..."

"I'm married," Zoe said and held up her hand, showing him the ring.

"Oh," Anthony said dejectedly. "He is a very lucky man."

Anthony sat gazing at the Acropolis. He had come up here numerous times before and enjoyed soaking in the atmosphere. He spied a look at Zoe who had a smile on her face. She took out a pad and a pencil and began to sketch, which really surprised him.

"You're an artist?"

"Yep. I work for the New South Wales Art Gallery," Zoe replied as she sketched.

"I love this place. It's so full of history," Anthony said, gazing at the tourists. "I miss having a culture that is so rich."

Zoe stopped sketching and looked at Anthony with a frown. "Australia has a rich history. The Aborigine culture is one of the most interesting."

"They're savages. That's not culture. This is culture," Anthony replied, opening his arms wide and indicating the ancient building.

Zoe shook her head. She could never understand why Australians looked down on their history. She couldn't figure out why they thought the history of the great southern land started in 1788 and not the thousands of years earlier when the Aborigine settled the country. She had seen so much beautiful artwork by the native Australians, and it was sad how her adopted country treated these people.

"Did you know that the Aborigine settled in Australia thousands of years ago, and their way of life was so gentle? I have a book about the 'dreaming' if you want to read it. It's–"

"No offense, Zoe, but their culture doesn't compare to the

accomplishments of Pericles, Sophocles, Plato, Philip, Alexander the Great. This," Anthony indicated the area, "is the cradle of civilization. You have a heritage I would love to call my own. I'm English, and the best that I can muster is a bunch of Celtic myths and Stonehenge. Big deal."

She couldn't believe that anyone would take their country's history for granted. She was a voracious reader and enjoyed learning about other cultures. It also helped her with art appreciation. "Anthony, when I was growing up in a little village, my brother told me tales of the Greek gods as well as other stories. I grew up loving my culture, but you have to look at what makes your country great as well," Zoe said to the young man. "You know about Queen Bodecea, don't you?"

Anthony snorted. "A woman who couldn't defeat the Romans."

"I guess you won't be a diplomat when you grow up, huh?" Zoe commented and went back to her sketching.

"So, where are you headed after this?"

"Larissa."

"Deadsville of Greece, huh?" Anthony laughed at his joke, oblivious to the scowl on Zoe's face. "I went there once with my father. It has to be the most backward little village on the map! No culture," the young man sniffed. "It's a farming community, you know. If we didn't have to drive through to get to Thessaloniki, I wouldn't step foot in the place. Dirty and backward."

Zoe rolled her eyes. "It's not bad for a place that's over 6,000 years old."

"Yeah, but it's not sophisticated like Athens. What's so special about it?"

"I was born there," Zoe said quietly.

"Oh," Anthony said, as he realised he had put his foot in his mouth. He'd wanted to impress the young woman with his knowledge of this beautiful country, but somehow it hadn't worked out that way.

"My parents were dirty and backward farmers, as were my brothers. We barbarians don't know much about the world, you see," Zoe grumbled. She wasn't sure why she let this boy's opinion matter to her, but it annoyed her that he disrespected her hometown. She was sure her brothers would laugh at her for even bothering to get upset. "My friend, Earl, has a saying which I think would be quite appropriate for you right now."

"What is it?"

"Engage your brain before your mouth." Zoe looked at him, got up, and went to look at the ruins more closely, leaving the young man with a flushed face.

Eva smiled and repeated the Minister's words to the middle aged man seated in front of them. They had been in a meeting with the Greek Immigration Minister for two hours. They had stopped earlier for the two-hour siesta, which totally aggravated Percy Hester, since he'd wanted to get on with his meetings. At midday, everything shut down–from shops to government departments. Hester was upset that a crucial meeting would be interrupted so they could go and have a nap.

When they resumed their talks, Alexandros Papas, a very difficult man, took an instant dislike to Eva and insulted her in Greek with a smile on his face. Her patience was fast running out with the Greek Minister. His arrogant tone was grating on her nerves. He kept referring to her as "the woman," as if she was a parasite. Percy Hester was beginning to lose his own patience with the Greek. Eva remained calm despite the difficult situation. She glanced at her watch, which read 9:00 p.m., and wanted to roll her eyes. Going around in circles was proving to be one of her least favorite ways to spend a day. She hoped Zoe had spent the day more productively than she had. Eva was looking forward to seeing her spouse at the end of this tiring day and cuddling up.

The meeting ended with a partial agreement on immigration, which wasn't what Hester wanted. They watched the Greek entourage leave, and Eva sat down and sighed.

"I don't think he liked you, Eva," Hester said, wiping his glasses with his handkerchief.

"Really? What gave you that idea?" Eva quipped as she saw the smile on the Minister's face.

"He called you a *skila*," Hester said. "I guess he doesn't like German accented Greeks," the Minister teased.

Eva grinned at the older man. "So, you know some Greek?"

"Only the swear words," Hester replied and laughed. His assistant and Eva joined in.

"Had he called you a *skili*, I would have translated it for you," Eva teased and ran her hand through her hair.

"So, how did that go, do you think?" Hester asked, pouring

himself some Turkish coffee. He didn't like the stuff, but it was the only coffee available. He tolerated it better when Eva told him not to drink the residue, which had made him gag the first time he had tried the beverage.

"About as good as a bodyline bouncer," Eva muttered. It was one of Zoe's favorite sayings when things went bad. Hester stopped mid sip and looked over his glasses at her.

"Are you a cricket fan?"

"No, my wife is," Eva responded without thinking and then looked up as she registered what she'd said. Hester didn't bat an eyelid and continued to sip the hot coffee.

"I knew I liked that kid for a reason," he grinned. "So does she play?"

Eva nodded. "She's quite a good batsman and can belt the ball around a bit."

"Do you think she might want to play for the Aussie Embassy against the English Embassy? We've scheduled a game in Thessaloniki."

"I'll ask her," Eva said quietly, pleased at the Minister's willingness to include her wife.

"I would like to have that little spitfire on my team," Hester chuckled and shuffled his papers. "Now I guess we have another round with Mr Papas tomorrow. I think we need to go over what we have before then so we can be prepared."

They went over the meeting and the notes they had made, and by the time they finished, it was way past 11:00 p.m. It was a quiet ride back to the embassy through busy streets. It was so different from back home, where the shops closed at 5:00 p.m. and everyone was home together with their families. The Athens nightlife was just getting started as the car weaved through traffic.

Eva was tired as she made her way up the carpeted steps, with Percy Hester just behind her.

"Good night, Eva."

"Good night, sir," Eva mumbled.

Hester stopped at his door and turned to her. "You did very well tonight, despite the boofhead's taunts. I understand some Greek, and he was a major oaf. Have you thought about going into politics?"

Eva snorted. She hated politics, and if it weren't compulsory to vote she wouldn't bother, but she wasn't going to share that piece of information with the Minister.

"No, I don't think I would make a good politician," Eva replied, getting a chuckle from the Minister.

"You sell yourself short, Eva," Percy said. "Good night."

Eva looked on as Hester closed the door, and she shook her head. Zoe would get a kick out of the fact Hester thought she would make a good politician. Eva smiled at what Zoe would say. Her thoughts turned to her young wife, who would have fallen asleep by now.

She unlocked the door to their darkened room, the only light coming from the full moon which bathed the room. Eva glanced at the bed and noted Zoe was fast asleep. She took off her jacket and left it on the chair.

Quietly removing the rest of her clothes, she headed for the bathroom where she ran the water and filled the tub. Leaning against the wall watching the water fill up, she closed her eyes and sighed. The trip and the long day had made her very tired, and a nice warm bath was going to ease some of the tension away. She settled into the tub with a sigh and let the water soothe her tired muscles. Letting her head rest against the rim, she closed her eyes.

Zoe woke with a start and looked at the clock that read 1:00 a.m. She looked over at the empty bed and scowled. Zoe pulled the covers back and put on her robe. It was only when she went near the bathroom that she saw the light showing from underneath the door. Opening it and peering in, she smiled at seeing Eva asleep in the bath. Zoe picked up the towel near the door and knelt beside the tub.

"Evy," Zoe whispered as she gently shook the sleeping woman.

Tired blue eyes opened and met her emerald eyes. "I fell asleep?" Eva mumbled.

"Yeah, love, you did. You're going to get all pruny. Come on." Zoe helped her partner out of the bathtub and dried her off. Putting her arms around her wife's waist, she looked up. "Time for bed, Mrs H."

"Hmm, okay, but I'm not sleeping in the other bed," Eva grumbled, leading her wife out of the bathroom.

Zoe shook her head. She gently pushed Eva to her own bed then went to the other bed and messed it up, pulling the covers down. She went back to Eva who was hitched up on her elbow, watching Zoe make the bed look slept in.

Zoe took off her robe and settled down next to her wife. "I

think the towel is a bit scratchy," she murmured and removed it from Eva's body and threw it across the room.

"Better?" Eva asked, giving her partner a kiss.

"Much better, now go to sleep," Zoe replied and rested her head on Eva's shoulder.

"I always listen to my wife," Eva whispered, obediently closing her eyes.

Chapter
10

The morning went very well for the Minister's team. The surly Greek Minister was in a better frame of mind and surprised them all by reverting to a mangled form of English. He told them he could understand the language, but speaking it was rather bothersome.

Eva sat back and watched as the two men began to talk in earnest. When Papas needed Eva to translate, he would look at her and indicate for her to interpret. Overall it was a very easy morning for Eva, one for which she was grateful.

That afternoon, seeing the sights, Eva took Zoe's hand as they stopped outside the Church of the Twelve Apostles to admire the architecture.

"I think it's rather funny to have a church here," Zoe said, putting her hand out and touching the stones.

"Why?"

"Well, we've just passed the Altar of the Twelve Gods, the Temple of Zeus, the Temple of Ares, the Temple of Apollo, and then here we come to the church where the God is real and not a mythical being," Zoe explained and looked up at her partner. "Don't you find it odd?"

"Odd, yes, but the Greeks have never been a logical people," Eva teased. "I don't think it would have served any purpose to demolish the old temples and obliterate the past to make way for the new," Eva reasoned.

"Hmm, true," Zoe agreed, as she looked around the area known as the Agora. It was an ancient marketplace where Greeks would trade and worship. The ancient site fascinated them both.

They continued to walk, occasionally stopping to read the map of the old city. Eva smiled as she watched her younger partner soak in the atmosphere. Eva had been to Athens before with her stepfather and was impressed by the historical aspects of the city. Zoe's enthusiastic approach to learning all about the city and its history didn't surprise Eva. Her wife's constant thirst for knowledge and her appreciation of history were traits Eva loved about her. She never stopped learning, always wanting to know more.

They wandered onto Areopagus Hill and climbed the steps, which were a little slippery from the overnight rain. Reaching the top, Eva put her arm around Zoe's shoulders and pointed to the view of the Agora.

Zoe looked around her in awe and then looked at Eva with a huge smile. Her brother, Mihali, had read her a story about how Ares, the god of war, was tried by the council of the gods for the murder of Halirrhothios, son of Poseidon. The council accepted his defense of justifiable homicide, on the grounds that he was protecting his daughter, Alcippe, from unwanted advances. Zoe remembered saying to her brother that if the council believed that lying, murderous god, then they were idiots.

"What's funny?" Eva asked, seeing Zoe's grin.

"Mihali told me the story about how Ares was tried here for the murder of Halirrhothios. I just found it funny that the others would accept his word."

Eva nodded. "Ares, the god of war and deceit. The old myths served a purpose you know."

"They did? How?"

"Well, when Saint Paul finally made it to Greece, he preached right here, and he spoke to the Athenians about an Unknown God," Eva said, looking around the area and trying to imagine the courage necessary to speak to the Greeks about a God they didn't know. "He stood down there," she pointed to the square down below, "and he preached about Jesus and about God. Imagine, Zoe, this place was filled with Greeks all wanting to hear this Roman preach to them."

Zoe took a deep breath and closed her eyes, letting the images form in her mind. They would often read the Bible together, and Eva would lead her towards having a better understanding of how events took place. They were always debating something they read.

"He was a braver man than I would have been," Zoe quietly said as she opened her eyes again.

"He did what he was commissioned to do, love. I'm sure if you were given the job he was, you would do it magnificently." Eva squeezed her wife's hand. "You put your heart and soul into everything, and I don't doubt it for a minute that you could do what Saint Paul did."

"I think the job would be easier if I had you by my side," Zoe said and cupped Eva's cheek. "With you, I can do anything."

Eva was deeply touched by her wife's love. They had only been together for five years, but she couldn't imagine life without her mate. "I love you, Zoe," Eva whispered.

"Evy, have you ever thought of what life would be like if we hadn't met up?" Zoe gazed at her partner while holding her hand.

"I don't think I would be alive, Zo."

"Really?"

Eva nodded. She had been at the lowest point in her life, and she hadn't wanted to face a future full of unhappiness. "I prayed to God that he would give me the strength to continue, because I knew I couldn't go on as I was."

"Oh."

"He answered my prayers," Eva said and smiled. "Getting hit by a rock is not usually the way one gets a revelation, but God moves in mysterious ways," Eva joked.

Zoe giggled. "You know, you keep going on about that rock. It was just a tiny rock, and it didn't hurt you!"

"I had a bruise for days," Eva mock pouted.

"Oh my poor baby," Zoe giggled and kissed Eva's arm.

"Thank you, a kiss makes it much better," Eva chuckled as Zoe gave her another kiss.

"Dad said that the house is waiting for us when we get to Larissa."

"Is that old place still standing?"

Zoe nodded. The house was indeed old, but Mihali had bought it so he could rebuild. He was never able to do anything with it since the war intervened and he hadn't survived to enjoy it. When she was old enough, Zoe shared the house with her friend Stavros. *Maybe it was God's hand in it*, Zoe mused to herself. It was situated directly opposite the house that Muller used for his residence.

"Why didn't you go back to the farm?" Eva asked.

"After Mama died, I couldn't bear to go back. All I wanted to do was curl up in a little ball and die. The farm had too many memories, Evy. I guess I'll have to go back and see what I can salvage from it." Zoe took a deep breath. Her heart still ached when she thought of her mother lying in her arms, dying. "Do you think we should sell it?"

"I don't know, love. It's your property."

"No, it's OUR property; and do you think we should sell it?"

Eva smiled. "Well, why don't we wait until we see it and then decide."

"Works for me," Zoe replied as her stomach grumbled. "I think I need to eat. Let's go and feed ourselves."

They stood and slowly made their way down the steps, Eva stopping every couple of steps while Zoe leaned on her. On the last remaining steps, Eva looked at her partner, grabbed her by the waist, and carried her down.

Eva lay back on the crumpled sheets and let out a contented sigh. She had missed being able to make love to her wife, who was burrowed against her side letting her fingers lazily trace Eva's bellybutton. Eva played with Zoe's unruly chestnut hair and put her arms around her.

"Oh, that was *so* good," Zoe mumbled and kissed her shoulder.

"Hmm, I enjoyed myself," Eva teased and got a little slap on the thigh. "Hey, stop hitting me!"

"Oh, my poor baby," Zoe cooed, leaning on her elbow. "Did I hurt you?"

Eva made a show of examining her thigh and looked down into twinkling emerald eyes. "You are such a brute."

Zoe chuckled. "You are such a wussy thing, aren't you?"

"That's why I have you to defend me...unless you're the one hitting me!" Eva teased. "Hey, I think Paula heard you while you were doing a little wall banging."

"Huh?"

"You hit the wall, love. Hard." Eva grinned as Zoe scrambled up to look for any damage to the wall beside the bed.

"Did not!" Zoe scowled and looked back at the wall.

Eva chuckled. "I'll just tell her you fell against the wall."

Zoe shook her head and lay back down next to her partner. "So, tomorrow we head for Larissa?"

"Yep. Flying up at 8:30 a.m., and we'll be there in half an hour. Our Thessaloniki meeting was cancelled. There's been some family emergency and the Trade Minister can't meet with us, so we won't be going there."

"Oh," Zoe whispered. "So are we heading to Italy earlier?"

"Nope." Eva shook her head and looked up at the ceiling.

Zoe smirked. "You are *so* bad." Zoe began to tickle the tall woman who yelped and tried without much success to grab the smaller woman's hands. She fell off the bed with a thud, landing on the carpet laughing. Zoe hung over the bed, grinning down at her wife.

"Are you going to explain *that* to Paula as well?" Zoe smirked and made room for her tall partner to climb back into bed.

"Oh, let's see. 'Paula, Zoe banged on our wall while we were making love for the first time in a week, and then she proceeded to ravish me so that I fell to the floor in a heap.' Yeah that sounds good. What do you think?" Eva grabbed Zoe's arms before she could be tickled again. "You don't play fair, Mrs H."

"If I give you a kiss, will you let go of my hands?" Eva nodded and her wife rewarded her with a quick kiss. "You are so easy," Zoe said, snuggling up against her wife and putting an arm around her bare waist. "So are you going to tell me, or do I torture you?"

"Tell you what?"

"Are we flying to Germany earlier?" Zoe repeated her question and watched Eva's grin widen.

"No, we are staying in Larissa for a few more days than planned," Eva replied. She was rather glad of the change in plans. It would allow them both to have some time with her father and Ally, catch up with Thanasi, and attend his wedding.

"Hmm," Zoe mumbled and put her head on Eva's shoulder. They stayed that way for a few minutes.

"You're nervous about going home?" Eva asked.

"Yeah, I am, a bit. I haven't been back to the farm in nearly eight years," Zoe sighed. "I sometimes wonder what life would have been like if mama hadn't died, if the war hadn't happened, if my brothers had lived."

"There would be one less happy soul in the world," Eva said quietly.

Zoe realised what she had said and looked up at Eva. "Oh no, Evy. We were destined to be together." Zoe tried to reassure Eva who held on to her tightly. "I think that whatever happened, I would be with you."

"You think so?"

"Absolutely. I think we are born on this earth for a reason, and I think God said, 'Zoe, my girl, you see that tall, gorgeous woman coming up that street? She's yours.' So you were mine from the moment you were born."

"Is that so?" Eva smiled.

"You bet. It just took me 8 years to figure out it was time to get myself born, that's all," Zoe replied as she settled back down. "Remember how you surprised me at the beach by taking your shirt off?"

Eva looked down at her wife and frowned. She didn't know where Zoe was headed with her line of thought. She couldn't make the connection between Zoe going home and her decision to let go of one of her fears by letting others see her scarred back. "I'm confused, Zo."

"Well, you made the decision to not let Muller dictate to you and to stop being afraid."

"Hmm, but what–"

"I'm afraid to go back to the farm," Zoe admitted quietly.

"Why?"

Zoe didn't answer for a short while and then looked back up into clear blue eyes. "On the day mama was killed, I had an argument with her. I said things to my mama that were hurtful," Zoe whispered, remembering the fateful day so vividly.

Zoe was fed up with feeding the animals and cleaning. The weather was foul, and it matched her mood. All she wanted to do was go down to the river, take a book, and read. Mihali had given her a copy of Oliver Twist *that he'd found in Athens. It was one of her most prized possessions, a well-read book with dog-eared pages.*

"Zoe Lambros, where are you child?" her mother's exasperated voice yelled out.

Zoe had gone behind the chicken shed for some quiet time. She groaned when she heard her mother's voice.

"Yes, Mama," Zoe muttered and got up from the ground,

leaving the book behind so that her mother would not see it and yell even more. She rounded the corner to find her mother glaring at her.

"Zoe, you know you have to help me get these chores done! I swear that brother of yours has put foolish ideas in your head!"

"I'm going to see the world one day, Mama," *Zoe muttered, repeating what she had told her mother many times before–much to the other woman's annoyance.*

"Zoe, the only place I want you to see right now is your room, to clean it up, and then clean the barn."

Zoe made a face. She hated the barn; it stank. "But, Mama–"

"Zoe, please, don't argue with me." *The older woman let out a frustrated sigh. She was alone, caring for a farm that she couldn't sow and harvest with a teenaged daughter whose rebellious stage had decided to show up.*

"I'm going to leave here one day, you'll see."

Her mother decided to humour the teenager who sat down on the ground and sulked. "Where would you go?"

"Away, far away from Larissa and Greece. I'm going to travel and see the world. I want to draw, learn, and become somebody."

"You are somebody, little one," *Ruth Lambros said and knelt beside her daughter.* "You are Zoe Lambros, a little too rebellious at the moment, but you are a good girl."

"I want to leave."

"And leave me alone?"

Zoe looked up into her mother's emerald coloured eyes. "Mama, I have to leave. I want to see what's over there." *Zoe indicated the mountains.* "I want to know what's out there beyond Mount Ossa."

"What's out there, little one, are the Germans."

"I hate it here," *Zoe mumbled as she picked up a stone. She looked at it and threw it against the barn.*

"Zoe..." *Ruth stopped as she caught sight of Stavros, his unruly black hair flying every which way. He braked his bicycle to a stop in front of the two and hopped off.*

"Auntie! I've been told to come and get you. The kraut commander wants all the village to be present!"

"Probably another one who likes to listen to his own voice!" *the older woman grumbled, getting up off the ground.* "Come on, Zoe. The sooner we listen to that oaf, the quicker you* *can come back and finish those chores!"*

"Yes, mama," Zoe grumbled and dusted herself off.

"What did you say?"

"I said I wanted to leave and see what was beyond Mount Ossa."

"That's not so bad, Zoe. At least you didn't lie to your mama," Eva said quietly, remembering lying regarding her whereabouts on the night her own mother was killed.

"I hurt her, Evy. I told her I didn't want to be with her," Zoe whispered. "Then she was dead. I didn't have a chance to apologize for my stupidity."

Eva sighed. "You told me you went to your mama's grave and spoke to her. Didn't you apologize?"

"I did."

"The dead can hear our thoughts, love," Eva said and kissed the top of Zoe's head and held on to her. Zoe's head rested on her shoulder. "Your mama would be very proud of you, Zoe."

"You think so?"

"I know so," Eva replied, scooping up her wife and holding her tightly as Zoe wept.

Chapter
11

Zoe closed her eyes tightly, gripped Eva's hand, and prepared for the landing of the plane. She hated the take offs and the landings. Her ears popped several times, and she found the whole experience distasteful. She opened her eyes to see a smirking Eva sitting next to her.

"I think my arm fell asleep," Eva said quietly, holding up a limp hand.

Zoe scowled at her. "Remind me again why I married you?"

"Because I'm adorable, and you can squeeze me tight and I don't break," Eva chuckled. They waited for a few minutes while the plane taxied down the runway and came to a stop. The short flight to Larissa was a godsend for Eva who didn't think she could take 5 hours in a car with Paula and Clarice chattering away.

Eva pulled Zoe out of the seat and gave her a small bump while she was picking up her bag.

"Behave yourself, Mrs H," Zoe mumbled.

"Yes, dear," Eva grinned.

They got off the plane to a cold, drizzling Larissa morning. "Oh jeez, Evy, the weather hasn't changed much," Zoe grumbled.

"Welcome home, love," Eva said and put her arm around her partner, surveying the airport which was quite small. They followed the rest of their group out of the drizzle. Zoe looked around and sighed.

"Did you tell Dad..." Zoe stopped when she saw a very familiar figure standing inside the tiny airport lounge. *He looks older*, Zoe thought to herself. His hair, what was left of it, had gone whiter. The long black robes and the golden cross around his neck were a sight Zoe thought she would never see again. Panayiotis had gone back to Larissa and, although he was married, he was allowed to resume his position in the priesthood. His congregation was very happy to have their favourite priest back. Beside him stood the woman that Zoe considered her adopted mother. Ally was bundled up in a parka and stomping one foot to try to heat up.

Eva looked down at Zoe with a grin. "Dad knows."

They entered the lounge and headed straight for her father, leaving the Minister's group. Zoe found herself engulfed in a big bear hug from her father-in-law, who then turned his attention to his tall daughter.

"Welcome home," the older man said and brushed away his tears. He hadn't seen his two daughters for four years. He squeezed his daughter tight.

"Hey, I need to breathe!" Eva chuckled and hugged her father.

Percy Hester grinned while he watched the reunion. He could see where Eva got her height and good looks. He wasn't aware that her father was a priest, and he didn't know much about the beliefs of the Greek Orthodox religion, but he assumed it was allowed. He let them get reacquainted while his assistant was organizing the travel arrangements to their hotel. Once that was done, he wandered over to the group to introduce himself.

"Good morning, I'm Percy Hester." Hester stretched out his hand which was engulfed in Panayiotis' large one.

"Good morning, and welcome to Larissa. I'm Panayiotis Haralambos," the priest replied in quite good English, much to Hester's surprise. "This is my wife, Alberta."

"Pleased to meet you, Mr Hester," Ally responded and shook his hand.

"You're an American?"

"Indeed. I was here during the war and I found a good reason to stay," Ally said with a chuckle.

"Has Eva invited you to the wedding?" Panayiotis asked. "The whole village will be there, and since you will be in town we would love to have you as well."

"Of course, yes, Eva did mention the wedding. I'm looking

forward to it." Hester turned when Michael signaled that the cars were waiting. "Eva, I want to arrange a meeting in an hour at this address." He handed Eva a piece of paper with the name of their hotel. "I'll see you then."

"Thank you," Eva said quietly and glanced at the paper. She frowned a little but put it in her pocket for later.

"It's been a treat to meet you, Father Haralambos. I'm sure we have a lot to talk about." He gently held Ally's hand and kissed it. "And you, Mrs Haralambos."

They watched him leave with the rest of the group in the convoy of cars. "Smooth," Father Haralambos mumbled and got a slap on the behind from his wife.

"He was being nice, Pany, now behave," Ally admonished him and gave him a quick kiss.

"So, you didn't mention in your last letter that you were back in the priesthood. Did you forget?" Eva teased her father.

"I wanted it to be a surprise," Panayiotis replied and grinned. "Surprise!"

Eva hugged her father again and helped him as they walked to where Alberta had parked the car. "So, where's the meeting?" Zoe asked.

Eva took the slip of paper out of her pocket and handed it to Zoe. Zoe's eyes went wide. "You're kidding me!"

Eva shook her head and sighed.

"Okay, so are we going to play charades? Where is the meeting being held?" Ally asked.

"Vinizelou Street," Eva said quietly.

"Oh, they must be staying at Kiria's new boarding house! That's a nice place, has beautiful views of the valley, and it's opposite where you will be staying..." Ally stopped talking when she realised that the two women looked uncomfortable. "What? What's the matter?"

"It's the place where Muller had his residence during the war," Zoe said quietly, and put her arm around Eva's waist and squeezed a little.

"Oh dear," Ally whispered. "What are you going to do?"

"Go to the meeting," Eva said, in a matter of fact way.

Half an hour later, Eva and Zoe were standing outside the rebuilt hotel. It was early morning still and a Saturday. The street was quiet and only a few people were out. They received a few curious looks but no one recognized them, which suited Eva.

She stared at the building as the memories flooded back, memories of a time she never thought she would come out of alive. Only because the woman standing next to her had saved her life did she get a second chance. She put her arm around Zoe's shoulders.

Zoe looked at the building for a few moments, and in her mind's eye she could still see the hated swastika flag flying over the entrance. She mentally shook herself and glanced up at her tall partner, who had a haunted look on her face.

Zoe leaned against her. "Are you okay?"

Eva sighed. "I have this urge to run."

"Yeah, me too, or torch the place," Zoe joked, trying to ease her wife's anxiety.

Eva looked down and smiled. She was interrupted in her thoughts when the servants' door opened and a portly woman exited, her grey hair trying valiantly to escape its net. She turned, screaming when she saw the two women.

"Oh my dear sweet Jesus and Mary Mother of God!" Despina cried out in joy and ran up to the two women, who both recognized the old housekeeper. Despina engulfed them in a hug and cried, "Welcome home, welcome home!"

Despina stepped back and looked them both over. She touched Eva's short hair and clucked a little. "I did so love that long hair! And you look a little skinny. I'm going to feed you while you are here. I'm sure you don't get enough good food in Australia."

"I'm fine, Despina," Eva chuckled. "Zoe makes sure I get fed."

"And you!" Despina turned to Zoe, who was giggling. "You cut your hair, too," the old woman smiled. "You look more and more like your mama." She cupped the young woman's face as tears fell down her own. "Does Father Haralambos know you are here?"

"Yes, he saw us at the airport," Eva replied quietly and got another hug from the old woman. "Are you still working here?"

"Heavens no! I own the hotel!" Despina said proudly. "Come inside. What are you doing standing out here?"

"Admiring the new paint job," Eva replied.

Despina frowned for a moment, and then it dawned on her why the two were out here and not inside. She wanted to smack herself on the head for her insensitivity, but it would have to wait. "It doesn't look the same inside. I remodeled it totally, and there is nothing left of the old house."

Eva smiled at the older woman. Despina had always looked after her when her stepfather employed her as a housekeeper during the war. She took care of her and listened to her when she was lonely.

"Even the kitchen?" Zoe asked, knowing the kitchen was one of the old woman's main grumbles when she'd briefly worked as Eva's maid.

"Especially the kitchen!" Despina chuckled. "I have a fresh batch of those nut cakes you like so much, too."

"Oh well, I have to go inside for those!" Eva replied and followed the older woman inside. She felt Zoe's hand on her back as they went through the servants' entrance and into the kitchen. The room was brightly lit with pots and pans on hooks above the bench top. It did, indeed, look different from the tiny, dark kitchen Eva remembered.

"This is nice," Zoe said as she looked around. "You're going to be late," she said to Eva, indicating the wall clock.

"Hmm. Despina, I'll come by later. I have a meeting with the Australian Minister."

"You're in his team?"

Eva nodded.

"Well go, child. You don't want to keep him waiting." Despina shooed the tall woman out of the kitchen, much to Zoe's amusement.

Zoe opened the door to her old house and held her breath. The house was clean, evidence of Ally's intervention. The door opened to the small living room, which held a sofa and a couple of old chairs. She'd spent almost three years in this house with Stavros, her dear friend. If she shut her eyes, she could remember the last day she saw her friend alive.

Stavros was late coming back, and Zoe was scared. The curfew was in place and that gave the krauts an excuse to shoot anyone they wanted. They could shoot anyone at any time, but for those that had an itchy trigger finger, the magical time of 6:00 p.m. seemed to cause their brains to burn out.

Zoe was very relieved to see the dark-haired young man come in with a bottle of illegal brew. They ate in silence until Stavros mentioned Father Haralambos, which only got Zoe upset since she didn't believe God cared anymore.

"He doesn't care anymore, Stav. He's forgotten us." Zoe munched on her dinner and frowned. "You know something, Stav?"

"What?"

"There is no God."

"So say the fools..."

"What?" Zoe exclaimed, looking at him sharply.

Stavros held up his hand in surrender. "That's what Father Haralambos said. He said that's what the Bible says! Personally, I think there are a lot of fools in Greece."

"We are so bright and cheerful!" Zoe smiled at him and gently hit him on the arm, and they both laughed. "You know, Stav, we are way too depressed to be Greeks...I think we are Russians in disguise."

"Ah, but we are Greek; and we do depressing well. We've had a lot of practice! Joy is for another time and another place."

Zoe stopped smiling and looked seriously at her friend. "And you are too young to be without joy. It makes your black eyes even blacker."

"I don't think that's possible, Zoe. As for the joy...we will find our joy after the war," Stavros promised. "Until then, we try and rid our country of the Germans."

"The krauts are gone, Stav," Zoe said quietly to the empty room. "And I've found joy, my friend."

Closing the door quietly behind her, she made her way up the stairs to her old bedroom. A part of her wished that it would be the same as it had been when they'd left, but she knew that wasn't going to happen. Too many years had passed; and as far as she knew, the house was used by Thanasi and others after the Germans had been defeated, while the internal fighting was going on–Greek against Greek.

The newly painted walls still bore the bullet holes where they'd hit the walls during the civil war. A little breeze blew through the open window and ruffled the plain lace curtains. A single bed stood beside the wall next to the window, and Zoe smiled. It was short, too short for Eva's long frame. Zoe went over to the bed, lay down, and looked up at the ceiling.

She had done that many times while she was here–her thoughts turning to her family and the war. It felt like a lifetime ago since all those tragic events had happened. She hoped what her wife said was right–about her mama being proud of her. She wanted to believe it.

"I'm sorry, Mama," Zoe whispered.

Chapter 12

The meeting was brief, much to Eva's relief. The layout of the hotel was indeed different, but Eva felt a little claustrophobic and wasn't too upset when the Minister broke up the meeting early. They were scheduled to meet the Mayor for talks about a sister state arrangement with Sydney, then lay a wreath at the war memorial for the Australian soldiers that were killed during the war. The stopover at Larissa was scheduled for only two days, but with the cancellation of the meetings in Thessaloniki, the Minister decided to extend it to four. They would then fly to Rome to continue their journey.

Eva sniffed the sweet aroma of baked goodies and smiled. Despina was making her favorite Greek sweet, *kadaifi*. It was flaky pastry with nuts and a rich syrup, and would make any diabetic go into a coma.

She pushed open the kitchen door and stood leaning against the door jamb. Eva had a severe case of déjà vu as she watched Despina take the cakes out of the oven. The rain splattering the window brought back memories from the close of the war.

Zoe was angry with Father Haralambos for not wanting to run away to save his life. Eva had just about given up hope, and had gone to the church to pray. Now, both were returning to the Muller residence. It had been a cold, wet day, and Zoe came in soaked to the skin.

Eva found herself attracted to the fiery young woman, think-ing she may have found a kindred spirit in the young woman. They marched into the kitchen to find an angry Despina.

"Oh my God!" Despina cried out as Zoe carried the mud from her boots onto the clean kitchen floor. Her spotless floor was now covered in water and mud. Zoe stood there with a sheepish grin and shrugged.

"Get out of here, NOW! You are..." the housekeeper yelled, stopping in mid-sentence when she saw Eva follow Zoe inside. "Fraulein Muller, I'm sorry..."

"Sorry..." She took off her muddy shoes, threw them out of the kitchen door, and looked down to find her white socks were now a mucky brown color.

"Get some hot water prepared for a bath, Despina," Eva said, ignoring the glare Despina was giving Zoe as they both trudged up the stairs.

It was, indeed, the day Eva had allowed Zoe into her heart and surrendered her soul to the young woman.

"Are you going to stand there holding the door up? I don't think it will fall down," Despina grinned, catching Eva with a smile on her face and a faraway look.

"I was thinking of a cold, wet night and muddy shoes," Eva replied, taking a seat near the bench.

"Zoe," Despina said matter-of-factly and got a chuckle out of the younger woman. Despina took the last batch of sweets out of the oven and set them down on racks to cool. She watched Eva for a few moments. "Are you happy, Eva?"

"Very happy, Despina."

"So, that little cyclone really did win your heart?" she asked, cupping Eva's cheek. "You needed someone to take care of you."

"She won my heart and my soul," Eva grinned and held up her wedding band. "Zoe takes good care of me."

"Her mama used to say that Zoe would make a good wife some day, and she was right," the older woman chuckled.

"What was Zoe's mama like?"

"She was about the same height that Zoe is, a little bit more meat on her than Zoe has. That child is too skinny. Ruth was a beautiful woman, with chestnut coloured hair and eyes that reminded me of emeralds."

"Sounds like Zoe took after her mama."

"Hmm, she did. Ruth was a talented artist as well. Do you remember you had a painting in your room of Mount Ossa, with the valley below shrouded in a mist?"

Eva frowned. She'd hardly paid any attention to the paintings on the walls at the time. She shook her head. "I don't remember it."

Despina half smiled. That didn't surprise her. She knew the young woman had been so alone, and her soul had been in need of tender loving care. "Wish I could show you, but the painting was destroyed when the place was bombed. Ruth painted it when she was a young woman and gave it to Kiriapseli."

"That was the woman that owned the house before Muller took it over?"

"Hmm, that poor woman." Despina shook her head. "Ruth got married and didn't paint much after that. She and Nicholas, that was her husband, had the large farm to take care of; then the three boys were born in quick succession, and then of course, Zoe was born. Zoe was such a difficult birth."

"How do you know so much, Despina?" Eva chuckled, amazed at the woman's knowledge about the town and the people.

Despina patted Eva's cheek and chuckled. "I was the midwife that delivered little Zoe. She came out shrieking and kicking. She was very annoyed at being born."

"You are full of surprises," Eva chuckled. "Do you know where Zoe went?"

Despina nodded. "She's across the street."

"Mihali's house," Eva said quietly and got up.

"Are you staying there tonight?"

Eva nodded. "I don't think I can stay here, Despina. It's just a little..."

Despina smiled and patted her on the shoulder. "I know, child, I know. Maybe you can come around for lunch. Do you still love *fasoulatha*?" Despina remembered Eva's love for the bean soup that was favoured by many Greeks, especially during the winter months.

"I do, but Zoe doesn't cook it; she hates it," Eva replied. Zoe did indeed hate making the soup or looking at it. Eva begged to get the soup made, but her pleas fell on deaf ears. Eva even tried making it herself, but it was a mess. Zoe once told Eva her mama forced her to eat the soup, and she vowed she would never voluntarily cook it if it were at all possible to avoid doing so.

Despina snorted. "Well, I want you to come for lunch, and I'll make you a big bowl of *fasoulatha*. I'll make Zoe her favorite food, too."

"You don't have to do two dishes, Despina. You have enough work with the guests..."

Despina chuckled. "You think I do all the cooking and cleaning?" She laughed when Eva nodded. "My dear child, I have a cook that does that. I'm just pottering around the kitchen because Kaliopi had a day off today. Don't worry about me."

"Okay, we'll come for lunch," Eva said and waved goodbye to the former housekeeper.

Zoe leaned against the house watching the rain fall. She smiled when she saw the servants' door open and the distinctive tall figure emerged into the street. Eva pulled her hooded coat around her head to protect herself against the rain and walked towards her.

"Well, fancy meeting you here, Mrs H," Zoe teased.

Eva took off the hood and grinned. "So, Mrs H, want to show me around?"

Zoe opened the door and was about to enter, when she stopped. She looked at Eva and then inside the room for a few moments. "You know, at times like these it would have been nice if I could carry you." Zoe scratched her ear.

Eva grinned. "You mean like this?" She picked Zoe up, cradling her in her arms and walking over the threshold, closing the door with her foot.

"Uh...yeah like that." Zoe looked up into her wife's blue eyes and chuckled. "You know, one of these days your back is going to yell at you for doing that."

"You worry too much, love," Eva whispered and gave her partner a quick kiss and let her down. "Okay, so show me around."

Zoe took her hand and led her to the window. She parted the curtains, pulling Eva to her. "You see the house?"

"Yeah," Eva said. She had a good view of Despina's hotel opposite.

"I used to sit here for hours looking at it and at you," Zoe grinned.

"You were watching me?"

"Hmm. You know, I could set the clock by you. You went to church at 8:00 a.m. every morning, you returned at 10:00 a.m. every morning. You seldom shopped, and I couldn't figure out why."

Eva chuckled. "Now you know?"

"Oh yeah, now I do. Back then I didn't know you hated shopping, so I couldn't figure it out." Zoe had spent many hours trying to understand why the woman didn't go shopping. When she did venture out, it was for only a brief period. "That saved your life, you know."

"Really? That I didn't like shopping?"

Zoe nodded and took her wife's hand. "The Resistance had a plan to kill you."

"They did?" Eva was surprised. She didn't think she had been important enough for anyone to waste their energy in getting her killed. She wasn't the problem; Muller was the problem.

"Yeah, but you seldom went out, so no one did anything."

"You see? Hating to shop saved my life," Eva teased her wife, who adored to window shop and usually dragged Eva along.

"Greek stupidity saved your life, love," Zoe countered. "I knew how to get to you."

"Really?"

"Oh yeah. My plan was to get in, lull you into a false sense of security, and then whammo!" Zoe fell against Eva and they both fell to the floor laughing. "It worked."

"Not really," Eva chuckled. "Did the plan call for you falling in *heavy like*?" Eva asked and kissed her. They lay on the wooden floor facing each other.

"Um...no." Zoe shook her head and grinned.

"Right. And did your plan involve me falling in love with you?"

"No."

"Uh huh. Your plan was not working all that well, Mrs H. I guess your plan didn't involve us spending a rainy night together?" Eva chuckled at Zoe's blush. "I didn't think so."

"I didn't say my plan was going to work."

"You know, I have a plan, too," Eva said and traced her finger down Zoe's cheek.

"Uh...really?"

"Yeah. It involves seeing how comfortable your bed is," Eva smirked.

Zoe jumped up and pulled her wife to her feet. "My bed is that way." Zoe pointed to the stairs and took Eva's hand.

"What do you want?" Panayiotis Haralambos was angry. He stood with his hands folded against his chest and a scowl on his face.

"Pany, that's no way...look, can I come in?" A tall, older man stood on the threshold of the church; he clasped his hands in front of him and waited.

"Why?"

"Because I want to speak to the village priest."

Father Haralambos snorted. "Not this village priest, old man. Go somewhere else," Panayiotis muttered and held his ground.

"Pany, please, I need to speak to you."

He wanted to tell the man to remove himself from his presence, but his conscience would bother him if he did. Panayiotis grimaced and opened the door. Shaking his head, he motioned the old man to enter the church. He closed the door quietly behind him.

The old man made the sign of the cross as he passed the image of the crucified Jesus and followed the priest into his office.

"So, to what do I owe the dubious pleasure of your visit?" Panayiotis asked, taking a seat behind his desk and folding his arms.

Petros Mitsos was a tall, distinguished-looking man. He had piercing gray eyes, his hair was silver with flecks of black, and he wore his tailored suit well.

"I'm sorry, Pany, I really am."

"So you said in your letters."

"You read them?"

"Of course I did. I thought you were dead. Imagine my surprise once I received a letter from you. Is there a reason you are here?"

Petros fidgeted. If anyone could tell him where his daughter was, Panayiotis was that man. He'd tried to track her down, but found she had left his cousin's place and they didn't know where she had gone. When he made his enquiries in the small village, a village he'd vowed he would never return to, he was shocked to find that the young man he had nearly killed was the village priest.

"I want to find Daphne."

"You're too late, Mr Mitsos," Panayiotis sniffed.

"What do you mean?"

"You abandoned her thirty years ago, you disowned her. *Now* you want to find her?"

"A man changes, Pany."

Panayiotis nodded his head. "Why?"

Petros looked down at his hands. "I made a mistake."

Panayiotis shook his head in disgust. "You made a mistake? A mistake is forgetting to do something; a mistake is something you didn't want to happen, Mr Mitsos. This wasn't a mistake. It was a monumental dereliction of your duty as a father and as a human being," the priest spat out. "You left your daughter, who was pregnant with *my* child, to fend for herself. You didn't give me a chance to see my child growing up."

"You have a right to be angry, Pany, but I want to make it up to her."

"You can't."

"Why don't you let Daphne decide that?"

"She can't, Mr Mitsos. Daphne was killed in Germany in 1938," Father Haralambos said quietly. He wished he could go back in time. He had wanted to elope and flee Larissa, but Daphne hadn't wanted to leave.

"Oh." Petros took out his handkerchief and mopped his brow. His chance to make things up to his only daughter was gone. "What about the child she had? Was it a boy or a girl?"

Panayiotis sighed. "You obviously didn't do much checking if you are asking me that question."

"Aren't you being a little hard on me, Pany? I am trying."

"Mr Mitsos, your *mistake* cost the life of the woman I loved, caused pain and hardship to my daughter, and, yes, you did have a granddaughter. She went through unnecessary pain because you were so full of pride."

"I have a granddaughter?"

"Indeed you do. You would have watched her grow up had you not decided that your image in the village would be tarnished by having a daughter who was pregnant and unmarried." Panayiotis took off his glasses and cleaned them with the bottom of his robe. "Was it worth it, Mr Mitsos?"

"It was a different time back then, Pany. You know it was."

The older man tried to justify why he had chosen to send his daughter away from the village when he'd found out she was pregnant.

"I would have married her, Mr Mitsos, but that wasn't the issue was it? I wasn't from a wealthy family. I was a simple man who made his living by being a shepherd."

Petros Mitsos could only bow his head. He knew what the priest was saying was true, and that his decision to send his daughter away had been based on the family's standing in the community. His wife had been appalled at the thought of having Panayiotis Haralambos as a son-in-law.

Petros looked up into ice-cold, blue eyes. "Is my grand-daughter alive?"

"She is," Panayiotis replied. He didn't want to deal with this man at all. Thirty years had passed since Daphne had been sent away, but the bitterness was everpresent in his mind and heart. As a priest, he knew he should forgive, but as a man, he felt unable to extend forgiveness to the older man.

"What does she look like? What's her name?" Petros leaned forward and held on to the desk, eager to find out everything he could about his only grandchild.

Panayiotis sat in silence for a moment. "She is her mother's daughter–tall with dark hair and blue eyes. She is a gentle, kind soul. I am very proud she is my daughter. I don't know why Daphne did it, but she showed that she still loved you both when she named her daughter Eva. I would never have named her that."

Petros was startled. His daughter, who he had disowned, had named her daughter after her mother. It was a bitter pill to swallow–that despite all he'd done, she'd still remembered her family. "Eva. Does she live here? Is she married?"

"She is married and she lives in Australia."

Petros sighed. He was never going to meet his only grand-child. Australia was too far away for him or his wife to travel. "Would you grant an old man's wish to at least give me her address so that I might write to her?"

Panayiotis was torn. Eva had the right to get to know her grandparents, even if they were responsible for her pain. Getting up from the desk, he picked up his coat and put it on. "I'll do better than that. Eva is here on a working holiday. I'll take you to her."

"She's here in Larissa?" The older man jumped to his feet in excited expectation that he would finally meet the grandchild he had almost given up hope of finding.

"Yes," the priest sighed. He wasn't sure if what he was about to do was right, but if Eva wanted to speak to her grandfather, then he wasn't going to stand in her way. "Come along."

Chapter 13

Zoe lay sprawled on the sofa, her legs over the arm rests, listening to the rain on the tin roof as she read. They spent an enjoyable, relaxing afternoon, talking and playing with each other. Eva went across the street to pick up some files she had to read, and she left Zoe on the sofa. They were going to go to her father-in-law's home for dinner and to catch up with Thanasi and meet his new bride-to-be.

Zoe turned to the door as she heard a light knock. She didn't think it was Eva, who would have simply entered the unlocked door. "Come in!" Zoe called out.

The door opened slowly, and Father Haralambos stuck his head inside and grinned. "Good afternoon, Zoe!"

"Hi, Dad. Come in." Zoe got up from her position on the sofa and watched as her father-in-law entered. Behind him came an older man.

"Zoe, this is Petros Mitsos. Petros, this is Zoe Haralambos." The priest made the introductions and, judging by the perplexed look on Petros' face, he was rather amused to see how this would play out.

"You have another daughter?" Petros turned to the priest and asked.

"Daughter-in-law," Panayiotis corrected and leaned against the wall holding his cane.

The older man was even more confused by this turn of

events. "You have a son?"

Zoe looked at her father-in-law and shook her head. "You are so bad, you know that? I can tell where Evy gets it from!" she gently scolded the older man with a grin.

"Wait a minute. I'm confused."

"Mr Mitsos, Eva and I are partners. We are married," Zoe said, watching the man's eyes go round as saucers. She sat back down on the sofa with an amused smile on her face. Whatever her father-in-law was doing, the look on his face indicated that he was enjoying himself over in the corner.

Mitsos was agitated by the news. "You are married to a woman?" He didn't think that was possible. He turned to the smirking priest. "What's the meaning of this?"

"Which part didn't you understand, Mr Mitsos? Zoe is married to my daughter."

"That's not natural!" Mitsos spat out. "You are a priest for God's sake! How do you condone your daughter being married to...to...a woman?"

"Excuse me, sir. Was there some reason you came to our home, or did you just want to insult someone today?" Zoe asked defensively. She wanted to get to the bottom of why her father-in-law had brought this man here.

"I am looking for Eva Haralambos."

"Why?"

"Look, young lady, I don't think you are showing the proper respect to me. I don't need to tell you what I am here for."

Zoe looked at the man for a moment and scratched her ear. "Hmm. You come into my home uninvited, you insult me, and you tell me to mind my own business. Is that about right?"

Mitsos was dumbfounded. He glanced back at the priest, who had a grave look on his face. When Mitsos turned from him and back to his very angry daughter-in-law, Panayiotis grinned.

"Is Eva here?" Mitsos asked Zoe, speaking very slowly.

"No," Zoe replied.

"When is she coming back?"

Zoe shrugged and sat down.

Father Haralambos decided he'd had enough fun at the older man's expense. "Zoe, this is Eva's grandfather."

Zoe's mouth dropped open. "Holy Mary, Mother of God!" Zoe exclaimed, then shrugged apologetically at her father-in-law. "*You* are Eva's grandfather?"

"Yes, finally." He turned to the priest. "Why didn't you say that to begin with?"

"So, what took you so long to try and find your granddaughter?" Zoe asked, clearly not impressed by the revelation. She was surprised, but not very impressed.

"What?"

"What took you so long to get in contact with Eva?" Zoe repeated.

"I don't think that concerns you," the older man said defensively.

"Here we go again," Zoe sighed. "Look, Mr Mitsos, despite what you think about my marriage or me as a person, your granddaughter is my concern."

"I need to speak to her–"

"Took you long enough," Zoe muttered. "Eva is not here."

"Yes, I gathered that. Can I wait for her?"

"I don't think so. I need to break the news to my wife that her grandfather, who couldn't have cared less about her for 30 years, has finally showed up. It's not something one just gets lumped with," Zoe said, giving her father-in-law a glare.

Petros was exasperated. Talking with the priest, and now this young woman, was grating on his last nerve. He would have some patience and play the game her way, for now. "All right. Can you please call me when you have spoken to her?"

"Sure will," Zoe said and watched as the two men walked out. "Dad, just a minute."

Father Haralambos stopped and turned to find Zoe putting her arm around his waist and looking up. "You enjoyed that way too much, shame on you," Zoe whispered and gave her father-in-law a hug.

"I don't know what you mean, Zoe," Panayiotis replied, giving Zoe a pat on the head as he left with the older man.

"Yeah, I bet you don't," Zoe muttered to herself as she closed the door. "And the trip was going so well," she said aloud, sitting heavily on the sofa. She got up and paced, trying to decide on the best way to tell her wife that her grandfather had just showed up.

The door slowly opened, and Eva walked in holding two fresh loaves of bread in her hands with the files tucked under her arm. "Hey, Zo, take these will you?" She handed the bread to her.

"Evy, we need to go for a walk."

"Huh? You want to go for a walk? Why?" Eva asked.

"I need to walk," Zoe insisted, taking her wife's hand and leading her out.

Eva frowned down at the odd behaviour, but she shrugged her shoulders and followed as Zoe wound through cobblestone streets. She smiled when she realised where they were going. They came to the clearing at Athena's Bluff. The lookout was a perfect place to see the valley with Mount Ossa looming over it. Zoe sat on the stone and patted the spot beside her. Eva sat down, her long legs dangling from the outcropping.

"So, this is nice," Eva murmured, beginning to nuzzle Zoe's neck.

"Oh, nice," Zoe agreed, forgetting why she had brought Eva to the bluff. "No, wait." Zoe pushed Eva away, much to her partner's consternation.

"Huh?"

"Eva...um...how do I come out and say this..."

"What?"

"You know your mother...how she left Larissa..." Zoe stammered.

"Zoe, did you get hit on the head while I was away?" Eva joked and playfully examined her wife's head for any injury.

"No!" Zoe gently slapped away Eva's hands. "Dad came over this afternoon."

"That's nice."

"And he brought someone with him." Zoe looked at her wife and took a deep breath. "Your grandfather is here."

Eva didn't say anything, simply looked out at the view before her. "Hmm."

Zoe was confused. She was quite sure Eva would have some more noticeable reaction to that news. "Did you hear what I said?"

"Yeah, my grandfather is here."

"And?"

"And what, Zo? What does he want?"

"I don't know. To see you. He wasn't very forthcoming about why he was here," Zoe muttered.

"Was he rude to you?" Eva asked. Zoe noticed her eyes went that icy blue that indicated her wife was about to get extremely upset.

"Well, he wasn't exactly welcoming me to the family."

"Forget him," Eva mumbled and took her hand.

Zoe watched her partner and sighed. As much as she disliked the man, she didn't want her wife to lose the only chance she might have to meet her grandfather. He was family, and family was important.

"Evy, he is family," Zoe said gently. Eva continued to stare out and frowned. "I think it would be good for you to see him."

"Why did he leave it all this time?" Eva asked quietly.

"I don't know, love," Zoe replied, leaning against her wife's shoulder. She put her arm around her wife's waist and watched the clouds drift along.

"When I was a teenager, I wondered where my grandparents were. I wanted to have some, but they chose to stay out of our lives, Zoe," Eva whispered.

Zoe didn't have an answer for that. She wanted to tell her wife that she should forgive, but she didn't think she would be able to, if their roles were reversed. Eva had suffered through a lot of pain because Petros Mitsos was a proud man and hadn't accepted his daughter's choice.

"Do you want to at least meet him?"

"Was Dad there, too?" Eva picked up a small pebble and threw it. She watched it bounce down to the rocks below.

"He was, and he deliberately hadn't told your grandfather about us."

Eva smiled. Her father's dislike of the man wasn't surprising, nor was it surprising he wouldn't be forthcoming with information about her. Eva felt sorry for the man if he was stupid enough to get Zoe angry.

"Do you think I should meet him?"

Zoe sighed. "Yes, I do. He is family, and you have a chance to tell him how you feel. Maybe you can find out why he chose to leave your mama."

Eva looked down at their clasped hands. "Will you be with me?"

Zoe smiled. "Try and stop me," Zoe replied. She tugged the tall woman's head closer and gave her a kiss, entangling her hands in Eva's soft, dark hair. Eva laid her head on Zoe's shoulder. "I'll always be with you," Zoe promised.

"It's been a long time, Eva." Despina wiped her hands on her apron and smiled across at the woman sitting at the table. Eva Mitsos was a tall, distinguished-looking woman with silvery

hair and piercing blue eyes. Despina looked at her old friend and
shook her head.

"Too long, Des, too long," the old woman said, shaking her
head.

"So, why did that idiot of a husband of yours take so long to
come back?" Despina had no respect for Petros Mitsos. She
thought he had been a proud and stupid man when he was young,
and she didn't think he had changed all that much.

Eva sighed. "You know how it is, Despina. He was a war
hero, and all of that rot."

Despina put the dishcloth down and looked at her friend.
"Eva, what he did wasn't right. Panayiotis would have married
Daphne. You know that."

"He wasn't–"

"He wasn't wealthy, and the great war hero didn't want a
simple shepherd as a son-in-law," Despina said and dared her old
friend to contradict her. She knew it was the truth, and that,
because of that, her friend and her daughter had been estranged.

"I did try and find Daphne without Petros knowing," Eva
said quietly. "She left my cousin's place, and I couldn't trace her
after that. What is my granddaughter like?"

Despina smiled. "You would be very proud of her, Eva. She
is a beautiful woman, both inside and out."

"Oh. Petros did such a terrible job this morning when he
went to try and speak to her. The man still thinks he is in charge
of the Greek army, the way he goes about things."

Despina snorted. "What did he do?"

"Well, he told me there was this young girl at the house that
gave him trouble. He didn't say what trouble or who the girl was.
He was rather irritable for the rest of the afternoon."

Despina laughed. Petros had obviously met Zoe, and she
could just imagine the sparks that flew when that happened,
since Petros had the finesse of a sledgehammer in talking to people. "Oh dear, that must have been something."

"Do you know who the girl was?"

"I sure do. Do you remember Alexandra's little girl, Ruth?"
Despina asked.

"Very quiet child. Didn't she marry Nicholas?"

"Well, Zoe is Ruth's daughter."

"Are this Zoe and my granddaughter friends?"

Despina didn't know how much to reveal to Eva's grandmother, but she would probably find out from someone else any-

way. From the description of how Petros had acted, Despina surmised that he already knew about Eva and Zoe's relationship.

"They are partners."

"In what?"

"Marriage," Despina said quietly and watched Eva frown for a few moments. "Eva, if you want to get to know your granddaughter, don't allow your prejudice to blind you."

"She's a lesbian?" Eva didn't know much about homosexuals. She tried to avoid them at all costs, although she did know a man that lived in the village that was rather effeminate. "Is she normal?"

Despina laughed. "Eva, sometimes I think you need a good slap on the head, my old friend! Of course, she's normal. She is a normal, grown woman."

"I don't know any lesbians. How would I know if they are normal!" Eva retorted defensively.

Despina scowled for a few moments and then shook her head. "Eva, your granddaughter is a wonderful, talented woman. Don't let your ignorance build a wall that will prevent you from getting to know her."

The two friends sat together eating sweets. Despina smiled and shook her head at how Eva and Petros were making life difficult for themselves, when all they had to do was admit they had been wrong. She knew they would love their granddaughter and her partner if only they would take the chance.

"What is Zoe like?" Eva asked quietly.

"You would like her. She reminds me a little of you, actually–very outgoing, a little quick tempered, but with a heart of gold."

"Do you think if we went over there, they would see me?" the old woman asked. She didn't want to leave the village without even having a chance to meet her granddaughter.

"I think you may get your chance," Despina chuckled as she spied Zoe and Eva coming towards them. Zoe's arms were animatedly flying everywhere, causing Eva to laugh as the young woman related a tale. They entered through the servants' door and stopped when they realized Despina had a guest.

Chapter
14

Eva laughed at Zoe's joke as they walked into Despina's kitchen. Her wife's jokes were getting better, with only the occasional really bad joke. She found she laughed even more at a good one, because they were sometimes so bad. They stopped prodding each other when they found an older woman sitting at the table along with their friend. Eva thought she looked very familiar, but couldn't place her.

"Ah, there you are," Despina said, getting up from the table to put a pot of water on to boil. "Tea?"

"Yes, please," Zoe said and sat down.

"Girls, I want to introduce you to someone–"

"Eva's grandmother," Zoe said and smiled at the shocked expression on the older woman's face. "I would recognise you anywhere." Zoe turned to Eva, who had also made the connection. She had her stoic face on, one that most people took to mean she wasn't interested. Zoe knew what was going on behind those blue eyes.

"How–"

"That's easy. Eva resembles you," Zoe said matter-of-factly, turning to her wife and winking at her.

Eva chuckled at Zoe's comments and turned to her grandmother. "This is Zoe Haralambos, my wife." Eva watched her grandmother carefully, then looked up at Despina who was smiling at her.

"As I was saying before Zoe beat me to the news," Despina said, chuckling, "this is Eva Mitsos, your grandmother."

"Hey, Evy! You were named after your grandmother!" Zoe said excitedly, getting a smile from her wife.

There was a tense silence for a few moments as the two women eyed each other. Despina decided it was a good time to see to her guests and left the three of them in the kitchen. Zoe was going to leave also, until Eva stopped her. She sat back down next to her partner, who held her hand.

"You look like your mama," Mrs Mitsos said quietly. Taking a deep breath, she added, "This is a little awkward."

Eva turned her head slightly with a hint of a smile on her face, waiting for the older woman to make the first move. Her grandmother fidgeted for a few moments, feeling extremely uncomfortable under her granddaughter's scrutiny.

Zoe looked between Eva and her grandmother and sighed. "Mrs Mitsos, do you like mangoes?"

The question startled the older woman, and she didn't know how to answer the young woman, so she remained silent. Eva turned to her wife and shook her head.

"Well I had to say something, you weren't doing anything," Zoe gently scolded her and gave her a playful backhand slap across her stomach.

"I was going to," Eva protested.

"You were not, you big chicken."

The older woman hid her grin at the playful banter between the two women. She could see how comfortable they felt with each other. Her granddaughter did, in fact, resemble Daphne so much that she thought she was seeing her own daughter walk in. The painful ache in her heart from having let her husband banish their daughter all those years ago made her want to cry for the daughter she had betrayed. Her granddaughter's German accent was a little jarring. She hadn't expected that, but then Daphne had settled in Germany so it shouldn't have been a surprise.

"How long have you two been together?" Mrs Mitsos asked. She watched as Eva glanced at Zoe, putting her arm around the younger woman's shoulders.

"Almost five years," Eva replied. "We met here in Larissa during the war."

"Did your mother come here with you as well?" Mrs Mitsos asked. She had asked her husband if he'd found out anything, but he hadn't been forthcoming. She wasn't sure if what he'd found was something he had not wanted to hear.

Eva looked at Zoe for a moment and then turned to her grandmother. "Mama was killed in 1938."

Mrs Mitsos' hand went to her mouth in shock. "Oh," she cried out quietly, as tears began to fall. Eva's resolve to remain a little aloof dissolved as her grandmother broke down. The older woman began to weep as Eva embraced her, her own tears tracking silently down her face.

"Are you okay?" Eva asked, accepting a napkin from Zoe to dry her grandmother's tears. Zoe dragged her chair to sit on the other side, next to the older woman.

"Thank you, I just wasn't...I...how did she die?"

Zoe decided she had better step in and answer that question. "She was killed during Kristalnacht. Someone mistook her for a Jewess."

"Oh. Did she marry? Was she happy?"

Eva nodded. "A German officer." Eva stopped for a moment. "Mama was happy with Major Muller," Eva lied. She didn't want the old woman to feel any more guilty than she already did. It was a white lie.

Mrs Mitsos looked at her granddaughter. "You don't lie very well, Eva."

"Uh..." Eva stammered. She'd been caught flat-footed and she turned to Zoe, who was trying valiantly to hide a grin.

"Your mother had the same problem–her eyebrows would twitch when she lied." The older woman was in a way pleased that her granddaughter tried to spare her some pain. She sighed when she thought of her daughter being unhappy and being married to a man that wasn't the father of her child. "Thank you for trying to spare my feelings."

"You really stink at lying, Evy," Zoe teased her wife, who turned a bright shade of red.

"Uh...mama wasn't unhappy all the time."

"No, just the majority of the time," the older woman guessed. "Eva, I wish I could go back in time and change things, but I can't. It was a different time back in 1919. Attitudes were different."

Eva sniffed. "Was my father so bad that mama couldn't marry him?"

"No, he wasn't bad," Eva Mitsos replied. How could she tell her granddaughter that they didn't want the young man because he was a simple shepherd and didn't have money or prospects?

"We thought he couldn't give your mother what she was used to."

"That's lame," Zoe said quietly. "He didn't have enough money to be *somebody.*"

Mrs Mitsos looked at Zoe. "Despina was right. You do speak your mind."

"One of her many lovable qualities," Eva replied as Zoe joined her. She took her wife's hand and squeezed it.

"You are right, Zoe. All I can do is apologize, but I know that won't change the past. I would like to be in your life, if you would let me."

Eva bent her head and played with her ring. "Does it bother you that Zoe is my wife?"

The older woman wasn't expecting that question and she looked at Zoe. "If I'm honest, I will say, yes, it does bother me. I won't lie and say it doesn't. I don't understand how you can love a woman."

"Why do you love your husband?" Eva asked.

Eva's grandmother frowned. No one had ever asked her that question before. "I love him because he makes me whole."

Eva smiled at Zoe. "Zoe makes me whole."

"I don't think it's the same."

"When Eva gets ill, I'm there to nurse her and usually scold her for being a bad patient," Zoe joked and then turned serious. "When Eva hurts, I hurt. When she's happy, I'm happy. I don't think it's any different for you and your husband, Mrs Mitsos. We give each other our love, and that isn't bad, is it?"

"Marriage is a big commitment, Zoe. Where do you see your relationship going in 5, 10, or 20 years?"

"I have absolutely no doubt in my mind that I will be married to Eva for the rest of my life," Zoe responded emphatically.

Mrs Mitsos was rather taken with the young woman. She could see the love she held for her granddaughter, but she didn't think that was enough. "Someone has to take the lead in a marriage, Zoe. I understand you want to believe that it's the same as for a man and a woman, but it isn't the same." Eva Mitsos didn't want to alienate her granddaughter now that she had found her, but honesty was the best way to deal with this issue. "Who is the head in your relationship?"

"We both decide what to do. We sit down and discuss it," Eva replied.

"What if you disagree? Who do you defer to when you have

a difference of opinion about what to do? How do you resolve it?"

"We pray about it and then sleep on it. Usually we find a solution in the morning," Eva said. Praying was a way they dealt with issues they didn't know how to handle, and it worked for them. Their prayers weren't answered all the time, but a solution to the problem was usually found. "We try and respect each other and resolve problems. I don't see anything wrong with that."

Eva Mitsos was impressed with the articulate way her granddaughter spoke. "Eva, I can't lie to you and say that what you have told me has changed my mind about your way of life. You are my granddaughter, and I want to get to know you and Zoe. I've spent 30 years regretting what happened with my daughter, I don't want to spend the rest of my life regretting that I didn't get the chance to get to know you."

"My brain hurts," Eva said as she laid her head on Zoe's lap on the sofa. Her long legs dangled from the armrests. They had walked back to their own house and were resting before going to dinner at her father's house to meet with Thanasi and his fiancée.

Zoe looked down at her wife, letting her finger trace a dark eyebrow. "It's been quite a day." Zoe brushed back Eva's bangs and let her fingers comb through the thick hair.

"Quite a day doesn't cover it, love," Eva murmured, enjoying Zoe's attentions. "So what is my grandfather like?"

Zoe pursed her lips. "I don't like him."

Eva chuckled. "Why?"

"He's full of himself and his own self importance."

"Most Greek men of that era are, Zoe."

"Dad isn't," Zoe reasoned. "My father wasn't. He was gentle and loving towards my mama and to us kids. I never heard him yell."

"Some men think they are important in the grand scheme of things."

Zoe looked down and met Eva's blue eyes. "In other words, they are full of it."

Eva laughed. "Yep." Eva took Zoe's hand and kissed it. "I wonder if things would have been different if they had let my father marry my mother."

"I guess your only daughter being an unmarried mother in

1919 was pretty bad for the image of a war hero," Zoe said sar-
castically. "You know, he could have just sent your mama to
another village, and then had Dad sent there too and just married
them."

"I don't think it was that easy, love. Having sex out of marriage was a big taboo back then."

"It's not a crime, Evy. You would think your mother had
committed a horrible crime by the way he acted."

"I don't know, love. You know, it's technically a crime if I
make love to you. I think sometimes it is more acceptable if a
person is a murderer rather than someone who loves another
human being in a way society doesn't approve of."

"Will that ever change, Evy?"

"I would like to think so, Zoe." Eva wanted to believe that
she would see a change in attitudes, but the realistic side of her
didn't think she would see it in her lifetime. "Maybe in 50 years
we could have a family without a Power of Attorney, or acknowledge our love without fear that someone would want to hurt us."

"Fifty years is a long time, Evy. I'll be 72 and you would
80! I guess it would be okay then if I kissed you on a bus, so I
could do so without getting dirty looks, huh?" Zoe joked.
"Speaking of good looking women..."

"We were?" Eva asked, not knowing how that tangent had
come about in their conversation.

"You are going to be one hell of a good looking woman
when you reach your grandmother's age," Zoe replied. The
resemblance was quite remarkable, and Zoe was intrigued with
Eva's grandmother. She was a very distinguished looking
woman.

"You mean I'm not good looking now?" Eva teased.

Zoe snorted. "You," she tweaked the dimpled chin, "are a
gorgeous woman, and I think you will age gracefully."

"Thank you, love," Eva smiled and closed her eyes.

"But if you don't, and you are toothless with no hair, I'll
still love you," Zoe finished, leaned down, and kissed her wife.
They both groaned when they heard a knock on the door. Eva got
up from her comfortable position and went to see who was there.

Standing outside with a bunch of flowers in one hand and a
bottle of retsina in the other was Athanasios Klaras. His once
dark hair was now sprinkled with white, and he smiled broadly.
Eva pulled him inside, taking the flowers and the wine and putting them down on the table. She turned to their friend and

embraced him. "Thanasi, you old dog!" Eva cried out and kissed him on the cheek

"Ah, Eva, you have grown more beautiful." Thanasi returned her kiss and hugged her.

"You flirt. Unhand my wife!" Zoe yelled, immediately being engulfed in the big man's embrace and lifted off the ground.

"Cyclone Zoe! Have you shrunk?" Thanasi teased his young friend and got the scowl he was after.

"I see the years haven't done much for your sense of humour," Zoe teased back. "So where is the future Mrs Panic God?" Zoe's nickname for her friend always amused the older man.

Thanasi chuckled. "You know, it was a mistake telling you my Resistance code name. You know that, right?"

"Did you just figure this out?" Eva chuckled. "So, where is she?"

"At your father's place helping Ally with dinner. I am to escort you two ladies to dinner." Thanasi bowed. "She really wants to meet you both."

"Uh huh. What stories have you been telling her?" Zoe asked, sitting down next to him on the sofa.

"The good ones, Zoe, the good ones."

"Now I'm scared," Zoe replied. "How did you meet her?"

"What's this? An interrogation?"

Eva grinned and replied in German. "We have ways of making you talk, Herr Klaras!" The three of them burst out laughing. Zoe knew that Eva loved their friend a great deal for her to joke in German. Zoe loved Eva's quirky sense of humour when it surfaced. It would surprise many people if they could see this side of her wife.

"I surrender! I surrender!" Thanasi put his hands in the air.

"Well it's a good thing you didn't get captured during the war then!" Zoe teased and ruffled his hair.

Thanasi chuckled. "So, you are a big deal with the Australians now I hear?"

"She practically runs the country, didn't you know?"

Eva snorted. "It's an interesting job."

"Yeah, so is sheep herding, but it doesn't send you on European trips," Thanasi joked and got Zoe giggling. "I know you're modest, but what are you doing with this Australian Minister?"

"Having an affair." Zoe couldn't help herself and guffawed at her own joke. Eva was chuckling herself at the image of her and the Minister.

"I'm an interpreter. I get to tell the Minister that the Greek Minister thought he was a total boofhead. My boss couldn't make the trip so he sent me instead."

"Boof...head?" Thanasi repeated slowly in English. "Is that a disease?"

"Aussie slang for idiot."

"Ah! *Vlakas!*" Thanasi chuckled. "So, do you want to meet the future Mrs Klaras?"

"Do we have a choice?" Eva asked, getting a playful slap on the head.

"Of course not! Come on, let's go to dinner, ladies!" Thanasi stood and captured a hand from both Eva and Zoe.

Chapter
15

The smoke rose and drifted in the light breeze as the roasting pig slowly turned on the spit. The evening was balmy for a winter's night, and they decided to eat outside. Eva shook her head at the preparations her father and her stepmother had made for a "small" dinner. She was sure her father must have spent a great deal of time trying to decide how "small" it should be. She was surprised that the whole village wasn't present. *He's probably saving that up for the wedding*, Eva mused.

The night had been one of the most relaxed Eva had spent since they'd arrived in Greece. Thanasi's wife was quite a nice woman who took an instant liking to Zoe. Eva grinned as she spotted Zoe through the kitchen window. In one hand, she held a dishcloth, and in the other, the plate she was supposed to be drying. The cloth never met the plate since Zoe's hands were going every which way, punctuating her speech.

"Zoe has charmed Althea," Thanasi said as he sat down on the chair next to her.

"Zoe can charm a rattlesnake if she wants to," Eva chuckled. "Not that Althea is a rattlesnake."

Thanasi laughed and turned from watching his bride-to-be. "So, how's life in the land of milk and honey?"

"It was a bit hard at first," Eva said quietly. "I think Zoe missed her friends and home."

"What about you?"

"What about me? If Zoe is happy, I'm happy."

Thanasi shook his head. "Didn't you miss your friends?"

Eva took a deep breath. "I didn't have any other friends, Thanasi. There was only you."

"That's no way to spend your days. Everyone needs to have a friend. You've been alone for too much of your life, Eva."

Eva looked up at the stars and smiled. "Maybe God heard my prayers."

Thanasi nodded. He loved both of them, although his first meeting with the tall woman probably wasn't the best way to be introduced. He smiled at the memory of how he'd held a gun to her head thinking she was the enemy, out to betray the priest he loved so much.

"What's so funny?"

"The day we met, Zoe calling me all sorts of names and Father H yelling for the first time that I could remember."

Eva grinned. She remembered that day; it was the day she finally acknowledged to herself that Zoe had stolen her heart. It was also a bitter day because she'd believed the father she'd found was going to be taken from her. "Funny how life turns out, isn't it?"

Thanasi bent down, cut some of the meat off of the roasting pig, and offered it to Eva who took it. "Who knows what's around the corner for us, Eva? Maybe there is this colossal plan for everyone."

"Thanasi, the philosopher now?" Eva teased. They were getting too serious, and she didn't want to think about the past.

"Hey, I'm a man of many talents!" Thanasi bowed. "Oh, before I forget, would you do us the honor of being our *koubara* at our wedding tomorrow? You and Zoe, together...um...I know it's short notice...uh..." Thanasi stammered. He had discussed it with Althea, and they couldn't think of two more deserving people to be their witnesses at their wedding. The position of *koubara* was an honor for any Greek since they also became godparents to any children of the marriage, a very serious responsibility.

Eva was deeply moved by her friend's request. "Of course we will. I don't think Zoe would say no. You know how much she loves you. It's a huge honor, thank you."

"Good, now I can relax!" Thanasi joked. He hadn't seriously thought his friend would turn him down, but the normal practice was to choose a married couple to serve as *koubaros* and *koubara* in the ceremony, and he'd wanted to get the asking out of the way.

Zoe watched her partner from the window as she finished drying some of the plates. Next to her was the young woman that would marry one of her best friends. She wasn't much taller than Zoe; her black hair was long and went down to her waist. Her brown eyes sparkled as she chatted to Zoe about Thanasi and the plans they had made for after the wedding.

"Zoe, can I ask you a question?" Althea twisted a towel in her hands.

"Sure."

"Thanasi and I would like you and Eva to be our *koubaras*...would you...uh..." the young woman stammered, unsure if her new friend would accept. She really enjoyed talking to Zoe and was at ease with her, which quite surprised her. She felt like she had known the young woman all her life. Thanasi often spoke about them both, and she'd heard stories about their time in the Resistance and in Egypt.

Althea hadn't spoken to Eva all that much, apart from the introductions. She felt intimidated by the woman's height and her German accent. Even when she spoke Greek, it was a little disconcerting. When she spotted the two chatting near the spit earlier, she was amazed at the loving way Eva looked at her partner and brushed away something from Zoe's cheek. Althea hadn't met many lesbians and didn't know what to think about it, but if Father Haralambos wasn't upset–and he was a priest after all–then she wasn't going to be. She'd watched them share a kiss and felt like she was intruding on a very private moment, so she'd gone into the house and left them outside.

Honoured by the request, Zoe screamed with delight and hugged the young woman to her. "Of course we will! Thank you. Does Evy know?"

"I think Thanasi was going to ask her."

Zoe turned and looked through the window. She saw her wife giving their friend one of her most dazzling smiles and a hug. "She knows," Zoe said happily.

"Zoe, can I ask you another question?" Althea asked. When her visitor nodded, she continued. "Is Eva shy?"

Zoe was mildly surprised. That wasn't a question she was

expecting. "Yes, she is. She's very quiet. We can't have the two of us being loud, now can we?" Zoe chuckled. She just couldn't imagine Eva being boisterous. "But she's great to have as a friend, Althea. She would give the shirt off her back if need be."

"That's what Thanasi told me. Wasn't it strange that she was the daughter of the German commander?"

Zoe leaned on the counter and watched Eva talking to Thanasi and her father. "Before I realized how I felt about her, that would have seemed strange. I had this image of a cold, godless, uncaring Nazi. I think her height added to that perception."

"The reality was far from the truth?" Althea was intrigued at how two such different people could come together. "I'm a little intimidated by your...um..."

Zoe smiled. "Wife. She's my partner, like you have Thanasi."

"I'm sorry, I didn't know what to call her...um..." the young woman stammered, feeling she'd made a total fool of herself.

"It's okay. As I was going to say about the reality being far from what I thought she was like–Eva is a warm-hearted, generous, God-loving woman."

"She just seems so quiet..."

"Get her drunk, then watch her talk," Zoe teased.

"Really?"

Zoe chuckled. "No, Eva goes even quieter when she's had a few drinks, so that won't do it. Look, don't worry. When she gets to know you a bit, she will start yapping and you won't be able to shut her up."

The arrival of the roasted pig interrupted Althea's next question. Thanasi and Eva brought the animal inside ready for carving, with Father Haralambos and Ally following right behind. This was the only family she had left, and Thanasi treated the two women as his sisters. After her little chat with Zoe, Althea vowed that she would make a special effort to talk to Eva and get to know her.

Three figures made their way down the quiet street, the full moon overhead making the walk easy in the darkness. The sound of their footsteps echoed off the stonewashed walls as they passed. Ally was between the other two women, hooking her arm around Eva's and the same for Zoe's. Ally wondered why her two daughters wanted the escort home, but judging from the way Eva was walking, she assumed it was to give the taller woman a massage.

The night had been one of the most relaxing Eva had spent on the trip. Thanasi's fiancée was quite a nice woman, who took an instant liking to Zoe. Once relaxed, the young woman had a good sense of humour. Althea reminded Eva of a very young Zoe, even though the young woman was also in her early twenties. She was quite surprised when Althea talked to her for most of the evening. Eva glanced at Zoe a couple of times and saw her wife looking quite amused.

"So, you want to take your shirt off and I'll get some warm oil," Ally suggested as they entered the front door.

Eva looked down at her stepmother with a puzzled frown. "Huh?"

"Your back. You want to have a massage, right?"

"Uh, no," Eva said and then looked at Zoe.

"Are you telling me your back doesn't hurt?" Ally said with disbelief.

"Uh, it's okay...a bit achy."

"You didn't tell me that!" Zoe was upset as she scowled up at her wife.

Eva wanted to grin at the sight of the smaller woman trying to intimidate her with a look, but she knew it would make Zoe even madder if she did. "Zo, it's nothing really...um..."

"You are so in trouble, Mrs H," Zoe muttered. She sat down next to her mother-in-law.

"Then if it's not your back, why did I escort you two ladies home? Not that I mind."

"We want your professional advice," Eva replied. She felt a bit embarrassed. She wasn't sure how she was going to ask her stepmother the rather delicate question about the different ways of conceiving.

Ally was confused. Her stepdaughter was looking very uncomfortable and her daughter-in-law was studying the floor. "Girls, what's the problem?"

"We want to have a baby," Zoe mumbled.

"Uh huh." Ally slowly nodded her head as the two women looked at each other for a brief moment. "You want to know how to go about it?"

"Uh...yeah," Eva confirmed quietly.

"Well, you get a woman, a man and then you leave them

alone so they can have sex. If everything works, 9 months later you have a baby," Ally teased. She knew what they wanted to ask and found it extremely cute. Both her daughters, who were naturally self-confident, were looking very timid.

Eva grinned sheepishly. "That's where we have a slight problem."

"You have no man."

"Actually, we have a man," Eva said, taking Zoe's hand and giving it a little squeeze.

"Earl?"

"No."

"Earl is such a wonderful young man, he would make a great father," Ally said. With his good looks and personality, she thought he was perfect father material. "So, do you have anyone in mind?"

"Do you remember Earl's partner, Pat? He volunteered."

"Oh my, yes, I remember Pat. He was the tall, good looking young man who looked–" Ally stopped and grinned. One look at Zoe's face told her why they had chosen Pat to father their children. Zoe was grinning at her and rolling her eyes towards Eva. "I'm going to have beautiful grandkids. Wait until I tell your father. He is going to be puffing out his chest and acting like he won the lottery!" Ally chuckled.

"Well, we have a slight problem before Dad can start celebrating. We both don't want to do it the normal way."

"Ah, I see. Well when I was back on the farm, we used to impregnate cows using a syringe."

"Would a turkey baster do?"

"No, a turkey baster is open at the top, and there is some likelihood you might spill some of the semen if you're not careful. I would say go for the syringe." Ally knew what the next question was going to be and was amused to see the two of them look at each other. "You want to know how you go about it?"

"Uh...yeah," Zoe said softly.

"Firstly, you have to make sure you are ovulating, because if you're not, it's going to be very frustrating. You can then use the syringe to impregnate Zoe."

"That's it?" Zoe asked. That sounded easy.

"Well, that's basically it. If you were to have sex with Pat it would be easier."

Zoe shook her head and looked up at her wife's twinkling blue eyes. "I don't want to do that. I would feel like I was cheating on Eva."

"If sex is out, your only option is to use a syringe."

"I guess we will call you when we have some good news," Eva grinned.

"Excellent. I'll have to stop your father from shouting it from the rooftops," Ally said as she got up from the sofa. "I'll see both of you in church tomorrow."

Eva opened the door and watched as her stepmother made her solitary way down the alleyway, having refused their offer for both of them to accompany her home. Eva lost sight of her in the darkness, and she closed the door quietly.

Zoe was standing in the center of the room, frowning. "You should tell me when you're not feeling well, Eva."

"I thought you were forgetting that..." Eva really didn't believe that her wife would forget, but it was worth a shot.

Zoe wrapped her arms around the tall woman's waist and looked up. "You are kidding, right?" Zoe began to unbutton her wife's shirt. "Tell me, if I was sick, would you forget that I was ill?"

"No," Eva replied. She had walked into that ambush and she sighed.

"Right. So how do you figure," Zoe took the shirt off Eva's broad shoulders and tossed it aside, "that I would forget about you?"

"You wouldn't," Eva replied, wrapping her strong arms around the young woman. She leaned down and nuzzled her neck, hoping to distract Zoe.

Her wife looked up and shook her head. "You are not playing fair."

Eva gave her a sexy smile leaning down and kissed her. "Zoe, I'm sick all over," she whispered in her ear.

Zoe chuckled. "Well, I'll have to make you feel better, won't I?"

"Uh huh."

Zoe took Eva's hand and they both went up the stairs, forgetting Eva's shirt in the living room.

Chapter 16

Father Panayiotis Haralambos smiled at the two young people before him. He had led them around a small table three times to signify their oath to preserve their marriage bond forever. He loved this ceremony, as it was most joyous. He quickly glanced at Thanasi who looked quite uncomfortable. The young man didn't believe in God but chose to get married in the Greek Orthodox Church to please his fiancée.

"May you love each other, take care of each other, and have God in your lives," the priest blessed Thanasi and Althea. Then he lifted the white crowns that signified that the newlyweds would receive the grace of the Holy Spirit and would be the founders of a new generation that would live their lives to the glory of God. He lifted the crowns off their heads and gave them a smile.

"I now pronounce you man and wife," Father Haralambos' deep voice boomed to the assembled wedding guests. They broke out in a cheer as Thanasi leaned down and kissed his new bride. Thanasi looked very handsome in his black suit. His bride wore a beautiful wedding gown of ivory white and looked radiant as she gazed up at her husband.

It was the first Greek Orthodox wedding Eva had attended, and she was quite intrigued by the white crowns that were placed on the groom and the bride. She thought it resembled something that athletes from the ancient Olympic Games would wear after

they won. She looked around the congregation and sighed when
she saw a familiar face coming towards her.

"Oh no," Eva whispered to Zoe, who turned to her partner in
alarm.

"What?"

Eva pulled Zoe in front of her. "Protect me, Zoe!"

Zoe frowned and turned to her taller partner. "What are you
talking about?" Zoe looked around the congregation to see what
had made Eva so agitated. By the way her wife was acting, she
was expecting to see Nazis come storming in. Seeing nothing out
of the ordinary, she turned to her partner. "What's wrong with
you?"

"Eva!"

Eva made a face and sighed. She turned toward the voice
and smiled at the petite elderly lady that called her. "Hello, Mrs
Elimbos," Eva greeted the old woman who had made her life a
little difficult during the war and who'd hit her with her cane the
last time they had met. The old lady was now stooped and fragile
looking as she made her way through the throng. Eva felt sorry
for the woman; she had outlived her husband and her sons,
who'd died in the war.

"Come down here, I can't even see you all the way up
there!" Mrs Elimbos tugged on Eva's jacket to get her to kneel
beside her. Zoe smothered a grin as her wife balanced on one
knee and was level with the old woman, as she sat on the chair
Eva had vacated.

"How are you, Mrs Elimbos?" Eva smiled.

"I'm old, living hurts. You don't want to hear about growing
old, do you?" The old woman patted Eva on the cheek. "I want to
apologise to you."

Eva was surprised and looked up at Zoe. "Why?"

The old woman sighed. "I regret hitting you, my dear child.
I didn't know you were working with the Resistance; I thought
you were the enemy."

Eva was deeply moved by the older woman's words. No one
in this small town had ever apologised to her for the way she was
treated during the war. Not that she was expecting any apologies.
She was part of the Nazi war machine, even if it was by associa-
tion.

The old woman took Eva's hands in hers and smiled. "When
you grow old, there are days when you regret half your life. You
have no idea how happy I was to hear that you would be coming

back." Eva tried to interrupt, but the old woman put her hand over her mouth, much to Zoe's amusement. "Father Haralambos was my saving grace during the war. It made me extremely happy to find out that you were young Daphne's little girl. I loved your mother like my own daughter."

"You knew my mother?" Eva asked, her voice breaking a little with the emotion.

"Your mother and my daughter, Kaliope, were best friends. It saddened me so much to see her leave. I didn't make the connection, but you certainly look like your mama." Martha Elimbos' eyes crinkled with fond memories of the two young women. "Will you forgive an old lady for hurting you?"

Eva didn't trust her voice at this point; she nodded. Martha cupped the young woman's face and smiled. "Well that's one thing I won't have to worry about anymore." She turned to Zoe who was hovering near Eva. "So, little Zoe, are you taking care of Eva?"

The two women looked at each other, wondering how much the old lady knew. Before they could respond, Martha laughed. "Just because I'm old, doesn't mean I'm blind. That's one thing old age hasn't taken away from me."

"We take care of each other, *Yiayia*." Zoe used the affectionate Greek term "grandmother" for the old woman. She had always been friendly with Zoe and would give her advice, whether she wanted it or not, after her mother was killed.

"Good girl," Martha said quietly and got up from her seat with a grimace. "Let me go and offer the newlyweds my congratulations before I get any older."

They both watched the old lady slowly make her way towards Thanasi and Althea. Eva hadn't moved from her kneeling position, too stunned at the turn of events.

"You know, Evy, I've never known that old woman to apologise for anything," Zoe said quietly and got a small smile from Eva as she rose and sat in the empty seat.

"That's never happened before," Eva said quietly, watching the wedding guests mill about.

"What?"

"I haven't had anyone apologise to me for what they did during the war. Not that I was expecting it, but it's nice."

Zoe stopped for a moment and wondered why she'd never asked her wife how she was treated during the war. Zoe only got to know her partner in the waning stages of the war. "Larissa isn't a happy place for you. I'm sorry, Evy, I didn't think-"

"Larissa is a very happy place for me, Zoe. All the bad things have been overshadowed by the good thing that happened to me here. You."

Zoe wanted to kiss her, but she restrained herself and leaned against her wife's shoulder. "You are the best thing to happen to me, love," Zoe whispered.

"What happened to her daughter?" Eva asked, watching the old woman greet Thanasi with the same tugging, until he went down on his haunches to speak to her.

"She was killed the same day mama died," Zoe replied.

Eva took a breath outside the church and squinted at the sun. It had finally warmed up and the rain had stopped, something she was sure made Althea very glad. The newlyweds were still thanking everyone who attended the wedding. It seemed like the whole village had gathered to see the former Resistance leader get married.

"Hello, Eva."

Eva turned around, met her grandmother's blue eyes, and smiled as the older woman embraced her.

"Where's Zoe?"

Eva looked around but couldn't spot her partner in amongst the crowd. "I think she helped Mrs Elimbos home. I'm not quite sure."

"Ah," Eva Mitsos said awkwardly, not knowing what to say.

"Eva, let's go." The gruff voice of Petros Mitsos announced his presence. Eva turned on reflex at the sound of her name.

"Wait a minute, Petros," his wife urged. The older man stopped and turned. "This is your granddaughter."

Petros Mitsos sniffed. "I know; she looks like Daphne."

His wife couldn't believe how stubborn her husband was. Well, having lived with him for so many years, she could believe it, but it was infuriating nevertheless. She had tried to talk to him about Eva, but the old man would not budge from his conviction that she wasn't normal.

"I'm pleased to meet you, sir." Eva offered her hand, which was ignored. Eva let her arm fall to her side and sighed. She looked around to locate her partner and was disappointed she couldn't find her.

"Come along, Eva, we have to be in Athens. There is no one here I want to see," Mitsos said gruffly.

The older woman was exasperated. "Petros Mitsos, you are an idiot." They'd spent so much time trying to find Daphne and her child. She had lain awake, praying to God for forgiveness for betraying her daughter. She wasn't about to let her stubborn husband walk away from their granddaughter now.

"Eva, you are making a scene." Mitsos gritted his teeth and glared at his wife.

Eva Mitsos rolled her eyes. "And you are becoming the village idiot."

"Excuse me, maybe I should go–"

"And you stay put." The older woman was now quite angry, and if it meant making a scene in front of the whole village, that was what she was going to do.

"I think it would be best to take this inside," Father Haralambos said as he stood behind his daughter, putting a reassuring hand on her shoulder. Zoe came up and stood next to Eva who looked down and gave her wife a smile.

The five of them went back into the church, Zoe taking Eva's hand and giving it a gentle squeeze. She had escorted Mrs Elimbos back to her house and had come back to find Eva standing near her grandmother, looking extremely uncomfortable. Her posture screamed that she wanted to be anywhere but where she was.

"Nice wedding, huh?" the priest said as he picked up some hymnals.

"Nice," Petros said gruffly. "That's what normal people do– get married, have children."

"And then abandon them if they make a mistake," Zoe piped up and glared at the older man.

"Zoe." Eva was not surprised by Zoe's remarks. She thought her partner had held her patience for quite some time, all things considered. One look into Zoe's eyes, and she could tell Petros Mitsos had stomped on Zoe's last patient nerve.

"No, Evy. I've had enough of this self righteous, pious, idiotic baloney."

"You don't respect your elders, young woman." Mitsos was angry at this slip of a girl who had the temerity to tell him off.

"And you, sir, have no respect for anyone. When you find some decency, let me know and maybe I'll show you the respect men of your age should get from girls my age," Zoe replied as she sat down next to her wife.

"How dare you?"

Eva stood up. She'd had enough of this as well, and her patience with this man had run out. She took a step towards her grandfather who was slightly shorter than she was. "You know, I've just about had a stomach full of what you think is right."

Zoe sat back, crossed her arms across her chest and grinned.

"What gives you the right to tell me how to live my life? You betrayed your daughter, left her alone in a strange country. You couldn't have cared less that she was alone with a child," Eva said, quietly but forcefully. "Did you know my mother married a German officer because he offered her a home? I don't know if she loved him, but I definitely know he didn't love her. He used her, Mr Mitsos, as one would use an old rag. Tell me, sir, how is that decent?"

The older man didn't say a word. He took a seat and looked down at the floor. He knew what he had done was wrong, but he wasn't going to admit that to this person who wasn't normal. She wasn't his granddaughter, not the one he'd envisioned and held out hope of one day meeting.

"My mother suffered a great deal at the hands of Hans Muller because she was too scared to come home, too scared that she would blacken the name of the great war hero. Tell me, sir, was it worth it? How does it make you feel to know that your ego was more important than your duty as a father?"

Petros' raised his head and met Eva's ice blue eyes. "You have *no* idea what you are talking about."

"Is that right? I remember my mother's tears, Mr Mitsos. I remember her crying at being alone, in a loveless marriage. Even when you abandoned her, she didn't curse your name. She told me stories about you and how you were a war hero. She named me after her mother because she felt I needed to have some family connection. She was so wrong about you." Eva unclenched her hands and took a deep breath. "She could have had a happy life with my father, but you chose to disown her instead of letting her marry the man she loved. My father is an honourable man. He risked his life during the war to save people he didn't know. He isn't a coward that ran when the Germans came to Greece."

Petros Mitsos' anger dissipated a little when he realized that she'd aimed that last barb squarely at him. He had taken his wife and fled to the United States to escape the war with the Third

Reich. Still, he didn't consider himself a coward. "I cannot condone your perversion, it's not natural."

Eva sighed and looked behind the altar at the crucified Jesus. "Is it wrong to love?"

"No, but it is wrong to pervert what you are. You are a beautiful woman, and you could have any man you want, but instead you choose to live with a loud mouthed little tramp!" Mitsos spat out.

"Hey!" Zoe cried out, but was silenced by Eva's hand on her shoulder. The young woman sat back down glaring at the older man.

"For a man your age, I am sorry to see that you are ignorant. This woman," Eva pointed to a scowling Zoe, "saved my life. She has more courage in her little finger than you have in your entire body. She has given me so much that you couldn't even begin to understand. Her mother was killed at the hands of my stepfather, Mr Mitsos. She had the courage to live through the horror of that, while you were sunning yourself in America."

Eva Mitsos was horrified at what her granddaughter was revealing. Her daughter had been extremely unhappy and had suffered greatly. She suspected her granddaughter had also suffered. She didn't understand why she had fallen in love with a woman, but she could see the genuine affection the younger woman held for her granddaughter. One look at Zoe and it was clear to her that it was more than just friendship that bound these two together. She didn't know if it was genuine love, but she hoped it was, in whatever context love occurred in a lesbian relationship.

"Do you know how it feels to lose your entire family and still able to find hope when there is absolutely no hope? Do you know what it means to reach out and trust the daughter of the man that killed your mother?" Eva took a deep breath. "To reach out to her and fall in love with her, to show her that she wasn't worthless because she was different?"

Mitsos glared at the floor and played with his worry beads.

"You don't know a thing. All you know is what you think is right, and you have a distorted view of that," Eva finished. She took Zoe's hand and they both walked out, leaving the older man astonished at the turn of events.

"She is usually such a shy person," Father Haralambos said and scratched his beard. He turned to the older man who looked up and followed his daughter's exit.

"Your daughter isn't normal! As a priest you can't condone homosexuality."

"My faith tells me that I have to love my neighbor, Mr Mitsos," Father Haralambos said to the older man, putting his hand on his shoulder. "As a father, I love my daughter for who and what she is. Your granddaughter is an honest, hard working, loving, gentle woman who has found love with someone who has all those qualities as well. She is her mother's daughter, Mr Mitsos. You are going to miss out if you don't get to know her."

Mitsos stood and gazed around the church. He looked at the priest with disgust. "You are deluded. I think you need to go back to the seminary and study what our Lord said. You are a disgrace to the priesthood."

Father Haralambos shook his head sadly and watched the old man leave the church with his wife. "You can't reason with a stupid man."

Eva and Zoe sat quietly on a park bench in the town square near the church. Most of the residents were taking their noon break. Eva was angry, angry with herself for losing her temper and allowing herself to lose control. She had a stomachache from the stressful confrontation.

"Are you okay?" Zoe asked, rubbing her back gently.

"No." Eva replied truthfully and leaned against Zoe. "I lost control."

"Eva, you didn't lose control. I know you hate to lose your temper, but that ignorant *blaka* wouldn't know what was decent if it fell on top of him." Zoe took her wife's hands and held them. Eva stopped shaking from her anger and was now trying to get herself together before she had to go to a meeting with Hester. They sat in silence watching the pigeons feed on crumbs littering the ground.

"Evy, does it matter what he thinks?"

"For a long time it did matter, Zoe. It mattered a lot. And it hurts that he doesn't want to acknowledge me."

Zoe now understood her wife's reaction to her grandfather. She was hurt that the old man denied who she was. Zoe wasn't sure how she could help her. "I'm not sure what I can do, Evy."

Eva turned to her and smiled. "Be yourself, Zoe. I have you, and that's all that matters to me. The ten year old Eva wanted to meet her grandfather."

"And the 30 year old Eva wanted to, as well. I'm sorry, Evy." Zoe cupped her wife's cheek and brushed away a tear with her thumb. Eva leaned down and let her head rest on Zoe's shoulder. She began to weep for the grandfather she'd dreamt up that didn't exist. Zoe held her tightly, unable to stop her own tears.

Chapter
17

The sound of the rooster crowing woke Zoe with a start. She raised her head slightly and immediately regretted it as the pounding in her head was keeping time with the rooster's crowing. She groaned and pulled the covers over her head to drown out the noise. Zoe wasn't sure what time they got in after the wedding reception; she couldn't even remember the last part of the party after having a little too much to drink. The homemade wine was strong and she wasn't aware of its potency. Her head ached from the overindulgence, and she selfishly wished for the rooster's immediate demise.

"It's too bad you can't kill the rooster," Eva mumbled, cuddling a little bit closer to her partner.

"Lucky rooster," Zoe said and opened her eyes to meet the sleepy blue eyes of her wife. "Tell me I didn't do anything stupid last night?"

"You danced for me." Eva grinned at the look on Zoe's face. Nearly everyone in the village attended the wedding dinner and it was a fun evening. Eva spent some time talking to people who recognized her and she'd quite enjoyed herself. She decided to take her partner home after discovering her under a table, sleeping soundly. As they walked home, Zoe began singing one of their favorite songs at the top of her voice and out of tune. It was fortunate that most of the village was at the wedding party so no one was around to be scandalized by the drunken young woman.

"Was I any good?" Zoe had no memory of it, but judging from the look on Eva's face it must have been rather interesting.

"Hmm, you danced the *tsifteteli* for me," Eva chuckled. It was one of the most erotic Greek dances she knew. It was a combination of belly dancing and some very suggestive hip thrusts and shaking. "You were very good. I didn't know you could dance it."

"It's my Eva Special," Zoe grinned and ran her hands through Eva's dark hair. "Did you enjoy it?"

Eva nodded. "Especially the part where you improvised. You took off your shirt and used it in a very inventive way."

Zoe's grin broadened and she waggled her eyebrows. "Did you join me?"

Eva shook her head and chuckled. "No, you wouldn't let me. You wanted the performance to be just for me."

"I am such a giving kind of girl," Zoe giggled and kissed her wife. "Did we make love?"

"No, you finished, said you were too hot, and then fell asleep." Eva laughed at the disappointed look on Zoe's face.

"What a waste of a dance!"

"I enjoyed it, thank you," Eva whispered and nuzzled her partner's neck. "How much did you have to drink?"

"Two glasses of the retsina! Honest! Only two!"

"My little two pot screamer," Eva teased. "What are you going to do today?"

"Hmm, I thought I might go to the farm," Zoe said quietly. She had put it off since arriving, and they only had one more night in Larissa before they would be heading to Berlin.

"Do you want me to come with you?" Eva brushed away Zoe's bangs away from her face.

Zoe desperately wanted her partner to be with her, but she knew Eva had to be at the meetings. "I would love for you to come with me, but you have to go to work. I think I'll be there for most of the day, so if you want to come over..."

"I'll come over as soon as I can." Eva kissed the top of Zoe's head and scooped her up in an embrace. "It's going to be okay, Zo."

"I hope so," Zoe mumbled and rested her head on Eva's shoulder.

Zoe's steps echoed down the quiet street. Most of the villagers were still asleep, recovering from the previous night's festivities. The local baker waved his greetings as Zoe passed the bakery.

Putting her hands in her pockets, she kicked a stone along as she walked, her pace slowing when she came to the village cemetery. Zoe stood there gazing at the wrought iron gates for a moment and took a deep breath. So much had happened to the little girl who, only eight years previously, had wished she were dead.

Walking quietly to her mother's gravesite, she was surprised to see a fresh bouquet of flowers placed near the cross. The weeds had been removed and the gravesite was well cared for. Zoe nodded her head and made a mental note to thank her mother-in-law for the loving gesture. She had once made a passing remark to Ally that the grave was going to be overgrown with weeds, since there was no one to tend to it.

"Well, Mama, I'm back home. Well, not really home, because my home is with Eva now, but you know what I mean." Zoe sat on the ground cross-legged. She plucked a blade of grass and twirled it around her finger absentmindedly. "You would like her, Mama. She has the same quirky sense of humor as Mihali. I wish you were still here." Zoe choked back the tears. "I told you I wanted to die when I lost you, but Mama, I found a reason to live."

Zoe lifted her head at the sound of two birds screeching overhead and took a deep breath. "I want to spend the rest of my life with her, Mama, every day of my life, like you did with Papa. I'm going to bring her over. Eva said that the dead can hear our thoughts, and I'm really hoping that's true, or else I'm talking to a pile of stones." Zoe shook her head and chuckled softly through her tears. "I know you can hear me and that one day I'm going to see you again, but Mama, forgive me if I don't want to join you any time soon."

Zoe brushed away the tears and lifted her head to see the village gravedigger going about his business. "You're still alive, Vangelli," Zoe muttered to herself. The old man had been the village gravedigger for as long as Zoe could remember. He never married, and Zoe always thought he was a lonely figure.

"I'm going to go to the farm and then bring Eva here,

Mama. I'm sorry I told you all those hurtful things. I never wanted to leave you alone, but I've learnt so much and I wish you were alive so I could take you to places you read about."

Zoe let out a sigh as she got up from the ground and dusted herself off. Looking again at the white cross that bore her mother's name, she crossed herself. "I love you, Mama."

The young woman turned and left the graveyard and headed down the road to the farm she had abandoned eight years before. Zoe stopped at the bottom of the road. Her heart beat a little faster, and her hands were sweaty. She wiped them along her khaki pants and took a deep breath. "Come on, you coward, move," Zoe chastised herself, putting her head down and walking purposefully up the hill. She stopped at the top and looked down at the place that she held in her heart and in her dreams. It was her home, her family, and her life before Eva came into her life.

The farmhouse was in a terrible state–part of the roof had caved in, and the walls that were once white were now a brown mucky color. Some of the paint stubbornly remained and clung on. Zoe grimaced at the house that her father had taken such pride in. He used to keep the house painted and well cared for. The once white fence around the house was peeling and the wood splintered. The gate hung at an odd angle from one hinge, the other long gone.

Zoe pushed the gate aside and it fell to the ground. She gave it a cursory glance and walked ahead to the front door. Zoe pursed her lips, looked at the old weatherbeaten door, and pushed. It swung open noisily to reveal the badly damaged living area.

The once cream walls were pitted with bullet holes and the paint scraped off. Zoe was angry that the war had made its presence felt in her home, judging by the bullet-riddled walls. She kicked away some debris in frustration.

"Goddamn it to hell!" Zoe cried out and kicked another piece of the fallen ceiling. She turned into a doorway, its door torn off the hinges. The only part that remained was one hinge, and that was rusting away. The once beautiful wrought iron bed was a rusty shell–the mattress had disappeared, and only the iron frame remained.

Zoe looked around her bedroom with disgust. Blotches of pale pink peaked out from mucky brown and like the rest of the house, the walls were filled with bullet holes. Blood was smeared near the broken window that overlooked the valley. Zoe sighed as her heart ached at the wanton destruction of her home. Stepping over fallen masonry, her eye caught the edges of a photograph peeking out of the rubble. She bent down and picked up the water-damaged picture.

Tears ran down her face and her hands shook as she gazed at the smiling face of a man with curly dark hair. He was laughing at the young girl seated on his knee who was cupping his face with her hands and laughing. With shaking fingers, Zoe traced the picture of her father. "Oh, Papa," she whispered. Taking a last look around the room, she spotted her favorite doll–its right leg was missing and the one unseeing eye stared up at the cloudy sky. Zoe made her way across the room and picked up the doll.

"Eftehia," Zoe said softly and kissed her doll. She continued to rummage around the room collecting old photographs and other personal items.

She stood at the doorway and looked back at the room. Taking a deep breath, she turned her back and walked away, out the back of the house. She was startled when she heard a noise behind her and turned to find a goat staring at her.

"It figures you would still be alive," Zoe muttered to the goat. The old animal survived the war, and Zoe wondered why he hadn't been caught and eaten by the soldiers or one of the villagers. The goat stared back at her, then snorted, turning and slowly walking away.

Zoe shook her head and walked around the courtyard, passing the chicken shed. She went around the shed, hoping that she would find what she'd left there many years before. Just under the brushes and the wooden supports for the shed was the book. Zoe stared at it for a few moments and then fell to her knees. With trembling hands, she picked up the badly damaged volume. Water logged, the pages stiff with mud, the book barely held together. She turned the pages over, barely able to make out the inscription written inside. The water had damaged the fine printing, but Zoe knew what it said. She tried to swallow the lump in her throat as she held the book in her shaking hands.

To my favorite sister, Zoe, may you always have more than Oliver did!

"Oliver Twist," Zoe whispered and closed her eyes. Mihali gave her the book before he left to fight the Germans. She held the book to her chest and began to weep.

"Zoe!"

Zoe looked up at the sound of her name. "Over here!" she called out. A few moments later Eva popped her head around the chicken shed and found her wife on the ground, her back against the structure. Zoe's tear-stained face gazed up at her, and Eva's heart broke at the look of heartache in her lover's eyes.

Eva dropped to her knees and pulled her wife into her embrace, stroking Zoe's chestnut hair as her wife wept anew. The meeting had gone on longer than usual though she had desperately wanted to cut it short.

Eva held Zoe slightly away from her and gazed into her eyes. "I'm sorry I couldn't come sooner."

Zoe nodded. "I want to sell the place and leave. I don't want to come back here ever again," Zoe whispered.

"Are you sure? Maybe you want to think about this and decide when we go home, love. I think you're too upset now." Eva brushed Zoe's bangs away from her eyes.

"There's nothing left, Evy."

Eva had to agree with that. It broke her heart to see her wife's childhood home destroyed.

"You have good memories, Zoe," Eva whispered and kissed her wife.

"I found this in my old room." Zoe took a photograph out of the book and showed it to her wife. Eva looked at the photo and grinned. There was no mistaking the mischievous look on the young girl's face and to whom it belonged.

"This is you?"

"I was eight and Papa just returned from Thessaloniki," Zoe said. She had driven her mother crazy by asking her every hour when her father would return. He had gone to Thessaloniki to sell some produce and promised his youngest that he would bring back a doll. The eight-year-old child stood at the gate from early in the morning waiting for her father to arrive.

"What was his name?"

"Nicholas," Zoe replied, gazing at her beloved father.

Eva liked the name. It fit the man she saw in the picture. "Zoe, if we have any boys, I think it would be good if we had a Nicholas in the family." Eva smiled at the look on Zoe's face. She wanted to honour the man that had shaped her wife's life, and she couldn't think of a more special way.

"Nicholas Panayiotis Haralambos." Zoe said the name a few times to get the feel of it.

Adding the middle name for her father made Eva's eyes shine, and she nodded.

Eva picked up the doll that looked like it had seen better days. The doll's clothes were dirty and torn, one eye and leg were missing. "Did she have a name as well?" Eva asked her younger partner. She was going to be very surprised if that doll didn't have a name.

"Eftehia." Zoe smiled and brushed her tears away from her eyes.

"Happiness." Eva translated the name and smiled as well. Pointing to the picture she asked, "Is that the same doll?"

Zoe nodded. "Papa bought it in Thessaloniki."

"Pleased to meet you, Eftehia," Eva shook the doll's hand and, much to her dismay, the arm came apart from the doll's body.

"Even my doll falls apart when you touch her," Zoe teased and kissed her wife. "I want to go home, Evy."

"Let's go." Eva got up from the ground and dusted herself off. She then reached down and helped Zoe to her feet. The younger woman put her arm around Eva's waist, and they walked away from the farmhouse together.

Zoe stopped and had a final look back at the old house. She gazed at it for a few moments then turned, and they walked down the dusty road back towards town.

"Evy, before we leave, would you like to visit my mama?" Zoe asked quietly. It was going to be the last time she would visit Larissa. Eva nodded and they turned in to the cemetery. Eva held her wife's hand as they stopped in front of a simple grave. A large white cross bore the name, Ruth Lambros, etched into the wood. Eva noticed the flowers at the base of the cross and looked down at Zoe.

"Ally takes care of the grave," Zoe explained.

Her stepmother's loving gesture touched Eva, and she made a mental note to thank her. Eva made the sign of the cross and bowed her head in silent prayer for a few moments. She then looked down at Zoe and held her hand.

"What did you pray about?" Zoe asked.

"I thanked God that your mother raised a very beautiful woman who has enriched my life," Eva replied. She leaned down and gave Zoe a quick kiss.

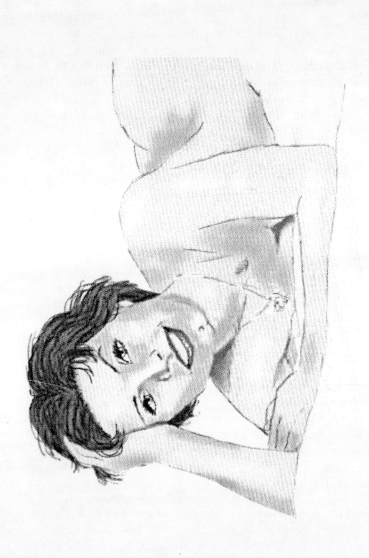

Chapter
18

Zoe leaned against the wall, watching the villagers pass through town and waving when they recognized her. The wind was blowing her short chestnut coloured hair into her eyes and she brushed away her bangs as she scanned the road, looking for her partner to come back from an unscheduled meeting with the Minister. A meeting Zoe had thought up to get Eva out of the way. It was amusing to watch her partner grumble about Percy Hester's need to dot every "i" and cross every "t." Percy Hester was in on the whole surprise birthday party, and Eva didn't suspect a thing.

Zoe was relieved she had finally gone back to the farm. It was difficult, and the sight of the destroyed home was heart wrenching, but she knew it would have been more painful if Eva hadn't been there to help her. Eva, the woman she'd wanted to kill eight years ago, the woman who fell in love with her, was her rock.

"Is she here yet?" Thanasi whispered through the crack in the door, interrupting Zoe's thoughts.

"Nope," Zoe said, scanning the street again.

Thanasi closed the door and went back to the preparations for the party. Zoe'd had the idea when they were still in Sydney. On their arrival, she asked her father-in-law to arrange it. He made all the arrangements, to his absolute joy. He wanted to celebrate her birthday to make up for all the times he hadn't been present. The toughest part of the plan was for Zoe to keep it a secret. The young woman wasn't sure how she was going to do that since she usually blurted out the news of the day to Eva, and she thought it might slip out. Much to her own surprise, she somehow managed.

A smile creased her lips as she saw a distant but unmistakable figure walk towards the house. Her tall body wrapped in her long cloak, a gift from Zoe on their arrival, Eva pulled the hood over her head, protecting her from the winds. Behind her walked Percy Hester and his assistant Michael Kremer, discussing the day's events.

"Oh wow," Zoe muttered as she got a severe case of deja vu from the scene unfolding before her.

It was the spring of 1944, and Zoe was standing outside her house glaring at the passing patrols. The wind was blowing her hair every which way as she watched the Germans go about their day to day business. Watching the house across the road had become a habit for Zoe. Her plan to kill Major Muller's daughter depended on a sound understanding of her movements, or so an elderly Resistance member told her. She pulled herself from her thoughts when the tall figure of Eva Muller slowly made her way up the street. A hood covered her head, but it was unmistakably the German woman. Zoe wondered if she went anywhere without her two shadows. She watched the woman pass and, without thinking, she knelt and picked up a small stone. She fingered the stone in her hand and threw it. The stone hit Eva in the arm, and she turned and met Zoe's stormy emerald eyes. Eva turned to her guards who were about to pounce on the young woman and prevented them from going to arrest her.

Eva put her head down and walked away while the guards gave Zoe glares. Zoe smiled back at them. She turned to go inside the house and opened the door, when she found herself pulled inside and the door forcibly shut.

"Zoe!" Thanasi hissed.

"*What?*" Zoe answered. She kept her eyes on her wife who stopped to discuss something with the Minister.

"Is she here yet?"

"Thanasi, you are beginning to sound like a little kid," Zoe teased. "She's down the road. It shouldn't take long."

The door closed again and Zoe stole a glance at it. She turned her attention back to the approaching woman. Zoe had a mischievous idea. Kneeling down, she picked up the lightest rock she could find. The Minister and Michael walked past Eva and went on ahead. Percy gave Zoe a wink and a tiny grin as they passed.

Eva stopped and watched Zoe for a moment, her own thoughts going back to 1944 and that fateful meeting. Seeing Zoe leaning against the wall as she was, made Eva remember the first time she saw the young woman. A great deal had happened to them since then, but Eva wouldn't trade one moment of it. Whether it was fate, destiny, or some cosmic force that brought them together, she would be forever grateful for having Zoe in her life. She gave her wife a smirk as she started coming towards her. Zoe was up to something, but she didn't know what. The look in her wife's eyes was a dead giveaway. A tiny rock sailed her way and Eva caught it. She looked at it and then glanced back at Zoe, who was grinning.

"What a nice way to greet your wife," Eva said, playing with the rock.

"It got your attention the first time, I thought it would again," Zoe replied, putting her arms around her wife's waist and looking up into twinkling blue eyes. "Have I ever thanked you for not letting the two goons that shadowed you come after me?"

Eva grinned as she looked at her partner's smiling face. "No, I don't think you did."

"Well, let me make amends," Zoe offered and brought her wife down for a searing kiss in the middle of the street. She laced her fingers through Eva's hair and whispered in her ear, "Thank you."

Eva was amazed that Zoe would kiss her in such a public place. She was sure several villagers passed them, although she wasn't even sure if she was still standing.

"Do you prefer that kind of greeting to getting hit by a rock?" Zoe asked. She was quite proud of herself for getting Eva a little flushed.

"Oh yeah!" Eva nodded enthusiastically. "Let's go inside. I think I have a way to thank you as well." The tall woman pulled Zoe towards the house and opened the door.

"SURPRISE!"

Eva stepped back in total amazement as she looked at the large group of people crowded into the tiny living area. The

crowd was comprised of her father, Ally, Thanasi and his new
bride, plus several former Resistance members she knew well—
faces of people she considered dear friends. She turned to find
Zoe with a huge smile on her face, rocking back and forth on the
balls of her feet, feeling mighty proud of herself.

Percy Hester, Michael, and all the members of the team
came around the corner and stood outside the door. Eva turned
and saw them as well and started to cry.

"Hey, you're not supposed to cry at your surprise birthday
party!" Zoe chuckled, putting her arm around the tall woman.

"You dreamt this up?" Eva asked and brushed away her
tears.

"Yeah, I got the idea in Sydney. Percy helped by keeping
you away," Zoe chuckled.

Eva turned to her boss, who was beaming at her, and shook
her finger at him. "I was wondering why you wanted to go over
yesterday's notes three times!"

"She made me do it." Percy Hester pointed at Zoe and put
his arm around the young woman. "You have a very loving partner there, Eva." He crooked his finger for Eva to lean down and
he kissed her on the cheek. "Happy birthday."

Eva was astounded at the turn of events. She had been hoping for a quiet night with Zoe, but her wife obviously had other
ideas. She turned to find her father standing next to her, his blue
eyes twinkling.

"Happy birthday, my child. I wasn't there for your birth but
I'm here for your 30th."

Eva fell into his arms and hugged him tightly as both of
them began to get a little misty eyed. She turned to find her wife
smiling at her. Thanasi threw party streamers and the music
started. Eva was oblivious to those around her. Her eyes locked
onto emerald green for a long moment. Opening her arms, Zoe
walked two steps and embraced her partner.

"Thank you, love," Eva whispered.

"You can thank me later," Zoe whispered and waggled her
eyebrows. She cupped her wife's cheek, brushing aside a tear.
"Happy birthday, Evy."

A resounding cheer went up when Despina rolled the cake
into view. Eva's eyes went wide when she saw the birthday cake.
The layers of chocolate made her mouth water just looking at it.
Zoe scooped a little of the chocolate frosting onto her finger and
offered it to her wife, who took the finger in her mouth and

sucked it a little before letting the finger go. Then she was inundated with gifts and well wishes.

The party was a success and Zoe stood to the side for a moment, sighing contently. She spotted Paula and Clarice standing to one side holding streamers. She wondered if Percy had ordered them to come. "Oh well, I hope they are enjoying themselves. I know I am," Zoe mused to herself.

Their guests left, and the two women found themselves undressed and lying in one another's arms in record time. Eva made a move to capture her wife's smaller figure under her own, but Zoe rolled and broke free, pressing her own body against that of her lover.

"Hey," the dark-haired woman pouted. "I'm supposed to be thanking you, remember?"

"Oh, you will, love, but I haven't finished giving you your birthday presents yet," Zoe said with a devilish grin.

The young woman reached down and captured Eva's mouth in a gentle kiss, teasing the older woman with her tongue until she heard Eva's breathless moan. Zoe broke off the kiss and stared down into her wife's sparkling azure eyes.

"You are so beautiful, Evy," she said, her voice hoarse with desire. "Do you know how lovely you are when you're excited?"

Zoe's eyes traveled the length of Eva's body, completely in awe that this woman was all hers, loved only her. She had to remind herself to take this slowly. A part of the young artist wanted to take her wife in a torrent of passion, but she wanted Eva to remember this birthday, this night, for the rest of her life.

Zoe leaned in for another kiss, this one intense, longer, and much more passionate. As she kissed the dark-haired woman, her hands began running over Eva's soft, warm flesh. Eva drew in a sharp breath and held it as Zoe's fingers barely touched the dark circles around her nipples. She released the breath with an audible exclamation when she felt Zoe's fingers, at last, pressing against the sensitive flesh.

"Oh yesss..." Eva moaned.

Zoe resumed her kisses, nipping at the sensitive skin of Eva's neck, her fingers continuing to trace erotic patterns along the length of Eva's body. The tall woman's hands ran down the length of her wife's back, ending up squeezing the flesh of a firm backside. Zoe felt her own self-control slipping a bit. She recovered quickly and moved her body lower, positioning her mouth over her wife's breasts, letting her warm breath caress them. Hovering just above the creamy flesh, her breath spilling across the tightened nub, she nipped at the skin lightly, pausing and lifting her head. Zoe smiled to herself, wondering just how much of this torture her lovely wife could take. She soon received her answer.

Eva whimpered and twined her fingers in the smaller woman's chestnut hair, urging her back down. Zoe brushed her lips against the already hard nipples, flicking her tongue across the taut flesh, and when Eva drew in a deep breath, Zoe licked her lips and took the pebbled flesh into her mouth.

Eva groaned loudly and tightened the grasp she had in her lover's hair, pressing the head more tightly to her breast, arching into the pleasure. Eva's heart beat faster as a fire began to smoulder between her legs.

All too soon, Zoe stopped, smiling at her wife's tortured groan at the loss of the intense sensation. She trailed soft warm kisses down her wife's body. Her hands skimmed across the entire surface as if trying to memorize her wife's form, igniting raging fires wherever they went. Eva's constant moans only served to encourage her. When Zoe let one hand slide down to caress a muscular thigh, Eva's legs unconsciously parted. Once they'd felt her lover's fingertips gliding along the skin, goose flesh erupted wherever those fingertips wandered. The taller woman fought to distribute, albeit unsuccessfully, the shiver that ran the length of her body.

By this time, Zoe's lips and tongue were weaving a sensuous path of pleasure down the flat plane of Eva's abdomen, pausing to tease with her tongue, just along the hairline that separated the smooth skin from the dark curls below. This time it was Zoe's turn to moan as the perfume of her wife's passion rose up to greet her. Zoe moved her mouth lower and licked around the edges of her wife's triangle of wiry curls, running her tongue seductively along the skin where thigh met sex. Zoe felt her lover spread her legs wider, her hips rising up in a silent plea for more contact. Eva's hands grasped the pillow under her head.

Zoe continued her deliberate seduction, all but ignoring the rise of her lover's hungry body. She wanted Eva crazy with lust. She wanted to hear her wife beg as she so often did during their lovemaking, and so, she continued the teasing strokes of her tongue. Zoe trailed soft kisses along the inside of Eva's thighs. She finally found herself poised before what she desired most. Zoe rested her cheek on the damp curls, breathing in the scent of her wife's readiness. She pressed against the curls, moaning as she did. "Oh, Evy...you feel so good. So warm...so wet." Zoe hummed against the flesh, causing Eva's hips to grind up in an attempt to generate more pressure.

Eva was nearing her breaking point, wondering how long the delightful torture would last before her wife simply took her. The dark-haired woman's need to control the situation was rising quickly. She could feel Zoe's breath against her sex, and she grunted with pleasure each time the young woman pressed her cheek against her.

"Zo," Eva husked out, entwining her fingers in the brown hair once again.

"Yes, love?" Zoe answered innocently, reaching out with her tongue and descending lower.

"Good Lord, Zoe...please, love...I..." Eva had never begged like this before. Usually, she was in the dominating position, unmercifully teasing her wife. She was both thrilled and frustrated at this new turn of events.

"One word, my love...all it takes is one little word." Zoe punctuated the statement by gliding her tongue lightly along the entire length of her wife's sex.

"Ohhh..." Eva groaned, desperately trying to get the word from her brain to her tongue.

"Zoe..." she thrust her hips up again. "Pleassssee." She drew the word out.

"Yep, that was the right one," Zoe grinned, but the smile was lost on her wife, whose blue eyes hazed over in a cloud of passion.

Zoe settled her mouth gently against the warm, wet center. She slid her tongue through the curls for a taste of her lover. Both women moaned loudly, Zoe's voice vibrating against her lover's skin. The feeling that sensation created was mind numbing. Eva thrust her hips up harder, rocking against her lover's mouth.

"Ohhh...yesss..." Eva held tightly to her wife's chestnut coloured locks. "Yes...yesss...there...like that..." she moaned and panted.

Zoe licked tenderly around the wet folds of flesh, eventually changing the pressure to long, deliberate strokes, as the rhythm of her wife's hips picked up its pace. She flicked the tip of her tongue against the engorged bundle of nerves. Eva cried out at the intense pleasure that action caused.

Eva nearly screamed in delight as Zoe increased the speed and the pressure of her tongue. The dark-haired woman could feel the pleasure rushing at her and she so wanted to make it last, to have this feeling forever; on the other hand, she could no more stop herself from rushing toward the edge of that proverbial cliff, than she could stop the sun from rising. Eva felt her lover's tongue slide deep inside of her, using the strong muscle to fill her. She jerked and convulsed as the powerful climax hit her, holding tightly to her wife's hair, pulling her closer, deeper into her.

Zoe felt herself jumping off the precipice right along with her wife. They both lost track of how many aftershocks passed through their bodies. She'd never thought Eva would ever let go this completely, but her wife surprised her by loudly shouting out her passion, then continuing to move against her after only a moment's pause.

For her part, Eva had never felt anything this intense before. As soon as her first orgasm began to fade, another rocked her. Zoe's continued caresses carried the dark-haired woman along on a wave of pure pleasure. The small woman pulled away to enter her wife with her fingers, and Eva immediately felt herself spiraling out of control again. She shook and shivered until she could no longer retain control of the muscles in her limbs. She let her arms fall limply to her sides, her legs weakly stretching out on the bed. Zoe crawled up to lay her head on her wife's chest, both women still panting and gasping for air. They lay in each other's arms for what seemed like hours, delightfully satisfied.

Finally able to find her voice, as well as some of her strength, Eva wrapped long arms around her wife and held her tightly. "Oh, Zo...I...I..." she stammered uncharacteristically.

The smaller woman lifted her head and giggled, emerald eyes shining brightly. "I love you too, Evy," she finished for her wife. "Oh, and by the way, happy birthday." Zoe smiled.

The two women were wrapped around each other, naked and thoroughly spent. Eva cradled long arms around Zoe, pinning her to her body. The young woman lay on top of her in absolute bliss.

"Evy?"

"Yes, love."

"I love you." Zoe kissed her between her breasts, causing Eva to giggle. She climbed up higher and looked into her wife's blue eyes.

"Happy birthday." Zoe leaned down and kissed her passionately. "I got you a birthday present."

"I thought you just gave me my birthday present," Eva chuckled as Zoe rolled her eyes.

"Tsk, you are so easy to please," Zoe teased and got off her partner and out of bed.

"Where are you going?" Eva hitched herself onto her elbow, watching Zoe go to their suitcases.

Zoe looked back and stopped. Eva's head was cradled in her hand as she hitched herself up on her elbow to watch her wife. Her dark hair was tousled. Zoe sighed when she saw the bed sheet fall. Eva looked so relaxed. Zoe smiled, knowing she was responsible for the tranquil state her wife was in. She found the camera near Eva's present and decided she couldn't pass up the opportunity.

"Don't move," Zoe ordered, picking up Eva's camera.

"Oh, Zoe, not again!" Eva complained, but remained where she was. She knew she was going to lose this debate, but she had to try.

"Oh come on, Evy. You look so gorgeous lying like that, and I have to paint you, pleeeasse," Zoe begged, knowing she had won her wife over long before she uttered the word.

Eva rolled her eyes. "How many times are you going to paint me, Zo? You have over twenty pieces!"

"So? Twenty pieces in five years, that's not a lot," Zoe reasoned. "Ah, but before I can take a picture, I need to add some color to the canvas," Zoe muttered and put the camera down. She found the present.

Eva frowned. "Zoe, what are you talking about?"

"Don't frown, you're going to ruin the shot," Zoe mumbled as she approached her wife and knelt beside her. "Hi there."

"Hi," Eva grinned.

"It's your birthday, and what normally happens on your birthday is that you get presents." Zoe stroked Eva's cheek. "And since it's a very special birthday, I thought I would make your present very special."

"I already have the best present in the world, Zoe." Eva tried to bring her wife closer for a kiss, but Zoe held her off.

"Ah, not so fast, Mrs Haralambos." Zoe laughed at Eva's pout. The young woman drew her hand from behind her back and opened the jewelry box that she held.

Eva's blue eyes opened wide at the sight before her. It was the most beautiful pendant. The base was gold, in the shape of a heart, with four sapphires and five diamonds. It took Eva's breath away as she gazed at it.

"The diamonds are for the years we've been together, and the sapphires remind me of your eyes," Zoe said quietly, reveling in the stunned look on Eva's face. She placed the gold chain around Eva's neck and let the pendant rest gently against her skin. "Do you like it?"

Eva took a deep breath. The pendant was beautiful, and she knew Zoe'd had a hand in designing it. "I love it, Zoe." She drew the young woman in for a passionate kiss. "Thank you."

Zoe beamed. She had designed and redesigned the pendant, driving Jack totally crazy with her ideas. She was sure he would throw her out after her last call to him. She knew she had to get this perfect because it was important. "I'm not finished just yet."

Zoe produced another small box and opened it to reveal matching earrings, sapphire with diamonds surrounding the gem. Zoe looked up from the earrings to look at Eva, only to find silent tears falling down her face.

"Hey, didn't I tell you that you shouldn't cry on your birthday?" Zoe lovingly wiped away her wife's tears and gently put the earrings on.

"You are gorgeous," Zoe kissed her wife, taking the camera and moving back a little. "Eva, stop crying, please!"

Eva was deeply moved. She loved her presents, but it was the spirit in which they were created that touched her soul the most. Zoe could have given her anything and she would have loved it. She brushed away the tears and looked down at the pendant.

Zoe grinned. She found the perfect picture and took it, much to Eva's surprise.

"Why did you take that?"

"Because you looked gorgeous, do I need another reason?" Zoe took another two shots and then laid the camera aside, settling next to her partner and putting her arm across Eva's bare waist. "I hope you like them."

"I love them, Zoe," Eva replied, kissing the top of her head.

They lay in silence for a few moments, relaxing in each

other's embrace.

"Eva, thank you for being there today." Zoe kissed her wife's shoulder as the tall woman hugged her closer. The broken doll sat in the corner, her torn clothes now gone, replaced with a toga that Eva made from a tea towel, much to Zoe's amusement. The empty eye socket was covered with a patch, which made the doll look like a refugee from Treasure Island.

Eva frowned a little and looked down. "Where else would I be, love?"

Zoe looked up and met her frowning partner. She smoothed away the frown lines on Eva's brow. "I felt like I was all alone out there, everything was gone," Zoe said quietly, resting her hand on Eva's belly.

"Zoe, do you remember what you said to me when I thought I was alone? You came to church and you prayed with me. Do you remember that?" Eva asked. That night was the turning point in her life, and the young woman in her arms was her saving grace. She couldn't envision a life without Zoe.

The church was dark, the only light came from the candles burning before the altar. Zoe stopped in the doorway when she noticed that Eva was kneeling in prayer. Not wanting to interrupt her, Zoe stood by a column and waited, but Eva was too emotionally overwrought to notice anyone as she looked up at the image of the crucified Christ.

"Lord, I can't believe that it could be your will to let Father Haralambos drink from this bitter cup." Her voice broke and she faltered. She wiped away the tears. "He's my father, Lord...I know you brought me here to find him and I know there is a reason for things to happen the way they do, but I can't see how this will benefit anyone. Please don't let him die. He has been my one saving grace in this nightmare." Eva choked on her words.

Tears welled up in Zoe's eyes as well, her heart going out to the older woman.

"I don't want to be alone again," Eva cried to the statue.

"You're not alone," Zoe said as she walked down the aisle and knelt beside her, taking her hand, "not anymore." Zoe tenderly wiped a tear from Eva's cheek.

"You're not alone," Zoe repeated her words.

"You're not alone, Zoe. I'll always be here." Eva kissed the top of her wife's chestnut coloured head as Zoe cuddled deeper.

"You are my life, Zoe. What you did today was hard, and I'm very proud of you."

"All I did was go home, Evy. That doesn't take much courage," Zoe replied.

"Facing something you're scared of requires courage, love. It's not always meeting a foe head on that requires nerve."

"I think having you by my side gave me the courage to go home, Evy. I don't think I could have done it without you," Zoe said, knowing in her heart that she could never have faced what she had if Eva hadn't been there. "I'm going to be with you when you go home, Evy."

Eva smiled down at the young woman nestled against her. "It will make what's coming up a little bit easier to bear."

"Are you nervous?" Zoe asked.

Eva sighed. "Yeah. I haven't been back since the night *Mutti* died," she said softly. The affectionate term for her mother always made Zoe feel sad and Eva seldom used it.

"How long has it been?"

"Eleven years," Eva replied. "I don't know where *Mutti* is buried..."

Zoe was shocked. "You mean, you didn't go to the funeral?"

Eva shook her head. "Muller had me taken away by a local doctor who drugged me. It was a couple of weeks before I was aware that I wasn't in Berlin anymore." The memories made her heart ache, and she closed her eyes. The pain and the humiliation that she'd suffered in the following weeks and months had made her wish Muller had killed her.

"Bastard," Zoe hissed. "He deserved what he got." The news from the Nuremberg trials had been very bleak for Muller and his associates. Rhimes had been sentenced to death for crimes against humanity, as was Muller. When Zoe read the letter to her wife, Eva was quiet and withdrawn. She didn't see it as a victory against the Nazi machine. Another chapter in her life ended, but the pain remained. She wanted to find her mother's resting place, to say goodbye.

"We'll find her," Zoe promised.

"It's been a long time, love."

"That's true, but I believe we will find her and then you can say goodbye to her." Zoe was adamant about the fact that she was going to find Daphne Muller's grave, even if she had to spend the next three days looking. It meant too much to her partner not to make every effort.

"Do you think we will?" Eva wasn't so sure. The war would make such things extremely difficult, and she wasn't even sure if the records were still available.

"Eva, we can't be in Berlin and not try. You've waited eleven years to say goodbye to your mother, I think the least I can do is try and find her while you're in the meetings."

"Thank you, Zo." Eva didn't know what else to say. Zoe's determination pushed Eva's doubts aside and made her look forward to their trip.

The roar of the engines made Zoe's head ache. She climbed the stairs to the plane and then looked back at Larissa for the last time. It was a beautiful morning for a winter's day; the sun peeked out from behind the clouds. Eva climbed the stairs behind her and stopped near the top step, watching her partner have one last, long look at her village.

"I didn't think it was going to be so hard to say goodbye, Evy," Zoe said as she looked around the airport. "Do you think we'll ever come back?"

Eva stepped up and put her arm around her partner's shoulders, looking out to where her father was standing. "I don't know, love. Australia is very far away. Maybe our children will make the journey."

"Oh, I forgot you're getting on in years," Zoe teased her. "For an old lady, you're not bad."

Eva gave her a playful slap on the behind and chuckled. "I can't wait for your 30th birthday, Zo."

"I can," Zoe said drolly.

Eva chuckled, took a last look at the village herself, and steered Zoe inside where they found their seats.

Chapter 19

The early morning light filtered through the windows causing Zoe to wake. She lay in bed for a few minutes with her eyes closed, listening to the cars outside and a whistle of some kind off in the distance. They were in Germany, a place she never thought she would visit willingly. The plane flight had been uneventful, with Paula and her friend Clarice actually speaking civilly to her. She wasn't sure why there had been an attitude change, but she suspected a tall, dark-haired woman had something to do with it.

Eva spent their first day in Germany in meetings–briefings with the Minister and his team–and then more meetings with bureaucrats, both the American and German variety. Zoe unpacked their clothes and read. She sketched a little but was extremely bored. Eva didn't get back to their room until well past 9:00 p.m.

They were sleeping in single beds as, much to their disgust, they'd discovered that they couldn't move the beds. Zoe was dismayed when she'd realised the bedposts were bolted to the floor. Eva just shook her head and went to have a bath to relax. They shared a bed until Eva's eyes closed and she was sound asleep. Zoe didn't want to leave her side, but she knew that they might get surprised early in the morning, so she reluctantly went to her own bed.

Zoe smiled and opened her eyes. The aforementioned tall, dark-haired woman was lying on her stomach, dead to the world. The sheet lay half way down her back and Zoe just enjoyed the view for a few moments. Getting out of her bed, Zoe debated with herself whether she should wake her wife or let her sleep in. She leaned over and grinned when she saw that Eva was wearing the pendant. Eva hadn't wanted to remove it, and the best solution that she could think up to avoid getting it impressed against her throat while she slept was to nestle it at the back of her neck. Shrugging her shoulders Zoe got on the bed and straddled her partner's hips. "Evy," she whispered.

"Hmm," Eva mumbled and continued to sleep, even with Zoe's weight on her backside.

"Evy, wake up."

"Don't want to."

"Today is your birthday!" Zoe said excitedly. Even though they'd celebrated her birthday two days before, Zoe didn't think it was out of place to have another celebration since it was the actual day of her wife's birth.

"Zo, why are you up?"

"Can't sleep in. Must be because I'm excited." Zoe lay on top of her partner and nuzzled her neck. She moved her knee in between Eva's long legs, eliciting a moan from her wife. "You know how I am when I get excited."

"Zo, I love you, but your knee is in a place where if you keep it there I won't be able to stop myself if the domestic staff waltzes in...oh..." Eva gasped as Zoe's fingers replaced her knee. "Oh God, Zo, that's some way to start a morning."

"Evy, you talk too much," Zoe gently scolded as Eva turned around and met twinkling emerald coloured eyes. "Good morning, birthday girl."

"Hi," Eva replied before getting another kiss from her wife.

Before either of them could go further, a tap on the door caused them both to jump. Zoe scrambled off her partner's body and dove into her own bed. A few seconds later, a middle aged woman stuck her head in.

"Lock door," Zoe muttered in Greek, pulling the covers over her head and trying to get her raging hormones under control.

"Good morning, Fraulein. I'm sorry, did I wake you?" The older woman stood in the middle of the room. Eva thought she didn't look too apologetic about disturbing them. "My name is Frau Wagner, and I will be your domestic help while you are here."

"Great," Zoe muttered in Greek from under the covers.

"I'm sorry. What did the young lady say?"

Eva stifled a grin and turned to Frau Wagner. "She said it was good to know. Do you normally come at this time?" Eva stole a quick glance at the clock and was quite surprised to find it was 8:00 a.m.

"Oh no, I'm running late today, and I thought I would give you two some extra time to sleep," Frau Wagner smiled.

"Of course," Eva mumbled and threw a pillow at Zoe. "Zo, wake up. Frau Wagner wants to clean up."

"Don't want to," Zoe muttered.

"Don't worry, I can do her bed later. Would you like me to run a bath for you?"

"Yes, thank you." Eva thanked the woman who nodded and headed to the bathroom. Eva lay back down and sighed.

"Evy?"

"Yes, love?"

"I want to go home," Zoe muttered and turned around to face a smirking Eva. "I don't think it's funny, birthday girl. I really, really, really want to make love to you, even with Frau what's-her-name in the next room."

Eva's only response was a groan as she turned over, pulling the covers over her head.

Once again, Zoe spent the morning reading and sketching. She wanted to go out to the Births, Deaths, and Marriages office to find out where Eva's mother was buried. That had been the plan, until Eva saw the condition of the city. The bombed out remains were very much still in evidence, even five years after the war. Eva didn't want her wife out all by herself and asked her to stay in. Zoe, having learned to listen to Eva when she specifically asked the young woman not to do something, remained at the embassy. She didn't need a repeat of what had happened in Egypt.

When Eva returned from her last meeting of the day, they decided to take in some of the sights, or what was left of them. They stood across from the official entry point into East Berlin and the Communist sector of the city. Barbed wire ran along the section deemed to be the border, and guards were posted. Eva shook her head at the state of her former town.

"Why are they doing this?" Zoe asked, not understanding the need for barbed wire or troops with guns.

"I guess so the people won't escape," Eva replied. "The university I went to is over on the other side."

"Did you live over there?"

"No. Actually it's not far from here."

"Do you want to go?" Zoe asked. She wasn't sure if Eva wanted to take that path.

Eva sighed as she watched the changing of the guards at the checkpoint. "Yes," she said and took Zoe's hand, walking away.

Zoe stole quick glances at Eva's face as they passed bombed out buildings. At one building, Eva stood for a long moment, staring at the charred remains.

"That was one of the oldest libraries in Berlin," Eva said quietly. She had spent many hours reading in the grand old library with its ornate ceilings and stained glass windows. It had had an old world charm about it.

"You know, I never really thought about what the war did to Germany," Zoe said as she gazed at the building, saddened by the loss. Three US soldiers walked past, laughing and making bomb noises as they passed the building. Though angered by their callous manner, Zoe stopped herself from saying anything. Eva watched the soldiers for a moment, then walked away.

They continued to chat as Eva played tourist guide to a city she knew so well, pointing out various buildings and landmarks. Zoe soaked in the history lesson with relish and asked questions, which made Eva appreciate the city even more, even though it wasn't at its best. Eva stopped talking when they reached an intersection and looked up at a burnt building, its roof caved in.

"What's this?" Zoe asked, not understanding why Eva had stopped talking. It was an unremarkable building, similar to other bombed out and burnt structures in the area.

"A synagogue," Eva whispered. Memories of *Kristalnacht* came flooding back. From this corner she'd watched the building go up in flames, watched as her friends beat the old rabbi.

The night was clear and she could see a thousand stars up in the heavens. The sound of running feet echoed down the alley as Eva turned to find Greta waiting for her. She was dressed in her Hitler Youth uniform, and she carried a plank of wood.

"What you going to do with that, Eta?" the young woman

asked.

"Smash some heads, of course!" Greta Strauss laughed and swung the piece of wood.

"Be careful you don't smash Eva's head!" Jurgen Reinhardt yelled out, and the group of teenagers laughed. The turn of events disturbed Eva. She wasn't sure why they were out, but Greta told her they were going to have fun.

"Come on, you two! Georg has found the perfect place to start our festivities!"

Greta smiled at her. "Come on, let's go and have some fun!" Greta took her hand and they both chased after their friends, ending up in front of an old synagogue. Someone started the fire before they got there, and the flames mesmerized Eva as they made a hissing noise and then a huge explosion.

An old man screaming in fear rushed out of the burning building. He gazed up at the fire that was ravaging the temple and cried out in German for them to put the fire out. The teenagers laughed, and to Eva's horror, her lover began to beat the man with the piece of wood she held in her hands. Eva was sickened by the sight of the old rabbi on the ground, trying to protect himself but unable to stop the beating. The fires made the night sky bright, and the rabbi's blood splattered onto the courtyard.

"Evy?" Zoe asked, concerned by the look on her wife's face. "Are you okay, love?"

"Old memories, Zo," Eva whispered and let her tears run down her face. She said a prayer asking for forgiveness for having taken part in such a crime.

Zoe put her arm around her tall partner's waist and tried to convey her support. She didn't know what to say to ease the woman's pain, but she would offer any comfort she could. Eva looked down at their joined hands and then back up at her wife. "About a block from here is where I used to live."

She took a last look at the burnt out synagogue and walked away and down the street until they got to a part of the city that was once pretty. Some of the buildings remained, beautiful old homes. Others were burned out shells.

"This is where I lived." Eva motioned down the street. "It used to have trees on either end of the pavement."

They stopped at a bombed out house. "What's left of my home, Zoe."

The once stately, two-story home was a shell. Fire and

bombs had done extensive damage to it, and Eva was saddened to see it, even though the place had spawned one of her worst nightmares.

"So much for our sightseeing," Eva tried to joke.

"Where do we go to find where your mama is buried, Eva?"

"I don't know. It used to be at the Registry for Births, Deaths, and Marriages." Eva took a last look at her former home and turned her back. Taking Zoe's hand, they made their way slowly back down the street. Eva stopped for moment, thinking she heard someone calling her name.

"Did you hear that?" she asked Zoe.

"Hear what?"

"I thought I heard my name."

"Nope, didn't hear it. So, are we going to go and ask some-one where it is?"

"What?"

Zoe sighed. "Where the births, deaths, and marriages records are kept."

Eva once again thought she heard someone call her name and turned around.

"Evy, what is the matter with you?" Zoe asked, concerned by the strange behavior her wife was exhibiting.

"Zoe, I think someone is calling my name."

Zoe frowned and looked around. There were people and sol-diers going about their daily business, but none of them was showing any sign they wanted to attract the attention of the two women. Eva shrugged and began to walk away.

"Eva!"

Zoe stopped upon hearing the faint voice. "Evy, I think someone is calling you."

"See, I'm not going mad."

"No, dear, you're not," Zoe teased.

They both turned to find an old lady valiantly attempting to run to catch up with them, her white hair all in disarray and a huge smile on her face.

"*Großmutter,*" Eva whispered not believing her eyes. "That's my grandmother!" Eva exclaimed and started to run, pulling Zoe with her, to meet the old woman.

"*Mein lieber Gott, es ist du. Mein kleines Eva!*" the old woman cried out as her granddaughter embraced her and lifted her off her feet. She couldn't believe it was her granddaughter. The young woman had been taken away, and her son wouldn't tell her where or what had happened to her. She had been very distressed. Eva was her favourite granddaughter.

"*Setzt mich 'runter!*" Elsa Muller cried for her tall granddaughter to let her down. She swatted the young woman on the shoulder and laughed. She thought she recognised the tall figure in the distance, but she wasn't sure; and she left her shopping and ran in case the woman might disappear before she caught up. Elsa was out of breath from all the running, and she was sure her heart would explode from happiness. "My little Eva, where have you been? I thought you were dead!"

Eva was crying; her beloved grandmother was alive. She'd sent letters to her, but they were never answered. She wondered if they'd ever gotten through at all, judging by the way her grandmother was hugging and kissing her.

Zoe stood to the side with a huge smile on her face. She liked the old woman. Anyone who greeted her wife like that was a good person to her.

"Oh dear, let me get my breath!" Elsa took several deep breaths and held on to Eva's hand.

"My God, I can't believe it's you!" She hugged Eva again getting a laugh out of the tall woman who hugged her back. "We are causing a spectacle here. Come to the house." The older woman pulled Eva by the hand and dragged her along. Eva turned to Zoe and grabbed her hand, and they went off down the road.

Elsa Muller looked at the dark-haired young woman and beamed. Zoe stood awkwardly and met the old woman's gaze and smiled. "Oh my God, my manners! Where did I leave my manners? I'm so sorry! Eva! Who is your friend?"

Eva looked sheepishly back at her wife. "I'm sorry, Omi. This is Zoe Haralambos, my wife. Zoe, this is my grandmother, Elsa Muller."

The introduction took Zoe by surprise. She hadn't expected Eva to introduce her this way and was now expecting a rebuff, but it never came.

The old woman came up to her and cupped her face in her hands. "Welcome to the family, little one!" Elsa kissed her cheek as Eva watched. "Zoe, what a beautiful name for a beautiful girl."

"Thank you...umm..." Zoe was at a loss what to call the older woman, "Mrs Muller."

"Ach! So formal!" The older woman playfully slapped her hand. "Call me Omi."

"Thank you, Omi," Zoe said shyly.

"So, you finally got rid of that vile Greta person, yes?"

Zoe coughed to hide her chuckle and the old woman looked at her with a smile.

Eva nodded.

"Good girl. I always thought you could do better than that upstart," the older woman said as she went into the kitchen to make some tea. Eva and Zoe followed her and sat at the table.

"You're not like any grandmother I know," Zoe said, watching the old woman try to reach a tin. Eva got up, took it off the top shelf, and handed it to her. She received a playful pat on the backside.

"Why is that?"

"Well, you didn't seem too surprised when Eva introduced me."

"Why should I be? Eva told me she didn't like boys, so she must like girls. She is my granddaughter, and I love her."

Zoe shook her head. It was a change from the other set of grandparents she'd met. "It's just that most people don't approve."

"Blah. Zoe, my sweet child, who cares what other people think! Do you love my Eva?"

The two women looked at each other and held hands. "I love her dearly."

Elsa put her own hand on top of theirs. "Well then, who am I to say you shouldn't. As long as she didn't get involved with that Greta person, then I'm happy." The old woman turned to make the tea.

"Omi hated Greta," Eva explained, and her grandmother snorted her disgust at the mention of her former girlfriend.

"She was a rude little child. I don't know why you went with her. What happened to her?"

"Sentenced to life in prison for crimes against humanity during the war, Omi."

The older woman turned with the teapot on her hand. "I knew she was bad. Terrible." Zoe got up from her seat, brought the tea and the cups to the table, and poured it. "Thank you, Zoe."

Elsa turned to her granddaughter. "I was so worried about you; and when Hans wouldn't tell me where you were, I thought I had lost you. I heard about the beating he gave you, my child. Did he hurt you badly?"

Eva sighed and looked down. Elsa lifted her granddaughter's face and met her eyes. "Don't answer me, little one. I can see it in your eyes. Hans was an idiot of a man. I don't know what was wrong with that boy. Are you all right now?"

"Sometimes my back hurts," Eva admitted quietly.

"Hmm, your grandfather had a back problem, and I used to put some tea to boil and would rub the tea into his back."

"Tea?" Zoe asked. She'd never tried that and made a mental note to herself to see if it worked on her wife.

"Oh yes, tea is very good." The old woman stopped in mid sentence and her eyes went wide.

Eva was alarmed and looked at Zoe. "Omi, are you all right?"

"Oh my dear God! It's your birthday today!" Elsa beamed and kissed her granddaughter. "God answered my prayers! I prayed that if you were still alive, I would see you again. Here you are, looking happy. I've gained another granddaughter. I think I'm the one getting all the presents! Your *Mutti* would have been so proud of you."

"I hope she would have been," Eva replied.

"I'm sure she would have."

"Omi, do you know where Eva's mother is buried?" Zoe asked. If anyone should know it would be this woman. She got a startled look from Eva who hadn't even thought to ask her grandmother.

"She wasn't buried, Zoe."

"She wasn't? What happened to her?" Zoe asked, a little perplexed.

"She was cremated. You didn't know?"

"No, he didn't tell me, Omi," Eva said quietly.

Her grandmother was angry and banged her fist on the table, causing the two women to jump slightly. "That dimwitted fool! How could he not tell you?" Elsa shook her head in disgust. "My little Eva, I am so sorry you didn't know. I have her ashes in an urn."

The two women looked at each other in surprise and then back at Eva's grandmother. "You mean you have them?"

"Of course. I wanted to give Daphne a proper burial, but

then the war escalated."

"Could I take them?" Eva asked. She knew exactly where she was going to put them. She turned to Zoe. "Do you mind, love?"

"Are you kidding? Of course, I don't mind! I reckon the best place would be under the jasmine," Zoe replied, getting a huge grin and a quick kiss from Eva.

"Of course, I can give them to you, but it's getting late and I don't want you to leave. Now, where are you staying?"

"At the embassy, Omi."

"Well, ring them up and tell them you are going to be staying here. I will make up the spare bed. You remember the room you used to sleep in?"

Eva did remember and nodded with a smile. She frequently slept over at her grandmother's house, and they would talk and eat the little cakes her grandmother would make. Her grandmother was the first person she told about her feelings for Greta. Elsa Muller never condemned her granddaughter for the way she was feeling, but talked to her about it. Her grandmother was the one who went to Daphne and explained how the young woman felt. For Eva's sake, they had all decided it would be best to hide the truth from Hans Muller.

"Go on and ring them up. I want you to stay here." Elsa pushed her granddaughter out of the chair and to the phone.

Zoe was bemused by the way the older woman was pushing her wife around. "Omi, do you have any good little Eva stories?"

"Hey!" Eva came back into the kitchen and waggled her finger at her wife.

"Don't complain, you asked Despina about me! Now shoo. Go and make that phone call!" Zoe pushed Eva out of the room and turned to her adopted grandmother. "So let's talk about little Eva."

Elsa laughed at Zoe's antics and patted the chair for Zoe to sit.

Chapter
20

Eva sighed as she slipped further into the warm water. The bath was so relaxing. She closed her eyes, letting her head rest on the rim of the tub. The day that had promised to bring up her demons had turned out surprisingly well. She'd found her grandmother and her mother's ashes, something she'd never thought would happen.

Eva chuckled to herself. Her young wife and her grandmother got on like a house on fire. She was sure she would regret the sharing of the information Zoe was prying out of her grandmother. Eva stopped and smiled. She'd never thought the trip back home would prove so wonderful. While it was true that it had been painful, both for herself and for Zoe, it was turning out to be the best thing they could have done. Eva lifted her hand from the water and let it dribble through her fingers. She turned towards the door, expecting Zoe to come and join her in the bath, but was quite shocked to see her grandmother.

Elsa came bustling in, oblivious to her granddaughter's shocked expression. She put the towels she had in her arms to the side.

"Omi!" Eva screamed, submersing herself in the bath.

The older woman snorted. "It's not as if I haven't seen what you have before, child." Elsa shook her head and put a clean towel on the rack. "Eva Muller, since when have you gone shy?"

"Since I grew up!" Eva muttered, scooping some of the water and flinging it at her grandmother, hitting her at the back of the head.

The older woman stopped and turned. She gave Eva a mock glare and waggled her finger. "You are not so old I can't take you over my knee, young lady." Elsa chuckled and ruffled her granddaughter's hair. Elsa noticed the scar on Eva's shoulder and scowled. "What happened?" she asked, indicating Eva's shoulder.

Eva looked down and sighed. "Do you remember Jurgen Reinhardt?"

"The one that use to mope around trying to get your attention? Mind you, there were a lot of boys moping about trying to get your attention." Elsa chuckled at the memory. Eva was a beautiful girl, and she'd had many of the boys trying to impress her with flowers and chocolates.

"Tall, blond hair, blue eyes...poster boy for the Aryan cause," Eva said. "There were a lot of them, too," Eva muttered and got a grin from her grandmother.

"So what happened with Jurgen?" Elsa sat on the rim of the bathtub.

"He tried to kill me," Eva said quietly. She didn't want to upset Omi with what her stepfather had done to her, but she couldn't avoid the subject either.

"*What?* Why? Because you spurned him?" Elsa shook her head in disgust. "It's not as if there aren't any other women around."

"Father told him to, Omi."

"Hans told Jurgen to kill you?" The older woman was not all that shocked by this news. Her son did have an explosive temper.

"He found out about my relationship with Zoe." Eva played with the water as her thoughts went back to 1944. Jurgen Reinhardt would have killed her had it not been for Zoe. She didn't know what Zoe had done to breach her defenses, but she'd allowed the young woman inside her heart. "Jurgen shot me."

Elsa was shocked. "That...that...pig!" Eva looked up with a stunned expression on her face. She'd never heard her grandmother swear. "How barbaric."

"Omi, you do like Zoe, don't you?"

Her grandmother looked down at the earnest face looking up at her and sighed. "Do you like Zoe?"

"That's not answering my question, Omi." Eva tapped her

grandmother on her knee, getting it wet.

"You are looking for a spanking, aren't you?" the older woman chuckled. "Answer my question first, young lady."

"I love her, Omi."

"The way you loved Greta?" Elsa Muller remembered the long conversations she'd had with her granddaughter and the doubts the young girl expressed. She was smitten with the older girl, but Elsa thought she had a bad case of hero worship. The older woman had seen many things in her life, but the fact that her granddaughter was a lesbian did come as a shock at first. Daphne was more shocked to find out, but there wasn't much the two women could do. Elsa initially thought Eva was just going through a rough time, as all teenagers did.

"That wasn't love."

"No?" The older woman's eyebrow spiked up and she gave her granddaughter a look. "I may be old, but I do remember a certain 17 year old telling me that this was, how did you put it?" Elsa closed her eyes in thought and then opened them. "Oh yes. '*Omi, I love her so much I can't eat!*'"

Eva chuckled. She remembered those words. Her grandmother was trying to get her to eat dinner, but the lovesick teenager was just not in the mood for food.

"So, my little Eva, now you are in love again?"

"Omi, what I had with Greta wasn't love. I don't know what it was, but it wasn't love. Zoe is so different from Greta in every way..."

"She's more respectful and a very nice girl. I can't place her accent. She isn't German, is she?"

Eva shook her head. "She's Greek."

"Ah." Elsa scooped some water and wet Eva's hair. Grabbing the soap, the older woman began to wash Eva's hair. Eva grinned at the way her grandmother did this without thinking. She'd missed her grandmother so much.

"Zoe is my wife, Omi, not my girlfriend or just my lover. She is my partner."

"I see," Elsa said, continuing to wash her granddaughter's hair. "Then it must be serious. How long have you been together?"

"Five years. We met in Larissa, in Greece."

"Are her parents still alive?"

Eva sighed. "No." Eva didn't want to upset her grandmother with tales about her son and the atrocities he had committed.

"She only has me and my father." Eva wasn't sure how her grandmother would accept that news. She looked up and was relieved to see a smile crease the old woman's face.

"I know Hans wasn't your father, my dear child. Your *Mutti* told me a long time ago, but that doesn't stop me from loving you as my granddaughter. Does it?"

Eva shook her head. Overcome with the emotions, Eva was afraid she would burst into tears if she said anything.

"Well that's good. Is your father a good man?"

"He's a priest, Omi. You would love him if you met him. He is a no-nonsense kind of man with a heart of gold."

"Then I would love to meet him."

"I love you, Omi," Eva said and leaned out of the bath a little and kissed the older woman on the cheek.

Elsa smiled back down at the granddaughter she thought she would never see again. "So, you love Zoe?"

"Yes, Omi, very much."

"How old is she?"

Eva knew what was coming and hid her grin. "She's 22 years old."

The older woman stopped and turned Eva's head towards her. "She's eight years younger than you!"

"Yeah." Eva grinned as her grandmother made clucking noises. "Do you approve?"

"Eva, my sweet child, it's not a matter of my approval. You're the one that will be with this woman, not me."

Eva was a little disappointed. She wanted her grandmother's approval, but it wasn't going to change the way she felt about her wife.

"Don't give me that pouty face." Elsa tapped her on the head. "If I said I approved of her, would it make any difference in how you felt about Zoe?"

"No, but...I love you and I want your blessing."

Elsa Muller closed her eyes for a moment and a smile creased her face. It had been a long time since anyone had wanted her opinion or her blessing. "I love you, Eva, and I don't want anyone to hurt you. If you love Zoe, and Zoe loves you, then you have my blessing."

Eva looked up into her grandmother's twinkling hazel eyes. "Thank you, Omi."

The old woman cupped Eva's cheek and kissed her. Straightening up, she put her hand behind her back and winced.

"Do you think you can finish your bath by yourself?"

"Yes, ma'am."

"Do you need me to send Zoe to help you?" Elsa teased as she went to the door.

"I don't think I would finish if you did that," Eva muttered to herself.

"I heard that." Elsa grinned and walked out of the bathroom, closing the door behind her. She stood watching the door for a moment and nodded a little. "Let's go and find out what this Zoe is all about," she said to herself, walking down the stairs.

Elsa came into the living room to find Zoe sprawled out on a rug with photo albums spread around her. The older woman smiled at the sight of her. She did like the young girl; she was more respectful than that she-demon her granddaughter had first chosen to be around.

"Would you like some tea, Zoe?"

Zoe looked up and smiled. Before the older woman could move, she got up from the floor. "I would love some, but I'll make it. Point me in the right direction."

Elsa chuckled and pointed to the kitchen. "So, did you find anything you like?" she asked, watching Zoe put the kettle on.

"Yeah, there's a lot of great photographs. I like the ones of Eva, but I also like the photographs of the Rhine Valley."

"I took those," Elsa said, feeling very pleased that Zoe took an interest. The photographs were special to her because the valley had inspired her, and it was where she'd met her husband, Johannes Muller, more than 60 years before.

"You're a photographer?"

"Yes, I love it."

"So that's where Evy gets her passion for it." Zoe nodded as she poured the water into the cups and made the tea.

"Yes. I remember I gave Eva one of my old cameras, and she would take some extraordinary pictures. She has a gift. Do you enjoy photography?"

Zoe blushed a little. "I love taking photographs of Eva. I'm an artist."

"Really? Do you have any portraits of Eva?"

"About twenty pieces. Would you like one?"

"Oh yes, please! Oh, I have one photograph I would love for

you to paint, if you don't mind."

Zoe put the tea on the table and watched as the older woman returned to the living room and came back a few moments later holding an old photo in her hand. She gazed at it for a moment, then handed it to Zoe.

Zoe took it and stared at it for a long moment. The picture was old and tattered a little around the edges. A tall woman stood with her arms around a tall, gangly teenager. Zoe instantly recognized Eva, her long hair pulled back and a twinkle in her eye. Eva resembled the taller woman, so Zoe assumed it was her mother.

"That's Daphne, such a beautiful woman inside and out."

"Like Eva," Zoe said quietly.

Elsa looked at Zoe and smiled. "Yes, very much so. Do you think you can paint it?"

Zoe nodded. "Did Eva's mother have blue eyes?"

"Exact same colour as Eva has."

"Ooh, I know those eyes very well," Zoe grinned, then blushed as she realized what she'd said. She looked up to find Eva's grandmother smiling at her.

"You are a character, Zoe," the older woman chuckled, getting up from the table and taking her tea into the living room. Zoe followed her and placed her cup on a nearby low table. She resumed her position on the rug and picked up a photo she had been looking at before the older woman came in.

"Uh huh, is that Evy?" Zoe pointed to a picture of tall young girl in running shorts. The look on her face was exuberant.

"Oh yes, indeed. All arms and legs, that's my Eva."

Zoe chuckled. The young girl was indeed all arms and legs; her dark hair was in a ponytail. "How old was she here?"

"Oh, let's see...that was in 1936 during the Olympic trials in Berlin, so she must have been 16 years old."

Zoe was stunned. "What?" She sat up and took the photo, looking at it more closely. "You mean to tell me that Eva went to the Olympics?"

"Oh no. She lost in the finals and didn't make it."

"Why is she looking so happy?"

"She was beaten by the German champion, I forget her name now, but Eva came close."

"Wow." Zoe couldn't believe it.

"Yes, she was quite good. I always knew she would be fast by the way she would run through my legs when she was three years old. A little terror."

"Eva, a little terror?" Zoe just couldn't picture her wife that way and began to laugh. "Eva is very quiet now."

"She didn't used to be, she was very outgoing." Elsa sighed. "I suppose the older one gets, the more serious one becomes."

"I don't think that's the reason, Omi," Zoe said quietly as she resumed looking at photos.

"Okay, enough talking about me!" Eva came into the living room and ruffled Zoe's hair.

"Hey there, Ms Terror Tot. Come down here," Zoe teased. Eva sat cross-legged on the floor beside her wife. "Omi, wants me to paint you."

Eva rolled her eyes and turned to her grandmother. "Omi, don't encourage her! She's forever trying to paint me."

"You would think I was trying to kill her or something." Zoe playfully slapped her wife on the shoulder.

The older woman chuckled at the antics of her granddaughter and her friend. "She was always like that, Zoe, never liked getting her photo taken." Elsa got up from the sofa and went back into the kitchen to get some biscuits.

"So that explains Miss Grouchiness," Zoe teased. She handed Eva the photograph that her grandmother had given her of Eva and her mother, and watched as Eva looked at it.

"*Mutti.*" Eva traced the picture of her mother with her finger. "She had black hair and the bluest eyes...and she always wore a perfume that reminded me of jasmine..." Eva said wistfully. Every time Eva went past jasmine, it brought good memories of her mother.

Zoe put her arm around Eva's waist and leaned on her shoulder. "I'll make it the best painting I have ever done," Zoe promised.

Eva sighed and gazed into sparkling emerald eyes. "Thank you, love." Eva cupped Zoe's cheek and leaned down to give her a gentle kiss.

Elsa watched the two women for a moment and felt like she was intruding on a very private moment. She walked back into the kitchen with a smile on her face.

Chapter
21

Eva laid back and smiled. The very familiar smell coming from the kitchen made her sigh with contentment. Zoe was curled up against her, her arm tightening her hold on her wife's waist. Eva was quite sure of what her grandmother was doing. She would be in the kitchen baking bread and cooking porridge for her breakfast. She hated porridge but ate it anyway, because she never wanted to disappoint her grandmother.

Zoe was quite taken with her former room. The walls were still a pale blue, her favorite color, and she chuckled at the response when Zoe walked in. Her wife took one look at the room, turned to her, and told her it matched her eyes. Her grandmother had taken great care with her awards and personal possessions, preserving them as they had been when she had left.

Eva didn't understand why the older woman had kept her old awards and trophies, the latter tarnished and in good need of some silver polish. Zoe had been like a kid in a candy store when she'd seen them. Eva looked down at the dark head resting on her shoulder. "Zo, wake up," Eva whispered and nudged the sleeping woman.

"Hm," Zoe mumbled.

Eva grinned and lifted one of Zoe's eyelids to reveal an emerald orb. "Hey, anyone home?"

"Evy, is the house on fire?" Zoe mumbled.

"Hmm...no."

"Is the world coming to an end?"

"No," Eva grinned.

"Are you sick?"

"No."

"Go to sleep." Zoe gave her a gentle slap on the belly and snuggled up.

"Zoe, come on, open your eyes," Eva pleaded with her.

Zoe opened her eyes and met the twinkling blue set of her wife. "Are you happy now?"

"Much. Good morning," Eva greeted her wife. She leaned down, looked into her wife's eyes, and smiled. Zoe put her arms around her wife's neck and brought her down for a long sensual kiss. "Oh I love waking up to that."

"Hmm, that's all you're going to get," Zoe sighed and closed her eyes again.

"Hey! Wake up!"

"Evy, your grandmother is downstairs. I am not going to make love to you with your grandmother within earshot."

When Zoe didn't hear anything, she opened her eyes to find a pouty-faced Eva. She had to laugh at the comical sight. "Come on, you know I can't. Anyway, you are not exactly quiet you know."

"I am, too."

Zoe snorted. "Eva Haralambos, you are not quiet. You wake the dead some days."

"Wake the dead?"

"Do I have to repeat what you did in Larissa when I gave you your birthday present?" Zoe smirked. She remembered that night quite well, and her wife's response to her "present" was quite vocal. She wondered if their neighbors had heard. She hoped they hadn't.

Eva blushed a little, much to Zoe's amusement. "That was some birthday present, Zo."

"Oh yeah."

Eva grinned at the memory of a few days before when Zoe surprised her, first with a birthday party, and afterwards by taking charge and making love to her. The day was made even more special by the pendant she now wore around her neck.

"I was thinking–"

"Should I worry?" Eva teased.

Zoe gave her a mock glare. "I was thinking...um...why don't

you ask your grandmother to join us in Sydney?"

Eva looked down at the dark hair resting on her shoulder and smiled. Zoe never ceased to amaze her with her generosity; it was one of the things she loved about her. "Are you sure?"

"Yeah, she's all alone here, and it's not very nice in Berlin now. I think she would enjoy it in Sydney with us. She would also make a good babysitter."

"I'll ask her, love. Thank you." Eva scooped the younger woman into her embrace and kissed her.

Zoe tweaked her wife's chin, getting a dazzling smile in return. "So, tell me, Miss Eva, are we staying here longer?"

"Well, we leave for Paris at midday, we have one day there and then we leave for home," Eva recounted. She was rather happy with that, since she would have the whole day off. The Minister spoke French, and he didn't need an interpreter. Eva couldn't speak French anyway, so that was fine with her.

"What about Italy?"

"Cancelled. The Minister has to return home because Parliament is sitting, and they have a foreign affairs brouhaha brewing."

"Really? What?" Zoe asked. She loved politics and the machinations of it. Eva didn't see the fascination, but Zoe enjoyed listening to the House of Representatives and Senate broadcasts on the radio. She would often find her arguing with the radio when a Minister was talking. Eva often wondered what kind of politician Zoe would make, and the thought usually brought a chuckle since she knew Zoe couldn't lie to save herself.

"Something about Russian spies or something."

"Oooh, the Opposition has been going on about that for months!"

"Yeah, thrilling," Eva said and yawned. She stretched to get the kinks out of her back, and Zoe looked on appreciatively.

"So, Mrs H, have you been to Paris?"

"Hmm, in 1935, with *Mutti*. It was one of the best holidays I ever had," Eva mused. Her mother took her on the trip and opened her eyes to the wonderful world of art. Eva was entranced by her mother's knowledge of the great artists and their background. "After we came back, I spent days trying to perfect the Mona Lisa smile." Eva chuckled at the memory. It drove her stepfather crazy until her mother explained what she was doing.

"I think you got it right," Zoe teased.

"You think so?" Eva asked and realised she was being teased when Zoe gave her a little smirk. "Not nice, Zoe."

Zoe was about to launch an all out tickling assault when the door opened and Elsa entered.

The older woman stood with her hands on her hips. "Girls, when do you think you are going to get up? Midday?"

"Uh...we just woke up...sort of," Eva tried to explain. She didn't know how to tell her grandmother that they normally discussed the upcoming day while snuggled together in bed.

"Uh huh. Well, can you two get up? I have breakfast made. I made some porridge for you, Eva."

Eva made a face that she couldn't hide from her grandmother. Zoe looked over at with a frown. She knew Eva hated porridge. "Omi, Eva hates porridge."

"You do? Since when? I always made it for you, and you never said anything."

"I didn't want to disappoint you, Omi, since you got up so early and–"

Eva was quite surprised when her grandmother snorted. "Young lady, are you telling me that I made porridge all those years and you hated it?"

"Yes, ma'am."

Elsa shook her head and turned to Zoe. "What does my granddaughter eat for breakfast?"

"Two eggs, sunny side up, with toast, bacon, and chamomile tea," Zoe replied.

"And what do you eat?"

"Same as Eva."

"Well, I can manage the eggs and toast, but I don't have any bacon or chamomile tea. Would normal tea do?"

"Yes, ma'am," Eva replied.

"And you will eat it?" Elsa asked, looking over her glasses at her granddaughter. Eva nodded. Elsa gave her a grin.

"Omi, we need to ask you something."

"Well I suggest you get dressed and come down to breakfast. You can ask me then."

The older woman left, leaving the two women to stare at the door in silence for a few moments.

"I would have eaten the porridge," Eva said quietly.

"Oh Lord, spare me," Zoe muttered and got out of bed. "Come on, let's get up!"

Elsa put the two fried eggs and the toast on the plate as her granddaughter entered, Zoe close behind. Eva gave her grandmother a kiss before sitting down.

Elsa tapped Eva on the head. "You should have told me you hated porridge."

"I'm sorry, Omi," Eva mumbled. "Zoe likes it."

"You do?" The older woman turned to Zoe who was nodding.

"I don't make it because Evy hates it, so I don't eat it either," Zoe said matter-of-factly.

"You don't eat it because Eva doesn't?" Elsa tried to work out that logic, but didn't understand it.

"Well, I don't eat *fasoulatha* and Evy loves it. So she doesn't eat it because I can't stand the smell of it." Zoe turned to Eva who was drinking her tea.

"That's convoluted logic, child. Must be a new fashion that I'm not aware of. Eva's grandfather hated chocolate, but that didn't stop me!" the older woman chuckled.

"Oh, well, if it was chocolate that would be different," Zoe replied solemnly.

Elsa shook her head and turned to get her own plate. She brought it to the table and sat down. The two women were looking at each other over the top of their teacups and giving each other little smiles. Elsa thought it was so amusing. *Ah young love*, she thought to herself.

"So, what did you want to ask me?"

"Omi, Zoe and I were wondering if you would like to come home to Sydney and live with us."

Elsa put down her teacup and looked at the two younger women. The invitation moved her deeply. "Oh, child, I would love to come, but it's so far away."

"You would love it, Omi. We have a big beautiful house. You can see the ocean from the back yard. And Eva built this great garden," Zoe said enthusiastically. "We would love to have you stay with us."

Elsa patted Zoe's cheek and grinned. "Zoe, you have no idea how much I would love to be with you," she turned to Eva, "and you, but I'm old and I wouldn't have any of my friends there."

"You can find new friends, Omi," Eva suggested.

The older woman chuckled. "Eva, I survived the war, and it

would pain me to leave. I know Berlin doesn't look like much at the moment, but it's my home."

"Who will take care of you when you get sick? I don't want to lose you again," Eva replied. She knew her grandmother wouldn't change her mind once she had it made up, but she had to try.

"Who took care of me before?" Elsa asked with a tiny grin. "Eva, Zoe, thank you for asking me, but I can't leave."

"Would you consider coming for a visit?"

"All the way to Australia?"

"And if you like it you might decide to stay," Zoe reasoned.

"She doesn't give up, does she?" Elsa asked Eva, who shook her head. "A visit...how long does the ship take?"

"Oh no, you won't be coming by ship. I'll send you a ticket to come over by plane."

Elsa put her hand over her mouth in shock. She knew it was very expensive to fly, and she didn't want her granddaughter to go to all that expense. "Oh no, Eva, that's much too expensive."

"Omi, remember what you told me when you got me that encyclopedia set?"

"I'm getting old, child, I don't remember everything."

Eva gave her grandmother a questioning look. "You told me that it was a pleasure to give, and that I should accept it gracefully."

"Yes, I did say that."

"Well, it's a pleasure to give, and you should accept it gracefully," Eva repeated and crossed her arms over her chest with a smug expression on her face.

Zoe looked at the older woman and grinned. "She's got you there."

"So it seems. Thank you." The older woman got up and kissed her granddaughter and then Zoe before sitting back down.

"Maybe you can come over before Zoe gives birth." Eva watched her grandmother stop mid chew and look up at Zoe, who was drinking her tea.

"Are you pregnant?"

"No, but I'm hoping to be soon."

"I don't understand."

"We want to become parents, and Zoe is going to bear our children. You're going to be a great grandmother." Eva beamed at her very confused grandmother.

"You know, there are days when I feel all of my 70 years,

and this is one of those days," Elsa muttered. "I thought you two were married. Do you allow Zoe to have male friends?"

The question caught Zoe mid swallow and she started coughing. Zoe looked at her adopted grandmother and shook her head. "God, no! Eva is all I need." Zoe realized too late what she'd said and blushed a bright shade of pink.

"I would hope so," Eva teased. "Omi, a good friend of ours is going to...um..."

"Donate his sperm?" Elsa supplied. She got over her initial shock about it and was quite interested in what her two granddaughters had planned.

"Yeah."

"And what does this friend look like? Is he a good, honest, hard working man?"

"He looks a lot like Eva, and he is honest, a great friend, and we think he is very special."

Elsa nodded and resumed eating. Eva looked at Zoe and shrugged. She didn't know what her grandmother was thinking, but she hoped she approved.

"Omi, would you like to come out before Zoe gives birth?"

"Of course I would, sweetheart. You're going to need all the help you can get," she said matter-of-factly and poured Eva another cup of tea. Elsa looked down and saw a book near Eva's hand. She picked it up and noticed the initials on the left hand side.

"Eva, did someone make a mistake with your initials?" Elsa indicated the diary.

Eva frowned and looked down. She picked up the diary and looked up at her grandmother. "No, Omi. My initials are EH now."

"What's the H for?"

Eva stole a quick glance at Zoe who was sipping her tea. "Haralambos, Omi."

"Oh dear, that's very Greek, isn't it?" the older woman chuckled. "Did you take Zoe's last name?"

"No. I adopted the name after finding out who my real father was," Eva said quietly, knowing she would wound the old woman with her words. She didn't want to upset her grandmother and tried to avoid the subject.

"I see." The older woman was quiet for a moment and then looked at her granddaughter.

"Were you ashamed to be a Muller?"

Eva knew whatever way she answered, it would be like a slap in the face to her grandmother. She took a deep breath and told the truth. "Omi, I *was* ashamed to be a Muller."

"Why, sweetheart? You were a very happy child, and you had the best of everything. Was life so horrible after you were sent away that you didn't want to be a part of this family?"

"Excuse me," Zoe said, quietly excusing herself from the table. She felt Eva had to talk to her grandmother alone.

"Zo, please stay."

Zoe stopped and looked back. She sat back down and folded her hands on the table.

"Omi, things happened to me that hurt me. Father tried to kill me, and I didn't want to be a Muller."

Zoe watched Elsa's face. Eva had never referred to Hans Muller as her father in the five years they had been together, and she knew it hurt Eva to even associate the word with Hans Muller.

"Do you still feel you don't have a family," Elsa asked.

"Omi, you would always be my grandmother, no matter what. I've never stopped loving you, ever." Eva went down on her knees. She knelt near her grandmother's chair and met her grandmother's blue eyes. "It wasn't you that I wanted to run away from. When things got tough and I felt all alone, I remembered how we used to go to the park and we would talk about everything and anything. I love you, Omi. I thought you didn't want me anymore either."

"Oh, child. What gave you that idea?"

"I sent letters, Omi, and I didn't get a reply." Eva let the tears fall. She'd sent letter after letter. She would wait near the letterbox, waiting to hear back from her grandmother, and nothing came. "I got a letter from Henrietta and she told me you were well, so I knew at least that you were still alive."

"Oh, my dear child!" Elsa gathered her granddaughter in her arms. "I didn't get any of the letters!" She cupped Eva's face in her hands and brushed away her tears. "I never forgot you, Eva. Hans wouldn't give me your address, no matter how often I asked. Then the war started, and I lost contact with Hans as well."

"When I found out who my father was, I changed my name."

"Are you ashamed of growing up German as well?"

"No, Omi. I'm not. I can't pass as a Greek with this accent," Eva tried to joke, getting a chuckle from her grandmother.

"Eva, I don't want you to forget your life here in Germany. I know what happened with Hans was a nightmare for you, but please, child, don't let that overshadow everything in your life. Will you do that for me?"

"I will try, Omi."

"That's all I ask. I have good memories of you growing up, and all I ever wanted was to see you happy." Elsa patted Eva's cheek and looked at Zoe who was resting her chin on the table watching the two women with a thoughtful look on her face. "I know you are happy with Zoe."

"I'm very happy, Omi," Eva replied, resuming her seat.

"Good."

"Does anything faze you?" Zoe asked. She was very impressed by the older woman's forthrightness. Zoe could also see where Eva got her no-nonsense style.

Elsa Muller sat pensively looking into her teacup. "Many things faze me, Zoe, but there are degrees of faziness."

"Degrees of faziness? Is that a word?" Eva teased her grandmother.

"I don't understand the word," Zoe frowned. She could understand the word for "faze" in German, but was unsure about the other word. Zoe looked to Eva, who repeated the word in Greek for her.

"I'm sorry, Zoe, I forget your mother tongue isn't German," the older woman grinned. "Maybe I should speak in Greek?" she said in Greek, getting Zoe's attention.

"You can speak Greek?"

"Who do you think taught Eva?"

Zoe looked at Eva who was smiling broadly. "I thought Eva's mother taught her."

"Omi was my Greek language lecturer at university," Eva said proudly. She had been very proud of her grandmother, but a little embarrassed that she was teaching the class. She soon got over her discomfort when her lecturer gave her additional help at home.

Elsa chuckled and got up from the table, collecting the plates and leaving Zoe open-mouthed at the news.

"Well, it's a good thing I didn't say anything bad in Greek then," Zoe muttered, causing Eva to nearly fall from her chair laughing. She got up still chuckling and put her arms around her wife.

"I love you," Eva chuckled and kissed her wife on the

cheek. "I should have told you, but it slipped my mind."

Zoe scowled at her. "I'm not even going to ask how that could slip your mind, but you are getting on in years, so I'll forgive you."

"Ouch, Zoe, that hurt," Eva grinned. "Do you want to go and see my old tree house?"

"I don't know, Evy. Do I have to climb a tree?"

"Yes, but I'll hold you."

"Oh well, in that case, lead the way."

Eva took her hand and gave it a kiss; and they both walked out into brilliant sunlight.

Chapter 22

Eva walked quietly down the street, her wife by her side and her grandmother's arm around hers. She smiled down at the older woman who gave her a brilliant smile in return. A dozen or so soldiers walked past them.

"Young boys," Elsa remarked, watching the men march away.

They crossed the street to the embassy building and entered. The lobby was warm, the fireplace giving the room an ambience that reminded Zoe of an old world hotel. Percy Hester was talking to his assistant near the elevator and turned when Michael indicated Eva had arrived. He waved them over.

"Good morning, sir," Eva greeted her boss and made the introductions. "This is my grandmother, Elsa Muller. Omi, this is Percy Hester, the Foreign Affairs and Immigration Minister."

"I'm pleased to meet you, Frau Muller." Percy took Elsa's hand and kissed it, getting an elevated eyebrow twitch from Eva.

"My, you are a gentleman," Elsa replied, surprising Eva with her English.

"*Danke,*" Percy replied in German. "So, it was a good reunion?"

"You brought my granddaughter back to me. For that I thank you a great deal," Elsa said and looked up at Eva.

"You should be very proud of her. Her linguistic skills are

superb." Hester looked at Eva who started to blush from the attention. "I do have to take her away from you for a moment, as I need to speak to her."

"Of course," Elsa replied. Eva leaned down and gave her grandmother a kiss before following her boss. The older woman stood watching the pair walk away, and then she turned to Zoe who sat near the fireplace. She looked up when the older woman sat next to her.

"Where are you headed after this?"

"Paris, then home," Zoe said with a sigh.

"Zoe, can I ask you something?"

"Sure," Zoe replied.

"Are you certain you are in love with my granddaughter?" Elsa realised too late how that question may have been misunderstood by the young woman. Zoe's shocked expression was enough to tell her she'd put the question the wrong way.

Zoe was taken aback. She wasn't expecting such a question from the older woman. "Mrs Muller, I have never been more certain about anything in my entire life."

"I'm sorry, Zoe. It's not the way I wanted to ask you that. You see, Eva is very important to me, and I know she loves you a great deal..."

Zoe looked away and into the flames, watching the burning log. "Omi, nothing is more important to me than Eva. I would never, ever hurt her." Zoe looked up into crystal blue eyes. "I would rather die before I would do that. She's all the family I have left."

Elsa felt quite stupid now to have doubted the young woman's love for granddaughter. "I am sorry, Zoe."

"I understand why you asked that question, Omi. I know what Eva went through, but I give you my word, I will never leave her."

Eva followed Percy Hester through to his commandeered office. She took the seat opposite the desk and was quite surprised to find that the Minister chose to sit next to her.

"So," Percy smiled, "how did you think this tour went?"

"We had some hiccups in Athens, but I think it's gone smoothly overall," Eva replied. She wasn't sure where the Minister was going with this, or why she'd been called to this meeting. Not having been on a previous diplomatic tour, she assumed it was done this way.

"Hmm, that's true." Percy played with the file on his lap. He smiled at Eva who sat there feeling quite uncomfortable. "You're probably wondering why I called you to this one on one meeting."

"Yes, that did cross my mind," Eva said with a chuckle.

"Okay. When this tour ends, I am going to be in need of a new personal assistant."

"Where is Michael going?"

"Michael has been promoted to assistant to the Defense Minister. He got the news a few days ago," Percy replied, loosening his tie. "So that leaves me with a position to fill."

"Right," Eva said, not knowing what that had to do with her.

"I want you for that position."

Percy grinned at the stunned expression on Eva's face. He did enjoy doing that to people. He respected the young woman a great deal, and she would be an asset to his department if she accepted. "You have handled your responsibilities quite well. I must admit I had my doubts at first, but I think you have proven yourself."

"Uh..." Eva was speechless. If she accepted the job, it would mean a promotion beyond what she thought she could achieve in the Interpreter section. It would enable Zoe to concentrate on her artwork and not have to worry about working elsewhere. "Will I have to move to Canberra?"

"No, my office is in Sydney. You would need to make the trip to Canberra occasionally when Parliament is sitting, but you would be based in Sydney."

"That's quite a promotion," Eva said quietly, still stunned by the offer. "Can I discuss it with Zoe before I give you my answer?"

Percy Hester gave her a smile. "Of course you can."

"Thank you, sir."

"Eva, I meant it when I said you did an excellent job. I wrote to Richard, complimenting you on your work and your patience with some pretty intolerable situations. You would have your own secretary and–"

"If I accept it, can I select the secretary?"

Percy nodded. "Is there someone you had in mind?"

"There is. Her name is Debbie Harrison. She is my secretary at the moment," Eva replied. She valued Debbie's friendship and her work. They had worked together for five years.

"Is she any good?"

"Yes, sir. She's an ASO1 at the moment," Eva replied. The pay scales didn't quite match the job designation, and Eva had often thought her secretary got paid peanuts for all the hard work she did.

Hester began to tap the pen on the file. "I see. Well, if you accept the position, I don't see it a problem. That would save a whole lot of interviewing for us. She would go from an ASO1 to an ASO5. Do you think she would like that?"

Eva grinned. "Oh, I know so, sir." Eva was definitely sure that her friend would enjoy the pay raise.

"Then it's done. Discuss it with Zoe and let me know after we reach Paris tonight." Hester put the file on the desk and got up from his seat. "Eva, I will tell you, some people are not going to like this decision."

"Yes, sir."

"You can stop with the sir. Call me Percy."

Eva's eyes widened. "Uh...okay."

"They will try and make an issue of your sexual preference, but as far as I'm concerned, I don't care. As long as you don't make an issue out of it, or provide any reason for others to complain to me, then I don't care." Hester pushed up his glasses. "At least they won't be able to say that I'm having an affair with you," the Minister chuckled.

"Uh..." Eva couldn't decide to be embarrassed or amused.

"Yes, I know those rumours about my wife and Richard."

"Uh huh," Eva replied, not knowing where to go with that piece of news.

"They are not true." Hester gave her a wink. "Now, I think it's time we head for the airport."

Percy Hester opened the door and let Eva pass before closing the door quietly. Eva walked quickly to the stairs to go to the lobby and stopped. Zoe was talking animatedly to her grandmother, who was laughing. With the promotion, she could give Zoe everything the young woman dreamed of. When the children came along, Zoe would be able to stay at home, take care of them, and not have to worry about childcare. Zoe would be able to do her artwork and not have to worry about asinine bosses.

❖●❖●❖●❖

Elsa Muller watched Zoe pack their suitcases with a shake of her head. The two suitcases were overflowing, and the older woman wondered how they would close them.

"Okay, Evy." Zoe beckoned her partner.

Elsa laughed when Eva came over and sat on the overstuffed bag, her weight allowing Zoe to zip the bag up.

"Oh yeah, Omi, I'm now the official suitcase sitter," Eva chuckled and sat on the other bag, allowing Zoe to zip it up. "Zoe packed like we were going away for three months."

"Oh funny ha, ha," Zoe muttered from the bathroom.

Elsa looked up at the clock and realized she had to get going. The last few days had given her a new lease on life. She turned to Eva, opened her arms, and embraced the tall young woman.

"You're going to be seeing us in nine months or so," Eva said in between brushing away her tears.

"I don't want you to spend your money–"

"Omi, please, we want to do this. I thought we already discussed this."

"All right, all right," the older woman agreed. She cupped her granddaughter's face and kissed her on the cheek. "I love you, Eva."

"I love you, too, Omi," Eva replied as she hugged the older woman.

Elsa turned and beckoned Zoe to her, then embraced the young woman, giving her a kiss on the cheek. "I want you to take care of yourself. Don't overdo things when you fall pregnant, and let Eva do everything."

"She does that already," Zoe teased.

"At your service, Mrs Haralambos," Eva replied.

"Have a good flight and remember when you get home, boil some tea if your back hurts, okay?"

"Yes, Omi."

The older woman gave them another hug. Eva walked her to the door and watched as she left their room and walked down the stairs. She closed the door quietly and turned. She leaned against the door, watching Zoe for a moment.

Zoe came over, put her arms around the tall woman's waist, and looked up into twinkling blue eyes. "So, tell me what's on your mind?"

Eva wanted to laugh. She hadn't said a word to Zoe about the Minister's job offer, but somehow her wife knew something was up. "What would be on my mind?"

Zoe snorted. "Evy, I can see it in your eyes, love. Ever since you came back from the meeting with Percy, your eyes have lit up and you look like the cat that ate the canary. So tell me."

"Is that right?" Eva teased. "What if I was just planning what I'm going to do to you tonight in Paris?"

Eva led her partner to the bed and lay down. Eva smiled when Zoe took her customary position, resting her head on her chest. She ran her fingers through the slightly wavy chestnut hair.

"Uh huh, and you shared this news with Percy Hester," Zoe giggled. "So, are you going to tell me, or are you going to keep it a secret?"

"Zoe, how would you like not to work? I mean, to work from home doing your artwork."

"Huh? Evy, I would love that, but we can't afford it with the mortgage and everything."

"Would you want to if we could?"

"Yeah, I would, but we can't. I don't want you to work yourself ragged like you did in the factory," Zoe replied, hitching herself up and leaning on her elbow. She watched her wife's face; a touch of a smile played on her lips.

"The Minister has offered me a promotion." Eva looked at her and gave her a huge grin.

"A promotion? But you don't work for the Minister."

"Michael is leaving, and he asked me to be his assistant." Eva wished she had her camera handy to capture the look on her wife's face. It was one of pure joy for the position offered to her. Eva knew what was coming next and wasn't too surprised when Zoe squealed with delight and brought her down for a kiss.

"Did you accept?"

"No, not yet."

"Why not? This is perfect for you. You can use your skills and everything!" Zoe jumped up and landed on top of her wife. "Evy, this is perfect! Why didn't you say yes right away?"

"I told him that I would ask you first and see what you thought," Eva replied.

Zoe's smiled broadened, if that were possible. Her face hurt from smiling so much. "I love you!"

"I love you, too, Zo." Eva chuckled at her wife's exuberant response to the news. "So what do I tell him?"

"Yes, of course!" Zoe couldn't believe the turn of events. It didn't surprise her that Eva was offered the promotion; her wife worked very hard and deserved it.

"I asked Percy if I could select my own secretary, and I told him I wanted Debbie."

"Debbie would love that, Evy. So that would jump you from an ASO2 to, what?"

Eva grinned.

"ASO8," Eva replied. The highest possible ranking that she could go. It was a huge financial jump for her. Zoe's mouth hung open at the news. "My pay could go to the mortgage, we still will have some left over, and we won't have to worry."

"I can still keep working-"

"Zoe, I don't want you to work. You can do your artwork at home, and you won't have to worry about the boofheads at the gallery. Unless you want to work."

"Are you sure?"

Eva nodded. "I have another reason, too."

"And that is?"

"Well, when you have our children, you would be able to look after them," Eva replied. "Is that all right?"

Zoe nodded. "You are something quite special, Eva Haralambos."

"You're not so bad yourself, Zoe Haralambos," Eva chuckled.

"So tell me, what do you have planned for Paris tonight?"

"You ask too many questions," Eva replied, moving out of Zoe's embrace and off the bed, amid Zoe's protests.

Chapter
23

"You know the Goddess of Love would have had better success if she'd had a head," Zoe said and gazed up at Eva with a grin.

They were standing in front of the Crouching Aphrodite statue. Her wife shook her head and chuckled. Eva was enjoying herself, showing Zoe around her favorite museum. Zoe was in her element, Eva thought, as she watched the young woman take in all the treasures the French museum had to offer. She was holding off on showing her the Mona Lisa. That was going to be special.

The Louvre was packed with tourists, but Zoe didn't mind. The plane had landed, at last, in Paris, something that Zoe was very grateful for since they'd hit some turbulence and her stomach was protesting a great deal. As soon as they'd settled into the embassy, they headed out. Zoe was quite adamant about there being only one place she wanted to see in Paris, and that was the Louvre. They gravitated to the Greek Art section and Zoe made some remarks about thieves, which Eva thought was quite funny, but the couple in front of them didn't appreciate.

Eva stopped where Zoe was looking at the statue of the Sleeping Hermaphrodite and wanted to laugh at the look on her wife's face. The naked woman lay draped over what looked to be a divan.

"Too big a bum," Zoe muttered.

Eva couldn't help herself and burst out laughing, causing the other tourists to turn to stare at her. She put her hand over her mouth to try and stop the giggles.

"Am I amusing you, Mrs H?" Zoe teased. "Are you having fun?"

"Oh yeah," Eva replied with a wink.

Zoe stopped in front of the Borghese Gladiator and stared at it for a moment. "Are all Greek men so well endowed?"

Eva completely lost her composure and moved a little further away to collect herself while Zoe grinned at having made her partner laugh. Her running commentary on the statues was getting to be a great deal of fun. Zoe didn't think the people around her were enjoying it, though. Eva got herself under control again and came back to stand next to Zoe with a serious expression on her face. "It's a good imitation," she said seriously while holding her chin and nodding. Zoe looked up at her and started to giggle.

Eva took Zoe's hand, much to her partner's surprise, and wandered around looking at other statues. They came to the Venus de Milo and Zoe whistled.

"What?"

"She's as tall as you are! I thought she was shorter," Zoe observed. "Are her hands supposed to be cut off?"

"Excuse me, miss, but do you have to give a running commentary on every piece you see here?" a haughty woman complained to Zoe, who gave her a blank look.

"Yes, you see my partner here is blind and I have to tell her what I'm seeing," Zoe replied, patting Eva on the arm.

"Oh." The woman was stunned and gazed up at Eva who had an amused expression on her face. "I'm so sorry. Please continue," she finished and walked away with a slight blush.

"Zoe, behave," Eva whispered.

"Yes, mum," Zoe replied with a chuckle and went to the next statue. "Have you noticed how all the women are tall, with or without arms?"

"Yes," Eva replied, not quite sure where Zoe was headed.

"You would think all Greek women were tall Amazons. I bet there were short Amazons as well, but do you see it in the art? Nooooo." Zoe shook her head. "What's with the no arms bit? Did a thief come along and say, 'Hey, this statue would look great if she had no arms?'"

"I don't know, Zo." Eva was trying very hard to keep a straight face.

"And all the men have big...you know..."

"You should see the statue of David in Italy," an older woman turned around and said with a grin.

"Exactly my point. I think all these artists created the statues with a lot of wishful thinking involved," Zoe told the woman, who smiled at her and moved off.

"You know, love, I've never experienced the Greek antiquities like that before." Eva leaned down and gave her a quick kiss.

"I live to serve," Zoe giggled. "So what is your favorite part? The Mona Lisa?"

"No." Eva shook her head.

"Are you going to show me?"

Eva nodded and took her hand, leading her out of the Greek Antiquities and to one painting that really impressed her, above all the others. They stopped in front of the work of art. The painting was *The Young Beggar* by Bartolomé Esteban Murillo. When Eva first saw it, she was taken with the way the artist had made the painting look so natural, the sunlight falling on the poor boy.

"Wow," Zoe mumbled and took a step closer to the artwork. "The detail in this is extraordinary; look at the expression in his face." Zoe was overawed by the artwork. "He looks so lost."

Eva nodded her head. When she first saw *The Young Beggar*, she was alone. She'd visited the Louvre by herself while her mother rested at their hotel. The slant of the sunlight hitting the boy and the detail in the artwork captivated the photographer in her.

"He is all alone, but that isn't the total of it. With the sun giving its warmth, he is able to enjoy some comfort," Eva said as she gazed at the painting.

Zoe looked away from the painting and up at her wife. She smiled and took her hand, giving it a little squeeze. "Okay, where is that Mona Lisa?"

"You have no patience, Zo," Eva teased.

"When I get to your age, Mrs H, I'll cultivate patience."

"You know, Zo, keep that up and I won't show you what I have planned for tonight."

"Is that supposed to scare me?" Zoe playfully slapped her wife on the bum and chuckled.

"Did it work?"

"No," Zoe laughed and walked on ahead, leaving Eva to shake her head and have a good chuckle.

Eva caught up and steered her young wife to the Italian art-work—16th century section. There was a crowd in front of the painting that everyone wanted to see. When they finally managed to get to the viewing area, Eva stood behind Zoe with her hands on her shoulders and leaned down.

"There she is, Zo."

The Mona Lisa gazed down at them from her perch, the enigmatic smile hiding her secrets. Zoe tilted her head to the side to gaze at the painting she'd heard a great deal about. She wasn't overly impressed with it. She'd thought it would be bigger, thought the smile was quite odd.

"You know, Evy, I know what's she thinking," Zoe said and looked up.

"Really?"

"Uh huh."

"Okay, I'll bite. What is she thinking?"

"She's got the same look you do when I'm painting you. She's thinking, 'Hurry up and paint me, Leonardo, my foot has fallen asleep!'" Zoe said seriously. The people around her started to chuckle, and Eva closed her eyes and tried in vain to stop laughing. "And you're right, you know."

"About what?" Eva managed to say before another fit of the giggles struck. She just couldn't get rid of the image of Mona Lisa chastising Leonardo da Vinci for taking too long.

"You have the same smile when you're trying not to strangle me," Zoe winked up at the tall woman.

Eva took Zoe's hand and led her away from the chuckling crowd. They wandered around several of the pieces until Zoe stopped in front of a Titian painting that took her breath away.

"Oh wow, Evy."

"Yeah, it's good, isn't it?"

"Good?" Zoe asked incredulously. "Good is a painting of a bowl of fruit."

"Hmm, depends on who paints the fruit, Zo," Eva teased.

Zoe gave her partner a mock glare at describing a master-piece as "good." They stood looking at the painting, *The Entombment.* Zoe marveled at the skill of the artist and the deep emotions it evoked at the sight of the dead Christ being entombed.

The announcement that the Louvre was closing was met

with a groan from Zoe, who was sure she would need at least a whole day to see everything. The fact that they were due to fly out the next day at midday didn't help.

Reluctantly, they made their way to the exit and stepped out into a cool evening. The wind was blowing, causing Zoe to pull on her jacket. Eva took her hand and they walked down the quiet street away from the crowds that were making their way home or to a hotel. Eva planned this night to be special. She wanted to make Zoe's Paris trip a memorable one before they left for home.

"Evy, where are we going?"

"Some place," Eva replied, giving Zoe a little smirk.

"Some place...is that the French name or the Greek?" Zoe teased.

"Patience, Zoe, patience."

They walked for a little while and came to a small restaurant near the River Seine. Zoe was stunned. It was something she'd thought only existed in the movies as she took in the view of the restaurant near the river, the full moon's shadow shimmering in the river.

"How long were you planning this?"

"Since I found out we were coming to Paris," Eva replied, quite pleased with her wife's reaction. It was a beautiful and romantic setting, the full moon adding to the romantic ambience. "Do you like?"

"Oh, Eva, this is...this is..."

Eva was amused to see her normally talkative spouse at a loss for words. Eva turned and spoke to the maitre d' that showed them to their table, which had a single rose in an elegant vase. Eva took the rose and gave it to her wife. "Happy Anniversary...a little early, but I thought this would be a really nice place to celebrate it."

Zoe took the rose and closed her eyes. Eva's surprise truly stunned the young woman. Their anniversary was a week away, but that didn't stop her spouse from giving her romantic streak a good workout.

"Evy, I love you." Zoe didn't know how to express the feelings she had for this woman and she didn't think a simple "I love you" would be sufficient.

"Zoe, I am looking forward to spending the rest of my life with you," Eva whispered, leaning over and giving her wife a kiss.

The waiter stood off to the side with a grin on his face and sighed. *Ah, young love,* he thought to himself as the two women kissed each other for a few moments. He really didn't want to interfere. He went up to them, took their order, and left them as quickly as possible.

Eva smiled at Zoe's stunned expression. "Are you happy?"

"Understatement of the year, Evy," Zoe said quietly, looking down at their joined hands and the matching rings. "This is one night I'll never forget."

Eva took her wife's hand and kissed it. "I want to give you the best."

"I already have the best." Zoe smiled and pushed her chair closer. She rested her head on Eva's shoulder and looked out at the calm water. "Everything else is icing on the cake."

Eva looked down at the dark head and shook her head, marveling at how life had turned out for the two of them. They had indeed come full circle, and she was looking forward to the next chapter of their lives. She was, without a doubt, a very happy woman.

Be sure to read the rest of this series by
Mary D. Brooks:

Out of Darkness

In a most troublesome period of human history, subjugated by the might of Nazi Germany, two women meet under extraordinary circumstances. This is the story of Eva Muller, the daughter of a German major, the commander of the occupying force in Larissa, Greece in 1944. Through the intervention of the village priest she meets Zoe Lambros. Zoe is a young Greek woman with vengence in her heart and a faith in God that's been shattered by the death of her family. They develop a friendship borne out of this dark time, and they help each other to learn to live and love again.

You Must Remember This

In this sequel to *Out of Darkness*, Eva, with the help of her step-mother, Alberta Haralambos, manages to get out of the factory and use her language skills in the ever busy interpreter division. Zoe Lambros sets out to fulfill her dream of studying for her arts degree. Then, from out of Eva's past comes a woman, Greta, who threatens their happiness. Greta hides a secret that when revealed will lead to extraordinary measures being taken to bring this woman to justice.

Available from booksellers.

And available this summer

New Beginnings

This fourth novel in the Eva and Zoe series starts a week after *Full Circle* concludes. Eva and Zoe have returned from Europe where they confronted their past and found new ways if dealing with their past experiences. New challenges await Eva and Zoe as they embark on a new chapter in their lives together.

Available Summer 2002

Available soon from

RENAISSANCE ALLIANCE

Cobb Island
By Blayne Cooper

Cobb Island offers not one but three romances in this novel set off the coast of Virginia. Marcy and Doug have had only sporadic contact since Marcy's family moved away a year ago. Their older sisters agree to supervise the lovesick teens during a week-long stay in an eerie island house that has been in Marcy's family since the late 1600s. But who will chaperone the chaperones? Sparks fly between them almost from the beginning, growing into lightning-size bolts when Liv notices that Kayla is answering her questions before she has even voiced them. It is Liv's training in translating foreign languages, however that proves to be the key that unlocks the house's secret history—and the story of a tragic love begun and ended four centuries earlier.

Echoes From the Mist
By Blayne Cooper

In this sequel to *Cobb Island*, paranormal researchers Kayla Redding and Olivia Hazelwood begin their professional and personal partnership as they tackle their first case together in the world's most haunted city—Edinburgh, Scotland. While in Edinburgh, the women visit the Cobb family ancestral home. The Cobb family historian takes the women on a journey back through time to 17th Century Colonial Virginia. He weaves the tale of Faylinn Cobb, explaining what happened to her and her family after her sister-in-law, Bridget Redding, was branded a witch.

Other titles to look for in the
coming months from
RENAISSANCE ALLIANCE

A Sacrifice For Friendship By DS Bauden

Valley of Dark Shadows By Mary D. Brooks

Broken Homes   By Lois Cloarec Hart

Words Heard In Silence By T Novan and Taylor Rickard

Printed in the United States
3603